BELTESHAZZAR

THE PALADIN PROMISE

a novel by

RUTH P. DURANT

Unless otherwise noted, all Scripture quotations are taken from the King James Version (KJV) of the Bible.

Scripture quotations marked (NKJV) are taken from the New King James Version. Copyright © 1979, 1980, 1982 by Thomas Nelson, Inc. Used by permission. All rights reserved.

ISBN: 978-1-935986-36-2

Lynchburg, Va.
www.liberty.edu/libertyuniversitypress

To all those who discover that His name is indeed Glorious, having lifted up their eyes to the hills.

To my husband, whose obedience to Him has made all things possible.

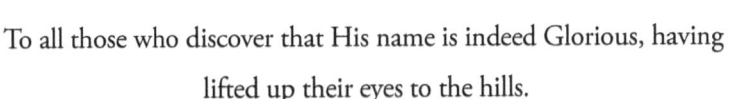

"He will not suffer thy foot to be moved . . . ."
-The Book of Psalms: 121:3

TABLE OF CONTENTS

God gave them knowledge and skill in all learning and wisdom.

KJV

Daniy-El 1:17

PART 1
The First Kingdom

PROLOGUE
Athens Circa 384 BC

The young Greek sat solemnly at his worktable, poring over the records of the scripted by the historian Ctesias of Cnidus. Transcripts lay strewn across every desk and shelf in the room. Polemus had spent two months searching the library in Corinth, but he was still dissatisfied with the knowledge that he had gained. In as many decades, he had accrued hundreds of similar documents from the provinces of Greece. The writings bore the titles of men of renown: Herodotus, Photius, Xenophon—the latter having fashioned historical romances for which his brother Daccarus had scoured the realm in search of, such that he might aid Polemus' study. Even within his treasure trove of Homeric epics and hymns, the vaunted heroes, Achilles and Odysseus, mocked him from the scripts, daring him to steer a course between their extremes: the first enmeshed in a world of moral disorder and his own human failings, whilst the second navigated a fantastical voyage, beset by his own patron goddess, Athena.

O Athens! The city of wisdom, and vice. He had stayed all these years despite his brother's urging, for he knew not where he would go to find what his heart desperately sought, a lack he could scarcely define himself. The city was crowded with altars and temples. He had listened quietly at the Areopagus, where his father, who held the office of Archon, presided over the assembly. Daily these august men spoke of divinities and rulerships, but none to his heart. Their speech poured forth much knowledge, but was devoid of wisdom. The magistrates recited all that was already known, but could say little of what was to come. Surely this cosseted life that he was afforded must amount to more than a repetition of theories and shallow offerings to gods of marble and bronze. He had been tutored at the famed Academy with its fountains and its groves of olive and plane trees. He had walked the marbled glory of the Mnesicles's Propylaea, and stood within the Erechtheum to gaze at the holy spring and the olive tree sacred to Minerva, yet his experiences had been empty of promise. So too, Phidias's statue of Athena Promachos, goddess of wisdom and good sense, stared lifelessly back at him. *What goddess sits docile, year by year?* he contemplated. *It is a farce! Worthy of one of my brother's whimsical plays. Whilst he had studied history, Daccarus had developed a penchant for the arts, spending much of his time writing or creating paintings.* At least, in his poetry and literary experiments, Daccarus always sought to capture and convey some essence of real hope. *But where is the hope in this life that I lead? Wisdom and good sense tells me that there must be something more than my vaunted knowledge.* He desperately needed an answer. Month by month, year by year he wandered the Agora, pausing to attend impromptu debates on history and theologies, hoping to find a nugget of new truth. He had studied in this city of death for many years but could find no-one to speak to him of life and its meaning. The debates always surrounded the same old philosophies of grandeur and Greek superiority of thought. *Is there no more to discover?* he groaned inwardly. *I am tired of forever looking back. What of the future? Would these gods who fashioned men have no purpose for their creations save the fulfillment of selfish desires at the expense of others? Were these wise and fruitful gods continually deaf to the pleas that were issued heavenward? Were the gods both deaf and dumb?* Polemus broke away from the harangue of questions, for he knew where they were destined to lead him. Nowhere! He had no answers within himself to assuage this turmoil that he felt. *Perhaps I should indeed have accepted Daccarus's offer to journey to new lands.* However, his older brother was a born traveler, whereas Polemus preferred to venture out with his mind and spirit.

He sighed and rose. The air had grown still with the foreboding of a storm. Polemus moved to the window. The sky was still clear and held prospects for a normal summer's day.

"You there," a voice shouted from the public court that abutted the magistrate's hall below. "Is one named Polemus within? If so, please inform him that a messenger from Styra's ship stands without. The merchants have arrived, and Master Fentus sends news."

"Fentus?" Polemus exclaimed elatedly. "A moment please! I will be but a moment," he shouted. Forgetting his aplomb and dignified stature, he vaulted down two flights of the small servant's stairs that opened to a hall directly off the forecourt. *Festus has sent! Daccarus must be well then!* Visions of his brother's journeys raced through his mind. He had spent over thirteen months in a state of worry, having heard no word since his sibling's departure the previous year.

The messenger returned from a horse cart that was stationed nearby. He bore a sizeable chest in his brawny arms. "My lord, the master sends greetings and a box." He gestured with a nod to the oak chest. It was bound with iron straps and sealed with pitch. "It was almost lost at sea, but good fortune was with you, young master."

"Thank you," Polemus said, grinning broadly. "Please extend my gratitude to the ship's master for his sacrifice. My father will be extremely pleased. Fentus has served our family well."

The man nodded in acknowledgement and departed. Polemus stumbled under the weight of the burden, but renewed hope lent him strength and he lumbered up the narrow stairs with the heavy load, eager to view its contents. He folded open a parchment that lay atop several other papers and tightly lidded jars. Joy surged through him again as he recognized the flowing script of his brother's hand. He smoothed the parchment then moved to the window where the sunlight streamed in warmly.

3

Greetings Polemus,

Be it known to you and father that I am well and prospering in my journeys. My passage through these eastern lands has stretched a much longer season than I had hoped, but I have spent my idle hours writing of the grand stories that I have heard told in this marvelous place. Before the long passage to Shinar, I spent many a season in the land called Judea. It is an entirely different place than we have been taught at the Academy. Its histories would enthrall one such as you. You still seek knowledge of spiritual things do you not, young brother? Having seen these lands, I am convinced that you spend altogether too much time in the company of those dusty scrolls. Common men here speak much of prophecies and holy writs with a dire passion that the scholars at the Academy lack. If you were not so in love with the libraries, I am sure that you would be at home there. Its people have taught me much, even beside campfires. They speak of a God such as we have never known, Polemus. Knowing of your love for both history and the arts, I have written to you of those things that I have heard there.

During the winter, a blessing must have been upon me, for I met one fellow who, seventeen years ago, himself traveled with the historian, Ctesias of Cnidus, of whom your colleagues speak at times. On the expedition they served as physicians to Artexerses Mnemon! Polemus, this place has hidden in the very stones much of the history of which you so often dream. You really should have taken me up on my offer, Little Brother. Nevertheless, enough scolding. It seems that Ctesias chronicled a history of Assyria and Persia—in six books, Polemus! Six! Astounding is it not, though some here do not give credit to his work. Yet it contains most compelling views regarding Babylonia. There is another who compiles like histories. His name is Berosus. However, I doubt that you have heard his title. All in all, Brother, who now can claim that literature is dead? You can say to your smug friend Hermocles that, alas, I shall boldly challenge his philosophies when I am again in Athens, for my eyes have been opened. This passage through unusual worlds, peoples and experiences has taught me more than I was granted those five decades that I was bound in

Greece. I believe you shall find the records that I have sent you utterly fascinating. Peculiarly, there is a common cord that binds the works of Ctesias to the knowledge that I gained in Judea. Hence, I have also placed within the box, transcripts of some ancient writings that I happened upon in the libraries at Achmeta. Through them, you may better understand those things I have encountered. It is one of several texts of its kind—we have no such prophets in Greece. . .'tis a pity. This particular text, the one bearing the gold seal, was passed to me by a dear friend, and on it I have based the record you now hold in your possession. It may be that this original transcript shall perhaps interest you more than my own attempts at literature, Little Brother, but I pray that between them both, you shall discover some glimmer of what you have yearned for so long. I believe that you shall find enough here to whet your appetite toward this 'life' that you have spoken of so often.

Now, do you recall the one whom Mother titled 'Strobos'—a Shadow—who could never himself be discovered, although his ill handiwork was always evident? Him I have secreted between the pages that I have written, for he is as the present darkness of this world, dissolving into obscurity as the light of a new day dawns, but evermore returning. Though threads have been lost in the histories that I have compiled, the weaving of Strobos's malice throughout is unmistakable. So here too you will find his hand upon the loom, though it seems that he is not destined to plague us forever. . . But that is enough for the present. I do not wish to disclose too much aforetime. For this, you will need to read on, Little Brother. May you find your way to this hope you seek.

Please tell Father to expect me in the spring whence his roving son shall return home. I regret that his seventieth year will have already passed, but the ship will not be returning before the next harvest. Styra aims to sail to Phoenicia after which we shall make port near Sparta. I shall lodge in the city with the ship's steward, Calis, before making the journey home. I shall have much more to tell you then.

Your Brother,
Daccarus

Polemus reached into the chest that held an array books and scrolls transcribed from nations throughout the Empire and found a carefully wrapped packet with a gold seal. He loosed the bindings and withdrew the papers reverently. The first read: *Words of Daniy-El, the Prophet.* Polemus frowned for the name was wholly unfamiliar to him.

Within the packet lay thick a book with a hand-sewn binding. It was his brother's script. He turned it in his hand, admiring his brother's handiwork. Daccarus had appended a short note to the binding. It was titled:

Belteshazzar—The Paladin Promise.

Slipped beneath the binding was a tiny square of parchment with a finely scripted note in his brother's hand. Polemus slid it out carefully and placed the paper close to the lamp. He squinted into the light that fell across the miniature page.

It is my only copy, Polemus, tend it well. You are at liberty to tell me what you think of my efforts when I return—Softly, of course!
Daccarus

Polemus smiled. Daccarus had always accused him of being a more discerning critic than Plato himself. The Academy had transformed them both. Whilst Spartan boys were plucked from their royal houses at seven years of age to be trained in the art of war, he and Daccarus had both been shuttled by a proud father into the vaunted halls of the Academy, despite the protests of a concerned mother who believed them too young to be inducted into the ways of power. Father nevertheless insisted. To him authority was born of increased wisdom. The training had served them well, but despite the lofty knowledge that was touted in the Agora, there had been some element of verity missing, and the brothers had each ceased to be satisfied with re-enacting the parade of magisterial acumen year by year. He craved something more—Something that, perhaps, Daccarus had found. He broke the string eagerly, and, drawing a cushioned bench to the window ledge, began to read.

JERUSALEM

The 17th Year of King Hezekiah

1

Reavers

Woe to them that draw iniquity with cords of vanity,

And sin as it were with a cart rope.

- The Book of the Prophet Isaiah

"No. *Nooooo! What has he done?*" The prophet Isaiah hoisted his robes and raced the length of the palace toward the king's audience chamber. Even now he could hear the pounding of hooves as the stranger's horses careened away from the palace courtyard. He had glimpsed the movement from a high window above the court as foreign voices rose on an ill wind that brought a chill to his flesh despite the searing heat of the day. *Could it have begun so simply?* What good would it do him now to make such haste? Yet he ran. *A cataclysm that starts as an innocent tribute meeting?* No. it was not innocent at all. The cloak of treachery was almost perfect. He was sure and yet . . . . *Would Hezekiah be willing to receive the word of the Lord now that the deed had been done?* There had been no time to forewarn the king. The vision had come as suddenly as the blast of a virulent storm across the desert sands, scouring away life and smothering hope. So it was with Yahweh. He came as He chose, for He alone *knew*, and men were scarcely privy to His wisdom of ages.

Isaiah burst into the hall just as the king was lowering himself wearily into his seat, a look of contentment and pride etching his powerful countenance.

King Hezekiah's advisors milled about him, relishing the aftermath of hosting their visitors. *Indeed it has begun,* Isaiah surmised slowing to a walk. *And he does not know. He does not know what he has done!* The dismay that rippled across the prophet's face as he entered the room drew King Hezekiah upright with a start. Only once before had the prophet found himself in such a state of consternation—that had been in the hour that he had come to announce to the king that he should set his house in order, for Yahweh had pronounced that the Israelite sovereign was destined for death. Hezekiah had wept sore on that day, fasting in sackcloth and ashes until, in His mercy, He had granted Hezekiah's petition to keep his life—15 more years, the time of which was not yet ended. Hezekiah was a prudent man, and Isaiah could see that the king already knew that the crisis was of some other making—something *he* had done. Hezekiah gulped a breath of air, his eyes widening in recognition that something had gone terribly wrong. Today, however, a reprieve was not foretold and Isaiah was delegated the unenviable task of delivering the daunting news. Though he may have wished, the prophet could not now turn back the sun as he had on that day as a sign to King Hezekiah that his life would be spared. The word of the Lord was sure, and now more than the life of the king hung in the balance.

King Hezekiah anxiously waved his counselors out of the hall. His brow furrowed as he strained to discern the cause of the prophet's anguish. "Everyone go. Leave us. Go!" The advisors looked in question at each other, and at the prophet, whose precipitous entrance had drawn anxious murmurs and stares.

The king extended his hand for Isaiah to draw closer. "What troubles you, my friend?"

Isaiah pointed in the direction of the forecourt through which the strangers had departed. "What did those men say? Where did they come from? What did you show them?" The questions poured out as a breathless whisper, so quietly that the king was compelled to lean forward to grasp the words as they escaped the prophet's lips. Hezekiah frowned, hesitating a moment. The king could clearly not decipher the source of the calamity. The king had surely thought them harmless, for such men would bear no air of destruction about them.

"They came from a far country, *even from Babylon*," he answered in a voice tinged with alarm.

Isaiah sighed heavily and slowly shook his head.

The king's voice rose in pitch, infected by sudden panic as the prophet's visage hardened with each word spoken. "All the things that are in my house they have seen. There is *nothing* within my house that I have not showed them . . . ." His words trailed away miserably. The men had come to steal the trust of the king whose generosity, on this occasion, had exceeded his good judgment. Hezekiah had viewed them through pure eyes, his discernment also clouded by the haze of ceremonial splendor and the dictates of royal hospitality. The king's hands flopped apologetically to his sides as the prophet expelled a pent up breath

"Hear the word of the Lord," Isaiah intoned, his tone as rough as gravel. "Behold, the days come, that all you have, and that which your fathers have laid up in store unto this day, shall be carried into Babylon: nothing shall be left, says the Lord." Isaiah paused, his lips buckling briefly before he could carry on. "And your sons, and the children of your loins, they will take them away, and they shall be *eunuchs* in the palace of the king of Babylon." As Isaiah finished his pronouncement, a wave of profound sadness crept over him. His words settled like a pall of death upon the sovereign.

Hezekiah slumped in his chair, his fist pressed to his lips as he assimilated the grim news that suffocated his elation. The seemingly humble emissaries had borne tributes and precious gifts in abundance, and in his pride, and folly, he had welcomed them.

Isaiah ascertained that they had been emissaries of Merodach-Baladan, son of Baladan, king of Babylon, who, having heard that Hezekiah had been sick, sent consolatory letters and presents. The same gifts and offerings now sat perched like poisonous serpents upon his dais. Hezekiah clasped his hands to his lips and straightened himself upon his throne.

"Good is the word of the Lord that you have spoken," he said simply.

Three years past Rabshakeh had descended from Assyria at the bidding of his king, Sennacherib, meaning to lay siege to Jerusalem. Hezekiah had defended the Children of Judah, slaying over one hundred and four score of the enemy. Now a new, more sinister foe would muster to besiege their walls.

It was not for Hezekiah's indiscretion, Isaiah knew, that ill would come to roost in their homestead. Rather, centuries of disobedience and rebellion by the Children of Judah against the God that had kept them hale for so long, though adversaries pressed thick to subsume them, would have fed the beast that would return to ravage their sanctuary. The ways of idolatry and variance had built in the people a false comfort, but Yahweh was not blind to the rebellion that had been cast up like a bank against the fortress of God's grace. As a result, the Hebrew seat of power—Jerusalem—was fated to be sliced asunder as enemies claimed it prize, and its people. Isaiah knew that his lifetime would pass before the deeds of the day bore its putrid fruit. A seer other than himself would tend the lamp on that day. May Yahweh extend His hand of mercy in that day, Isaiah prayed, for he had seen much more than he could convey to the sorrowful king. Isaiah understood the pain that the king shielded within his bosom, but he, like Isaiah, had learnt to turn his will over to his Lord, ever trusting Him. Nevertheless, there was a boon—there would be freedom from war throughout the days of Hezekiah. The king understood this, and he gave thanks. *Until that day Lord . . . .*

BABYLON

The 2nd Year of Nebuchadnezzar

2

The Decree

And the city was broken up,

And all the men of war fled by night by way

of the gate between two walls. . . .

- *The Fourth Book of the Kings*

"Impossible!"

"He *insists*, my lord."

"But it cannot be done! *It cannot!*"

"It must, Sarsechim-Nebo. Our lives are at stake."

"No." the chief magi shook his head. "Never has a king given such a horrific command. And in only his second year. Does he mean to ruin the kingdom?"

"Quietly, Sarsechim-Nebo. Do not forget yourself. Guard your speech. Such words may be taken for treachery. We must find a way to stall the king's judgment. We have always been able to depend on Felioch to cast an alignment of the stars in our favor—"

"That will not be satisfactory at such a critical time as this. Felioch's readings and predictions are undependable, and most oft fantasy. The king is losing confidence in us. Something must be done soon . . . before the decree takes effect!"

The buzz of whispers that had been flitting through the council room became an angry hum at the mention of the king's fearful order.

"It is plainly preposterous. Can we read his mind? He must surely withdraw his decree—"

"A decree cannot be withdrawn. Either we give the king what he wants or we will be put to death. He said it as simply."

"The king has surely gone mad. He—"

"Quiet. *Quiet my friends!* Take hold of yourselves. The walls have ears. Be wary. Do not provoke the king to take our heads prematurely. There is yet time for us to agree on a remedy. If each of us searches for the answer, we will be successful. Perhaps the king has made mention of the dream to his chamberlain, or one of the eunuchs. Seek Ashpenaz. He can—"

"The prince of the eunuchs will divulge nothing to us. He opposes our ways and will do us more harm should we allow him to see our need."

"Then we shall question his aides, discreetly, in a hope of recreating the vision. Until then we shall dismiss."

The council of magicians broke apart reluctantly.

"Nergal-Sharezer. May I speak with you—privately? Please." A voice called to the chief magi as he exited the broad doors to the hall. He halted his departure to a slow walk as a lithe man emerged from the sea of faces moving along the corridor. His demeanor was calm and sharply contrasted the haze of anxiety that had pervaded the council room. News of the decree had dispelled their usual equanimity.

"Nergal-Sharezer. We must talk," the man hissed.

"Not now, Strobos," the counselor ground out between his teeth. "We shall speak. But tonight—in my quarters." He moved away abruptly before a response could be given.

Strobos quirked his lips as he watched the older man shuffle away. He would wait, but not indefinitely. If Nergal-Sharezer would not act, then he would seek an alternate recourse. The master was adept at the arts, but shortsighted. Someone needed to have a vision beyond the confines of the council. If he needed to be removed, then so be it. Strobos was certain that the king would relent. Then they could proceed with the expulsions as the council had approved. *Tonight then, it would be decided.*

The pounding vibrated the thin timbers of the chamber door. Rising from his prayers the young man hurried to release the catch before the frame was dislodged. After two years in captivity, he had been accorded increased privileges owing to his favor in the king's court. Yet he was not fooled. His status remained that of a slave. Amongst his own he was sometimes referred to as a 'free-captive'. He could travel throughout the city but he could never leave. It was forbidden. He was allowed the privacy of his chamber, where he prayed and worshiped alone. He was also permitted to visit with a few of his brethren who were also free to traverse the confines of the palace. But their status could as easily be rescinded. He was no fool to allow the pampered halls to make him complacent, nor to forget that he was a prisoner at the king's behest.

This was all the more evident by the way the door shook upon its hinges.

"In the name of the king or we shall break it down."

Soldiers. Who else would be so uncouth?

"Belteshazzar!"

The sound of his given Chaldean name still grated like the stones of the mill grinding without corn. *Hrmph.* He wished no affinity with their accursed god. *'Favored by-Bel'* and *'Keeper of Bel's Treasure'* they had said. Despite his aversion to it, the ill-conceived name would be his throughout his captivity. His friends Azaryah, Miysha-El, and Hananyah had suffered the same indignity. Still, having each other was some comfort amidst these Chaldeans who changed gods like flitting locusts.

Miysha-El would sometimes joke about his new title. "Meshach—Guest of a King? If this is the manner in which their guests are treated who would want to be a slave? Or you, Hananyah. What 'royalty' have they ascribed to you? And Daniy-El. What 'treasure' have they bestowed upon you, or any of us, among eunuchs, eh?"

However, for Daniy-El the loss was external only. In his heart he was, and always would be, Daniy-El—and he would be true to his name, for with Yahweh as his judge he would need fear no man within these provinces.

"I come," he shouted, lifting the catch just before a spear butt descended to ram the meager hasp. The soldier halted his strike and staggered to regain his balance in the open portal.

"On the king's order, the decree is to be executed immediately—Or should I say, the Men of Wisdom shall be." The soldier chuckled maliciously. "No wizardry will dull the gaoler's axe, you can be sure. Come." Others of the king's guard crowded the threshold, their fierce scowls demanding compliance.

The soldier ignored the bewildered expression that was returned from the doorway.

"What decree is this? Where are we going? Where is Arioch?" His questions were brushed aside like the fluttering of an errant moth as muscled arms closed to seize their prisoner.

A rumbling voice reverberated along the corridor outside the room. "I am here, Belteshazzar. Come quietly." The soldiers made way to admit a large man who bowed through the low doorway. Straightening, his head brushed the low ceiling in the chamber. "The king has commanded the enactment of his decree."

"What decree is this, Arioch? What is this about? I have no wish to resist but I should at least know the cause."

Puzzlement carving deep furrows in his brow, the king's captain regarded Daniy-El with mirrored incomprehension. "You do not know? How could you not? The Men of Wisdom have held council for the entire day on the matter."

"You should know as well as any that I am not welcome in the council—I am a slave, remember. It is the truth, Arioch. I am aware of no decree."

Arioch motioned the soldiers outside of the small room and pulled the door closed.

"Belteshazzar. The king is adamant. No one has succeeded in dissuading him. I cannot save you from this!" he whispered urgently.

"From what, Arioch?" Daniy-El threw his arms wide in growing frustration.

The captain of the guard exhaled slowly. He crumpled his lips as though deciding whether an explanation would be prudent.

Seeing his hesitation, Belteshazzar pressed for an answer. "Arioch. What decision could the king have made in such haste?"

The captain finally relented. "This morning the king awoke in a pall of sweat. He summoned Nergal-Sharezer and his following, the sorcerers, the astrologers, and the Chaldeans. He said that he had suffered from a horrific dream, but that it was lost to him when he awoke, and he can find no trace of its journey through his mind. He ordered that the dream be told him, and also, he requires its interpretation."

Belteshazzar's eyes widened.

"Yes. The dream is gone, and yet the king wishes it revealed again. But no one has been able to discern a way to meet his need. Nergal-Sharezer and the Chaldeans have entreated him to speak of his vision that they may unravel its interpretation. They hoped to buy enough time for them to work their sorceries but the king was livid. He knows their constant ploys. He has charged them all with deception. Some think the king has been a fool to hearken so diligently to the wizards but he is not always deceived. He abides much, but misses little. Nebuchadnezzar knows that they are not above speaking lies and corrupt words to their king. His dream has afforded an opportunity to prove them. And so, he has demanded both the dream and its reading. Of course, none could oblige such a request."

Arioch ran his hand through his hair, recalling the tension that had charged the throne room.

"At long length Nergal-Sharezer held his peace, for he did not wish to stoke the king's fury further. The king was wroth."

"I am sure." Belteshazzar mumbled. "They are clever, that lot. But this is beyond them."

Nebuchadnezzar issued a writ this evening, which states that unless one of the Men of Wisdom comes forward with the answers each of you will be beheaded. You are to be imprisoned to belay flight."

Belteshazzar smiled ruefully. "Where would I run, Arioch? What resources have I?

"I am sorry Belteshazzar," he replied, shoulders slumping. "You have been through so much already."

The young man knew that the captain spoke of more than the day's occurrences. "I will speak with the king," he said firmly.

Arioch's gaze lifted in surprise. "It will bear you no fruit. When the Chaldeans broached a reprieve we thought the king would have beheaded all who stood in his presence had some unknown thing not stayed his hand. It will do you no good."

"I will go to the king. Will you help me?"

Arioch sighed. "I suppose there can be no further harm done."

"Thank you."

"It's your head, Belteshazzar."

"Indeed," the young man agreed. "Indeed."

The king's audience chamber was unusually cold, and no servants tended the candles, which sputtered in pools of hot wax. Nebuchadnezzar sat uneasily, watching Belteshazzar approach. If he could have spared any the intended fate, it would have been this one. He was not a vulture as were the majority of his heralded Men of Wisdom. His lips curled in annoyance. A deceitful lot were these sorcerers and magicians, but Belteshazzar, he was somehow—different. The king had noticed that he never pushed himself forward in matters to which he attended, yet he freely gave his advice. Much to their dismay, Belteshazzar eclipsed the sorcerers and wizards in knowledge and understanding. He spoke quietly, and always with discernment, never scrabbling for a reward as did the governors in the king's court. Nether did the three Hebrew men with whom he kept company.

Perhaps I was too rash in my decree. No. A king cannot entertain regrets. An unfortunate casualty then. . . . .

The king broke off his ruminations as Belteshazzar came before him. He stood circumspectly, awaiting the king's gesture to draw near. Yet the king delayed. *Such self-command for one so young. A pity to lose him. Nevertheless—.* "Come." He raised his hand to signal the approach.

Belteshazzar again waited.

The king reclined, feigning nonchalance.

"What report could you bring at this hour, Belteshazzar? A petition perhaps? Arioch was very insistent."

"My king. It is said that you have dreamed—"

The king sat up suddenly. "Yes! What of the matter? Are you here to reveal it to me, and to interpret?" He spread his hands questioningly. He continued through Belteshazzar's helpless silence. "If not your time is wasted. I can give no mercy in this. I have already confirmed it by edict. I cannot gainsay my own word. Cannot, and *will not!*" He sat back again.

"Perhaps the king would consider—"

"No." Nebuchadnezzar interrupted. 'I have already denied Nergal-Sharezer his petition to forestall my judgment."

"Unlike the Chaldeans, you know that I speak only the truth, even at my peril. I ask only a short period of forbearance. Grant me this and I *will* show the king this dream and its meaning."

The king stared at him for a long time before raising his hand in capitulation. "Very well. Your petition is granted. I shall expect your return on the morrow. Do not disappoint me Belteshazzar." The king's voice grew low and grave. He raised a finger in warning. "There shall be no further allowances in this."

Belteshazzar nodded. "Thank you, my king." He bowed and removed himself from the audience chamber. Now more than ever he would need the support of his friends, for the greater petition was yet to unfold.

Hananyah and Miysha-El stood aghast. Each paced the room, considering the implications of Daniy-El's report.

"We are to be killed? Without speaking in our defense?" Azaryah questioned. His lifted arms flopped to his sides.

"Our defense is in Yahweh. We shall petition *Him* for the answer," Daniy-El affirmed, pointing upward. "It has always been that way. We cannot allow ourselves to panic because the circumstances are dire."

"But to know the king's dream in its entirety? You are certain that Yahweh will reveal this one to you tonight? Has it not always been for interpretation alone that you have been given His voice?"

"What choice do we have Azaryah? You know Yahweh can do all things. And we have been faithful, have we not? He may show His mercy yet again and deliver us. . . ."

"As He has before!" Miysha-El added, striking the table in conviction.

"Yes. As he has done countless times since we were dragged here in shackles. How else could we have risen to such an estate in this land of our enemies? Many of our brethren have perished through the desolation, yet from the advent of this terrible sojourn we have receive consideration in the court of the king. We remain, amongst a few others who have rejected the ample pleasures of the king's court in order to keep to His word. We remain to carry the standard until this sentence is completed by Yahweh, or we die."

Miysha-El nodded in agreement. "We shall take heart. Yahweh shows His might in such times."

"He has endowed me with the blessing of interpreting men's dreams. Is it too great a task for Him to render to me also the dream itself? I do not believe it is. I will ask in earnest and He will answer at His choosing. First, however, we must purify ourselves, and fast. Did He not say that He would honor those who honor Him? It may be that His glory will be manifested through this abomination. No more can be said this night. Nebuchadnezzar has given a brief stay of the executions. Let us not abhor the gift. We shall go to our quarters and seek the One who can aid us."

Shuffling feet carried his friends in opposite directions along the corridor. A few hours was now all that remained to him before dawn drew back its shimmering mantle. *Yahweh strengthen me.* This place—Its men harbored such evil. *Yahweh keep me. Let me not go down to their pit.* He would pray—he would wait—And the morning would unveil its secrets as it willed—whether of life, or of death, none could know.

Tempers flared within the dim chamber that housed the king's chief magician. Nergal-Sharezer was not used to being challenged by one lower than he on the ladder of power.

"Your neck is not the one bared to the executioner's blade, Strobos."

"Isn't it? It may as well be so, for all the success you have had with the king of late."

"Watch your tongue," Nergal-Sharezer growled. He was in no mood for Strobos's callous indifference. "Let's just make it through the next day. Then there will be every occasion to renew our plans. *Please.* It is vital that you hold your peace with the counselors. We need, every one of us, to dedicate our arts toward finding an answer to the king's dreams. He—"

"He asks too much and you know it!" Strobos interrupted in annoyance. "When we have secured the council we will be better placed to guide the king's hand. As for this *decree*, the king shall never go through with the executions. You are too valuable to him. He does little without consulting the gods, *and you.* I am sure that—"

"Save the discourse, Strobos. I have heard enough opinions on the matter. Let me assure you, the king will keep his word. You were not there to see the hardness in his face. He will not balk at spilling our blood."

"Could you not then depart the palace until the king calms? You have coin. Use it."

"Leave. To go where, Strobos? And to do what? When I lack for fine food, do I plant fitches to harvest for the winter? Should I scratch for miserable grain even as the peasants do? Do you not realize? On the day that I abscond, I will be barred from making use of the riches that I have stored so assiduously these last decades. You of all people should know that the moment one trades in coin the little birds fly back to the king, chirping their little songs. No! I would rather be dead than live out my days in ignominy."

Nergal-Sharezer moved away wearily toward his large desk, which was arrayed with pitchers, bowls and jars of all descriptions. Large urns of liquid also sat on the floor nearby. Turning his back to the younger man, he selected two small containers and sat heavily. Removing their lids, he withdrew two spoons of dark powder. "If I were you, I would be every bit as concerned over this distressing development as the Order, for you will find yours also to be a much less gratifying life should we be disposed of." The magician gestured brusquely. "Leave me now," he commanded. "I have spells that I must cast urgently, and I will bear no intrusion."

Strobos's mouth worked angrily but he said nothing. He stared at his back a long time before finally speaking. "Very well. But we shall speak again."

As the door closed softly behind him Nergal-Sharezer replaced the clay jars that he had been fiddling with pretentiously, for he had been eager to be left alone. H exhaled a pent up breath and stared unseeing across the chamber. The web that he had been so carefully weaving with the counselors was in danger of unraveling at the whim of a precocious king. Nergal-Sharezer gritted his teeth in frustration. Nothing was transpiring as he had anticipated. So many loose threads that he could not now control upon an ever-widening loom. *One measure at a time*, he counseled himself. *First, the king's business. . . .* Hopefully they would be allowed to live through the night.

Nergal-Sharezer resumed his conjuring. Surely Bel-Merodach would answer for the sake of the king! He watched expectantly, yet nothing occurred even as his casting reached completion. Suddenly, he was gripped by a spasm of fear. His arts were proving useless, and with that failure, hopelessness had begun to tighten a grip on his heart. *Come on Nergal, think of something!* However, no solutions unfolded to extricate him from the entanglement of a king's stubborn will. He laid his head in his hands, beseeching the other for inspiration, if not for himself, then one of the others, for without the unveiling of some merciful remedy, and quickly, there would be no reprieve to be gained them across all the heavens.

3

Petition

There is no God like Thee in heaven above or on earth beneath,
Who keepest covenant and mercy with thy servants
That walk before Thee with all their heart . . . .

- King Solomon

Daniy-El lay prostrate on the floor of the small but neatly appointed bedchamber. His prayers echoed softly off the stones that sheltered him against the thick darkness beyond. His lamp offered a vibrant light to quell his lingering restlessness. *The Word of Yahweh will never fall to the ground. His promises to his children will be upheld. I need only be faithful and believe.* . . . Daniy-El rose and blew out the lamp. He returned to his palette on the floor, staying still while his eyes roved the familiar gloom. A silver blue light pierced the slatted timber of the window above his head. The night hours held no terrors for the young man. His days, whether waking or asleep, had long been dedicated to Yahweh and His service. He had proved his Lord repeatedly throughout his sojourn in this isolated place. His visions confirmed something that men spent their lives questing to discover—the wonder of a personal God, who sometimes spoke to chasten, but also to comfort and to enfold.

The visions that were imparted always gave direction and clarity to matters that puzzled other men, and defied the wiles of the enchanters who vied to capture the fleeting glory of the king's court. They stirred potions and cast baubles to glean wisdom through dark arts.

However, Daniy-El had no need for mystical devices or bloodstained rites. The Word of Yahweh was not limited by vile sorceries nor celestial alignments. Neither did He reverence the audience of kings above the bowed ear of a humble-hearted slave. When He spoke, none could gainsay His wisdom.

Although Daniy-El felt the press of the need upon his neck like the heavy arm of an enemy soldier, he resolved to dispel the air of anxiety that sought to envelop him. *In God's time*, he reminded himself. He pulled his knees up and bowed himself beside his bed. He relaxed tense muscles that fought against his will to be calm and took a deep breath. Still the claw of uncertainty scrabbled to take hold of his mind. *Wisdom and might are His*, he reassured himself. Silence loomed in the shadowy chamber, its noiselessness urging him to doubt. He dispelled the quiet onslaught with an intense litany of praise that blazed the consuming dross away from his spirit. He raised his unseen hands and drew solace from the promises of his Lord that had been read so daily in the Temple. As a boy, he had wrapped himself in their splendor. Now, many of these same scrolls lay buried amidst the piles of rudimentary texts in the library at Shinar—a travesty often mourned by the children of the Captivity, the woeful day still fresh in their minds.

Daniy-El considered himself fortunate to have been granted access to the large volume of writings held hostage in Babylon's vast library. Its vaults contained psalms scripted in wonder, along with other sacred blessings that had flowed from the quills of prophets and scribes like rivers of grace.

Daniy-El shook his head and looked about with a sigh. Whereas the words of the ancients bathed his own mind in peace, their value was lost upon these nobles of Chaldea. Even now a song of worship streamed from his memory to his tongue. Uttered quietly, the words hallowed his passage from the daunting surrounds and the clamor of earth-bound thoughts to the majestic Presence that was his true sustenance—his sanctuary.

Amidst his whispers, the vision unfolded gently from the embrace of the night, slowly revealing the vibrancy of a future disparate from the dimness of the closed room. Gruesome images of death were interwoven with myriad wars that foretold centuries of grim violence. Tears coursed down his cheeks yet he remained immobile, absorbing the visual pulses that enlightened his eyes and— *What was this?* Daniy-El rocked back on his heels, the impact of a new vision slamming against senses that had been overwrought and subdued by the shackles of what had seemed to be the triumph of evil. The revelation that followed careened him into an unfettered future—peeling back the tapestries shrouding his mind to unleash a majestic kingdom of power, and unchallenged supremacy.

With it came a holy balm that spread like a cool river, imbuing peace, and life. Despite the claims of a governing Evil, its scourge was swept into darkness by an emblazoned banner of light. Daniy-El sucked in a breath. *It would happen.* The sorrow of ages would be made to hearken to the new promise which none would be able to oppose. The Hand of Yahweh would not be dissuaded from its course. Daniy-El raised his fists to the heavens and suppressed a triumphant laugh that sought to erupt and sunder the solitude that masked the palace. He arose with a surge, arms still upraised in victory. He had come on behalf of the king, but in so doing, he had also been granted a glimpse of a conquest that the world would wait lifetimes to see. The world *will* have its King of Kings. The burden of his imprisonment shifted to infinitely broader shoulders than his—shoulders that had borne the weight of innumerable centuries of disappointment and pain. He had received an invaluable gift this night. *Blessed be the name of Yahweh forever.* He would serve this pagan king, for it was not over, but had only just begun.

The victories foreshadowed by the waking dream emptied a wellspring of hope within Daniy-El's bosom. The interpretation, though meant primarily for the king, had an import that reached far beyond countless generations. The solidity of the triumph of an immoveable God—'*He removes kings, and establishes kings. He gives wisdom to the wise, and knowledge to them that know understanding; He reveals the deep and secret things; He knows what is in the darkness and light dwells with Him*, Daniy-El rejoiced. He spun in an arc, his face upturned to bathe in the warmth of the unseen Presence.

Their deliverance was at hand. *Yahweh be praised. Thank you. Thank you*, he mouthed to the heavens.

Now, to seek the king.

"You clearly have good news," Arioch observed at Daniy-El's brisk steps. The young man nodded in excitement. They stood in the antechamber beyond the king's bedchamber.

"Can you answer the king's request?" Arioch pressed eagerly. "Have you at least some guidance to impart? If not, in his present mood I fear I may be joining you on the executioner's block if your tidings are poor," he added in a more serious tone.

"Better than that Arioch," Daniy-El said, grinning. "I have been shown everything."

"Everything? Do you truly mean you have seen the dream itself?" Arioch stood open-mouthed.

"Everything." Daniy-El confirmed with a hint of amusement. "Yahweh has no limit to His power. It was His will, and so He has blessed me with the understanding to reveal this thing."

"Come, then. Come. *Come!*" Arioch urged. "The guardsmen are assembling even now. They will shortly be dispatched to fulfill the edict were you to fail. Come. The king awaits. He has been unable to sleep and sits brooding. I will be glad for this blight that has encompassed him to be driven away."

Arioch went ahead of Daniy-El. The chief's respect had blossomed over the years for this counselor whose circumspect conduct became more and more evident with time; his prudence was especially notable in contrast to the behavior of the other Men of Wisdom whose pride was exceeded only by the girth of their ample bellies. Favor followed Belteshazzar and also his three Hebrew comrades. Despite their affable dispositions, however, they had made enemies within the court. These closely guarded halls did not value honor and truth. The majority of the princes and governors relied upon superior influence amongst the rulers to institute their will. Otherwise, the capacity for violence, whether overt or cloaked in disingenuous shrouds, became the gauge of success. Subversion and deceit were close friends behind thick chamber doors. Unlike these men of power, Belteshazzar courted neither. He was forthright, yet humble in offering his opinion. His lips framed no boasts nor did he practice the kissing of rings. His allegiance was known to be first to his God and subsequently to his king, and there had thus far been no conflict of duty. In fact, King Nebuchadnezzar had prospered in whatsoever area lay under Belteshazzar's jurisdiction.

Owing to all this, Arioch was encouraged to aid the young man now. An infidel's death was not fitting for one of such integrity and rare promise.

"My lord." Arioch bowed at the threshold to the king's chamber. "Belteshazzar of the Children of Judah bid give you urgent tidings."

Nebuchadnezzar motioned for them to attend his side.

Arioch waved Belteshazzar forward, accompanying him to the opposite end of the table at which the king sat poring over a myriad of scrolls.

The king gestured to the writings. "I was seeking my own explanation perchance you did not come."

"I am here, as promised."

"To render me all that I have asked?"

"And more." The counselor stood erect, his answer showing that he felt no trepidation at provoking the king's displeasure.

The king held Belteshazzar pinned with an eagle's unflinching gaze. Nebuchadnezzar was familiar with assessing his prey. "I shall know well enough if you speak the truth. Go on"

"The astrologers, magicians, and soothsayers cannot show the king this secret," Daniy-El said plainly, his tone carrying no hint of scorn at the insufficiency of the other counselors. "But there is a God in heaven that reveals secrets and has chosen to tell you what shall be in the future, and kingdoms to come."

Nebuchadnezzar straightened at the last words, for it was known by all that the king harbored no greater love than for matters of kingship and the legacy of his nation. A king needed fear many things: sweetly disguised poisons, the maw of war, plotting insurgents who spied incessantly—each lead to its own finality of death. Suppressing the initial show of enthusiasm the king sank back in his chair, his eyes though, still glistening at the unspoken prospect.

"And it is not that I am wise beyond other men," Belteshazzar continued evenly, "but that the king might be delivered his answer."

Arioch was convinced that, were it not for this man and the unashamed relationship that he demonstrated with a God that no one else could see, the gruesome fate of the Men of Wisdom would have been sealed. He knew firsthand that for the sake of a good servant an attentive master would lend his ear. Arioch had heard mention of miracles evidenced amongst these young men who had been brought as captives from the land of Judah, but he had never experienced even a vague semblance of the like, until now. Over the years he had spent in the king's court he had been intimately appraised of the magician's tricks and the subtle devices that overlaid the sorceries of their counterparts. But for a man to glean the unknown from the very air, and with an eerie consistency—for Arioch had heard of prior instances of readings that the young man had offered—to him this was a miracle.

Even now, Arioch considered, taking the measure of Belteshazzar's relaxed stance, *with the king's ear and the lives of many in his palm, he has not exalted himself in glory. A marvelous attribute to discover in a slave—meekness without obsequious ingratiation.*

Belteshazzar outstretched his arms. "You, my king, saw a great image, in the likeness of a man. It was shining and terrible to behold. Its head was formed of gold and its breast and arms were of silver. Its belly and thighs were of brass. It stood on legs of iron, with feet partially of iron and clay. Then you saw an immense stone, held by invisible hands, bashing the legs until they were broken. And when they snapped, the body stumbled and disintegrated. The stone that smote the image then became a tremendous mountain that eclipsed the earth."

Arioch studied the king who was now leaning forward rubbing his chin. The king's eyes bored into Belteshazzar with increasing intensity. The guardsman hoped the king's razor sharp scrutiny would be rewarded with a favorable explanation to the dream which appeared to be a blatant condemnation of the man to whom the dream was sent. This perhaps, now accounted for Nebuchadnezzar's inexplicable alarm and extreme reaction to the vision, for the impression that such a dream would have stamped into the king's mind—the brutal obliteration of the man's visage and an erosion more virulent than a cankerworm—would have been strong enough to leave the king with a residual fear of his own destruction at the hands of a future enemy. The dream, then, would seem to be a judicious warning from his own gods. And although the king had forgotten the account, the seed of dread had been sown to eat away at his composure and good sense—the edict being a reflection of his lingering distress.

Even now the misery had begun to creep back over the king's features. Nebuchadnezzar's unpredictable temper was too often unleashed to sear flesh and bone—if not in the kilns then at the taut end of a gallows.

"Be careful, Belteshazzar," Arioch uttered under his breath.

The young man glanced his way as though he had heard the cautionary whisper, and smiled in reassurance.

"You, my king, are a king of kings," Belteshazzar continued, undeterred, "for the God of Heaven has given you this kingdom, power, strength, and glory. He has given you supremacy over everything. You will have dominion over all. *You* are the head of gold!" Belteshazzar extended his hands toward the king whose countenance softened perceptibly at the revelation.

"There shall be three kingdoms following yours. These have been likened to the brass and iron that you saw. The kingdom of iron will be strong, and shall break the others, but will be divided and weakened by its disparities; this failing is represented by the clay. The God of Heaven, the terrible stone that crushed the towering form, shall establish His kingdom which will consume all those that came before. None shall be able to destroy it. This is a certainty, my king," Belteshazzar finished, his voice raised animatedly.

Nebuchadnezzar surged to his feet and rushed toward Belteshazzar. Arioch's gut knotted in that brief instant, but dissipated as suddenly when the king's lunging stride carried him to Belteshazzar's feet where he fell prostrate before the stupefied counselor. An effusion of gratitude poured forth from the king's lips—his expressions of thanks mingled equally with unabashed exclamations of wonder.

Arioch caught Belteshazzar's eye and they exchanged stunned looks. Finally the king arose, laughing. He grasped Belteshazzar by the shoulders and, shouting for his servants, he pulled the young man close.

"You have earned a great honor, my friend, for you have made my heart light this day. Truly your God is a God of gods and a Lord of kings, for you have been able to uncover my secret, even to me."

Nebuchadnezzar turned to Arioch, his excitement too great to contain. "Such tidings, eh Arioch? My kingdom is secure and I shall reign unchallenged. What more could a king ask?" Nebuchadnezzar shouted in exuberance, his delight infecting Arioch who grinned broadly. The melancholy that had pervaded the king's chamber was dispelled in a twinkling. Arioch saw nothing now of the murderous despair that had enveloped the king in its suffocating web. The king's face shone with renewed vitality and power. Arioch suspected from the telling that, beyond Nebuchadnezzar's fear for his own safety on the first morning following the dream, that the king's distemper had also been colored by a perceived threat to the sanctity of his kingdom. The nightmare was of his own making, though sufficiently real to have provoked the king to take countless lives to assuage his anger at their inability to relieve his mental anguish.

Arioch might have welcomed the extermination of a few notable vermin amidst the cadre of wise men that had caused his guardsmen untold difficulties with their mounting secrecies and plots. But not at the expense of the others. Yet he would have carried out his duty. The salvation of several of these undeserving men had now been wrought at the hands of the man whom they despised for his reticence and discrete conduct.

Many things Arioch was forced to guard close to his breast lest his intervention provoke internal strife and premature deaths. He would protect Belteshazzar where he could in this den of asps. At least the young man's position with his sovereign was secure for the moment, Arioch's brooding gave way to a smile. He could not have anticipated such a peaceable outcome to the whole affair. He was even more pleased that the remedy had been wrought at the hands of the Child of Judah, rather than one from the closed orders, for their secrecies were a constant thorn in his side.

The king's sudden elevation in reverence for Belteshazzar meant, however that he would need be even more cautious than before in safeguarding this one's life against the treachery that would inevitably find its way to his door. Magicians, sorcerers, soothsayers, astrologers . . . . There was no scarcity of troublemakers meddling in the king's business. He had already unearthed a seed of discontent that was germinating within the sorcerer's hold. Arioch purposed to increase his vigilance for the kingdom may be destined to stand through Nebuchadnezzar's reign but dull wits were apt to be sharpened on the edge of a traitor's blade and Arioch had no capable heir to his throne. *Best to keep the king alive. And to do that I will need loyalty at the king's back, and mine.*

4

Priests of Bel-Merodach

The wicked have laid a snare for me, yet erred
I not from Thy precepts.

- King David

The king returned to his private chamber and sunk heavily upon his
cushioned bed. He held tight to the thick bedpost that was overlaid with ivory
and gold, and rested his head against it. Its cool touch soothed him, and relief
flooded his bones. He laughed freely then, as he contemplated his good fortune.
That a God he knew not would favor him above all kings!—To the extent that
he would bless his kingdom for the duration of his reign! The intensity and
strange power that had suffused his dreams gave him no cause to doubt the
signs, nor the interpretation given by the humble Hebrew. *It was a good day*
for my kingdom when I sought the finest of Judah's sons. I can do anything now!
Anything! he surmised. Who could halt his domination.? *No-one!* He laughed
even more loudly as his mind flooded with images of wondrous exploits. *What*
a season this has been. Would I truly have killed them all? Yes, he admitted to
himself. Their sly words and vague interpretations had worn his patience to
a frayed thread. They wearied him so, day after day, with their speeches of
greatness for the empire. But could they show him aught? No. *None—except*
Belteshazzar. Nebuchadnezzar threw his arms wide and looked at the ceiling

draped with linens and thick embroideries of purple and gold. He pondered the young counselor—he was impressive for one so young. *The Jewish slave was his prize. I would do well to bestow upon him some honor. And there were others within the court who had shown themselves equally trustworthy.* One, he knew, was called Abed-Nego. He would have Ashpenaz send the names of the others.

Nebuchadnezzar rubbed his chin thoughtfully. There would be unpleasant consequences though. *Nergal-Sharezer will seethe with jealousy. . . .* The king folded his hands behind his head. *Let him. His arrogance galls. It may serve to sting him from his complacency, along with the other sheep that tread in his wake, bending my ears with their petty wrangling.* Most times their internal dissension was not a disturbance to him for their scrabbling to gain a foothold to higher glory was kept at a safe enough distance below his throne. Now, with the dread of the dream expunged, he was released to renew his plans for even greater exploits. All in all, what aspiration was left to a king who owned and ruled the breadth of the Assyrian plains, and who had subjugated all foes beyond? What new wonder could a king imagine amidst such splendor as he already possessed?

Nebuchadnezzar bolted upright on the bed, scattering the pillows in his excitement. His eyes flitted as he searched for the mental key that had suddenly sparked an awareness deep within. Had not a God over god's just declared him the head of all nations, supreme and unchallengeable? Was it not worthy of celebration?—a celebration worthy of *my magnificent stature? Of course*—the dream had given him the answer. His chest swelled with pride as he mused over his inspiration.

"It will be magnificent. That smug little Egyptian Pharaoh will grow purple with envy," Nebuchadnezzar gloated. "No, unlike he, I will not be immortalized in common stone for I am a man worthy of the finest." He congratulated himself on his impressive vision. He would charge Nergal-Sharezer with overseeing the construction. *The pompous fellow will be kept out of my hair for a while and he dare not fail me in this. I may not be around to see this last King of whom Belteshazzar has spoken with such animation, but here I am now, and Assyria will be gifted with a marvel beyond compare in the entire world, and in it my glory will rival the dawn!*

Access to the plain of Dura had been restricted by order of the king for over three months. The four friends gathered atop the south-east corner of the city wall, eager to quiz each other on the mystery that had surfaced rather unexpectedly.

"What is Nebuchadnezzar up to now?" Miysha-El questioned. "I thought at first that he prepared chariot races, but now I am not sure . . . ." Hananyah and Azaryah returned blank stares and shrugged. Daniy-El remained silent, looking out over the wall in the direction of Dura. His reserve drew a sideways glance from Miysha-El, and though he did not comment, he watched his friend surreptitiously.

"Thanks to the king's burgeoning love for you, Daniy-El, Nebuchadnezzar has gifted us with honorable places over the provinces. But although this province lies within my ambit, yet I cannot be certain what the king has ordained. I know only that he has commissioned goldsmiths from as far as the northern borders. The forges work day and night but no-one is permitted to commune with the artisans. The plain is secured by more of Arioch's guardsmen than the royal treasuries, or even the regent himself. The treasuries are being emptied of gold with alarming rapidity, whether to buy supplies or to go to the forge I cannot determine. That quantity of gold could buy two winters worth of corn for all Assyria. Nebuchadnezzar must be building something or why keep everyone so far away? Or it may be to enact a ritual of some sort. Nergal-Sharezer surely knows the heart of the matter. I think he blames us for his order's fall from grace and his animosity chokes his reason. He is as tight-lipped as a dead crocodile. He will tell me nothing."

"Nor I," Miysha-El informed them.

There have been no wagons traversing my district," Azaryah said. "If he is indeed constructing something what could it be? And why the terrible secrecy? This unsettles me. What do you think Daniy-El? *Daniy-El!*"

Three pairs of eyes turned in puzzlement to seek the face of their friend who had remained curiously quiet since their meeting.

"What is it Daniy-El?" Hananyah asked, drawing close. "Do you have any idea what the king plans?"

"I—I cannot be certain," Daniy-El replied in hesitation, a frown etching his brow. "I believe I may know but it would be such folly, and—," he paused again, his visage reflecting a myriad of conflicting thoughts. "This is not what I anticipated from giving him his wish. This—*it would be blasphemous!*"

"What Daniy-El? What would be blasphemous in this place that already flaunts its debaucheries?'

"I believe that he means to make an idol—"

"But Assyria has many idols already," Azaryah interjected. "What difference would one more make? And why would he need to empty the treasuries to do it?"

"For the sake—" Daniy-El began.

"Of vanity!" Miysha-El finished, grasping the enormity of Daniy-El's conclusion. They looked at each other, sharing an understanding.

"Yes," Daniy-El confirmed dejectedly.

"So he has an idol? What of it?" Azaryah asked, still bewildered.

"I believe the king may have taken away a slightly different interpretation of the dream than I had meant to convey. How could I have anticipated this? Perhaps I was too excited to read that deeply into his effusive praise. That gleam in his eye. I should have suspected a man of his nature would take such a thing too far. This is the last thing that I would have wanted to happen."

"Are you referring to your interpretation of his dream? You cannot turn a man's heart. The king has many idols in his palace. If he wants to damn himself with one more, we can do little to dissuade him."

"It's not that simple, Hananyah. Consider it. How many carts of gold has the king commissioned so far?"

"Almost one hundred and sixty," Hananyah said. "With at least thirty more to come."

"And the smiths?"

"Seventy-nine," Hananyah informed. Sudden realization popped his eyes wide. "It could not be!" he shouted, as Azaryah simultaneously placed a hand to his own mouth. "An idol made with that much gold would be—"

"*Enormous!*" Azaryah concluded simultaneously, now looking as mortified at the prospect as Daniy-El and Miysha-El had been.

"Too huge to fit in the palace for the private admiration of one king and his household."

"Then he means for Babylon to bow down to a false god."

"I fear he intends the entire realm to bow down to *him* in the form of some contrived deity!" Daniy-El corrected. "In the dream he was only a head of gold but he will see himself having complete dominion without the taint of subdued nations. Nebuchadnezzar is a god in his own eyes and my interpretation of his dream would have served to confirm his own supremacy."

"But no man is above Yahweh. Would He allow this?"

"In everything He has a purpose. We need only trust Him," Daniy-El said.

"Perhaps we are being hasty," Azaryah postulated. "There may yet be some other explanation."

"I doubt it," Hananyah sniffed. "Self-deification would not be beyond such a man. Considering what we know of the king's conceit we shall be fortunate if the thing is not as tall as the palace roof!" he chuckled.

Miysha-El nodded. "We shall know soon enough." Returning to their earlier joviality the trio moved away from Daniy-El who stood gazing off toward the plain. He alone was not laughing.

Weeks later the three Children of Judah stood gaping as they gathered at the edge of the plain of Dura, looking across the expanse to their destination. The invitation from the king had been issued to all palace administrators one month after the friends had ventured the king's purpose. Miysha-El was dismayed that their speculation had not been erroneous after all.

"That thing must be colossal to be seen so clearly at this great distance," Hananyah observed."I was joking about the palace roof but that monstrosity surely must tower above it."

"This bodes ill for us," Azaryah mourned.

"May God have mercy on us this day, for if it is as we surmise, the repercussions will be severe when we decline," Miysha-El said bluntly.

"Perhaps we will not be asked to bow down to it, but merely to attend a feast or something," Hananyah whispered hopefully.

"After all the king's effort," Azaryah snorted. "Not very likely. Sooner or later everyone will be paraded before it to kiss its vile toes or some other insanity."

No-one spoke for several moments as their eyes remained fixed on the gargantuan gold effigy that stood atop a broad pedestal. It dwarfed the large crowd that milled at its feet. They swarmed like ants before the towering image of Nebuchadnezzar, its golden shell blazing like the sun at noonday.

"We will not go down there then," Hananyah stated with grim finality. He shielded his eyes from the glare as the sun moved from behind a cloud, its fiery rays igniting brilliant reflections off the massive statue.

"No," agreed Miysha-El.

"But we will surely be missed among the officials," Azaryah lamented, raising his hands to his head in consternation. "What do you two propose we do then?"

"We shall proceed to the edge of the procession to be certain, though I am persuaded of the outcome. We shall leave the plain with the others from the earlier procession, but on pain of death we shall not bow down," Miysha-El growled. "Praise be to Yahweh that Daniy-El was spared this by his duties in his province." As chief governor the fourth of their number was designated to oversee the palace affairs whilst the princes and other high officials attended the splendidly planned festivities.

The three Children of Judah were nearing the end of the crossing, just as word of the worship ceremony began to spread via excited whispers from those trailing back to the main city. Sufficiently convinced, the Hebrews veered westward on the vast plain, moving to the rear of the swirling multitude.

Whilst they hurried away, all other heads turned in unison as heralds announced the king's arrival at the makeshift, tented entablature located at the center of the buzzing throng. Trumpets blared incessantly during the royal procession. Chariots bearing the princes bore down on the crowd who hastily made way for their passage. Several of the king's aides completed the swarm of satraps who descended on the dais to jostle for position amongst Nebuchadnezzar's encircling attendants.

There were many within the king's purview, but he ignored the fawning administrators and spoke. Pausing to look around, Miysha-El shook his head sadly at their public display that demonstrated an embarrassing lack of self-possession. At that moment, a musical cacophony rose in the distance, signaling the start of the dedication ceremony. Tabrets rang throughout the multitude, drawing attention to the forefront of the proceedings. Young dancers, perfumed in spikenard, wove dexterously through the gathering, drumming the taut skins against their hands and causing the jingles in the small tambourines to clash in unison. The heady scent of the precious ointment spread through the gathering, gripping the onlookers more cruelly than barbed flesh hooks. The thrumming pulse escalated to a feverish pitch. The twirling celebrants held their timbrels aloft as they spun enthusiastically, reveling in the conjured heat of the festivities. The clashing of cymbals was followed by the jaunty intonations of a bevy of priests. Their voices carried on the light breeze that stirred across the plain, however their words were indistinguishable over the buzz of the throng.

"What are they saying?" Azaryah asked, straining to peer above the heads of those before him.

A stiff wind rose up, carrying the insistent cries farther afield and the masses quieted to a dim hush, all assaying to catch the elusive pronouncement.

"Can you hear anything?" Miysha-El questioned Hananyah urgently.

"It seems that the king has issued a command . . . ." He paused, listening intently, before continuing ". . . that at whatever time or place the cornet, sackbut, or dulcimer is heard . . ." He hesitated again, inclining his ear to catch the repeated phrases, ". . . we are to bow down and worship the idol!"

Miysha-El sucked in a sharp intake of breath. "Just as we feared."

Azaryah was disconsolate. "Why would people ascribe wholeheartedly to such blasphemy?"

"You forget that we are no longer in Jerusalem, friend. What matter is this new *god* among so many deceivers?"

Hananyah stilled their conversation with a raised hand. "Here's why," he said, shaking his head in dismay. "There is a penalty."

"What penalty?" Azaryah exclaimed. "He would impose a penalty? Surely not! Is it not enough to be trapped amidst such defilement?"

Hananyah raised his palms beseechingly. "Be still, my friend. He is the king and disobedience is invariably treated harshly."

"What penalty then? Tell us."

Hananyah's shoulders drooped and he released a measured breath. "Any person who refuses to comply with Nebuchadnezzar's command is to be burnt alive. He plans to—"

"Are you certain," Miysha-El interrupted, frowning in disbelief. "Burnt alive?"

Hananyah's grim silence was his confirmation.

"Well," Miysha-El said, his visage becoming as intense as Hananyah had ever seen it, "the King shall need to stoke his furnace, for I shall never commit this abomination."

"Indeed. Nor I!" Hananyah joined resolutely. "What do you say Azaryah?"

The two turned to regard Azaryah who stood rigid, eyes staring fixedly at the image that towered before them. "We have been through so much already. And the judgments of the king are assuredly harsh, but the reckoning of Yahweh will be even more so if we were to capitulate now. I too say no!"

"We are agreed then," Miysha-El said firmly. "Good. We know not what shall result from this decree, but our unity will give us strength, and Yahweh will comfort us whatever the outcome. Let us now go quickly before this becomes a common peddler's show." His companions nodded in agreement, and they turned to traverse the plain that now burned like Nibshan of the Engedi. The small group hurried away past the storage flaxen tents bounding the provisional worship court. By half-light the friends had passed by the last of the festivities and were well on their way to the palace.

Their hasty withdrawal was observed from the murky depths of a tent bearing a cache of *asis* for the post-worship festivities to toast the new god. The man receded further behind a crate stacked with large clay flagons, eager not to be seen as he watched keenly to discern their intent. After they had hastened by he waited a few moments more before emerging into the light. He squinted in the direction of the departing companions, then, unbeknownst to the three friends they were shadowed for half of a mile by the cloaked figure. After the sun had crested in the sky and passed its zenith, the pursuing form dissolved into the teeming mass of devotees, many yet arriving in a constant stream. A satisfied smirk crossed the man's lips and he curled his fist in triumph. *It will be so simple,* he thought. *So very simple.*

"At last! We have what we need," Nergal-Sharezer rejoiced. He smiled maliciously, already savoring the victory. "And caught in a snare of their own making besides. *Public defiance?*"

He would wager anything on the Hebrews's stubborn adherence to some futile faith in their unseen God. *The self-righteous slaves will never capitulate, even if afforded the opportunity.*

"I congratulate you Strobos. You have outdone yourself this time. The king will be unable to contain his temper when he discovers that his beloved trio has acted against him. I know him well. He shall be driven beyond even the rage that consumed him when the Order was unable to decipher his visions. He will not abide this infraction, regardless of how useful these Hebrews may be to him. Nebuchadnezzar's pride is often greater than his good sense."

He rubbed his hands together, and then focused his gaze upon the artful young man whose aid was both a blessing and a bane. Strobos was to be lauded for his sharp wits and disdain for danger. Those traits allowed him to seek avenues that others would cast aside as unmerited. His latest proposal may prove to be the most useful that he had conceived. '*He was born to be a spy*', Rab-Mag had often said. Yet Strobos had shown a distinct dissatisfaction with his life in the shadows. Nergal-Sharezer knew all too well that the man wished to be recognized amongst their number—to be a Master of the Arts, but his true talents lay elsewhere—in absolute subversion, and Nergal-Sharezer used all his powers to persuade the apprentice to focus on his strengths and let the gods honor him accordingly. He was aware, nevertheless that despite Strobos's current congeniality and submissive demeanor, an untamed weasel was dangerous to befriend, and treacherous at best. Still, they needed him, and Strobos understood this all too well. He had thus improved his station over the years since he had come to their notice as a boy. Nergal-Sharezer knew that his value was unmistakable to men whose higher breeding made them unaccustomed to such levels of subterfuge. Strobos had progressively allied himself with officials of every rank, offering his services privately as he wished. Yet Strobos was wise enough not to pit himself against the Order, for it was by their hands that he would ultimately be elevated to the position of honor that he so craved. Without them, Strobos was nothing, for he could not cast spells, nor could he read the stars, nor mix virulent portions, but his dexterity at sedition was unparalleled and oftimes proved to be more potent a tool than all their wizardry and craft. Such a trait was precisely what the Order required in order to rid themselves of the menace that had sprung up from the slave quarter, of all places. Who could have foretold that bonded men would rise so highly in the king's favor, to the point where they could threaten entrenched alliances and invaluable coalitions that had taken the Order decades to establish? Nergal-Sharezer spat upon their vaunted chastity. *Who were they but slaves at their master's pleasure?* Yes, he would use Strobos whilst the man's eyes glittered in anticipation of the silver and gold-trimmed cloak, a revered emblem of power throughout the kingdom. Strobos's lust was often only evident in his eyes, which Nergal-Sharezer had learnt to read. The creature that gnawed with fangs of fire within that young man would not be assuaged unless he was granted some prize. . . . And it was time now to dispense some reward, lest the beast break forth and ruin their hard-earned security. He and his counterparts would agree a suitable recompense for Strobos's services. Another rung on the ladder should suffice for now. Strobos could at last ditch the title of apprentice and become a lord within the court. He would see to it personally, also ensuring that his services remained within reach of the Order.

There were so many plans to be made, but at last, after the years of unwanted scrutiny and meddling in the affairs of the high officials and princes, he could see a glow of light emanating just beyond his reach, and optimism once again blossomed within his bosom.

"One small matter to which I need now attend with the king, and our problems will all but disappear," Nergal-Sharezer surmised, drawing a vigorous nod from Strobos.

In a veil of smoke, the magi thought to himself, and laughed heartily. *Smoke and ashes.*

He shared his mirth with his younger companion who, inferring the source of his glee, joined freely in the banter.

"As if by magic," Strobos jibed, twirling his hand in affectation.

The magi ignored the taunt. "Your kind of 'sorcery' has its place, I will admit. You will be rewarded of course," Nergal-Sharezer assured.

"Of course," Strobos said, suddenly growing somber.

"We shall discuss the matter further, *after* I have visited with the king." Nergal-Sharezer rose to leave and moved to usher Strobos out.

Strobos resisted the urging hand that pressed insistently upon his back. He turned to face the magician. "I will be waiting," he said quietly.

"I am sure," Nergal-Sharezer replied. "After you," he offered, gesturing to the open door.

This time Strobos exited, and moved casually down the corridor without offering further comment.

The magician huffed and closed the door to his chamber, making a check of the lock before moving on. Caution was always mandatory with the likes of Strobos about. He made a mental note to search out another to watch his back. Matters were coming to a head, and this course would be wise, he decided. Magical powers or no, he still needed to sleep, and flesh had never been known to turn back the bite of steel.

5

Ensnared

. . . Hearken thou to the supplication of thy servant . . .

- King Solomon

The king's court reverberated with a boisterous trammel akin to the hay market. Miysha-El could sense the raging animosity emanating from the sequestered court attendees even before they entered the brass-paneled doors. He suspected that their peremptory summons to the king's audience hall was not for the purpose of dispensing good graces. His gut roiled, but he calmed the unsettling sensation with a silent prayer. *Defend us. O God, from the wrath of this enemy to whom we are given in service.* He straightened his back and led the way forward, flanked by Hananyah and Azaryah, who, in turn, were bracketed tightly by six soldiers.

"Meshach!" The shout arrested everyone in the room and the fracas subsided quickly in deference to their sovereign. At the sound of his Babylonian name Miysha-El raised his gaze to the top of the dais where the king sat, leaning forward with his hands braced on his knees. Nebuchadnezzar's glower scythed across the room, bringing Miysha-El up short for a moment. He overcame the stutter in his step and returned an even look to their sovereign who watched them approach with a cold fire in his eyes. He surveyed the three before him.

"Shadrach! Meshach! Abed-Nego!" Nebuchadnezzar's accustomed elation at seeing the trio, whom he generally had held in high esteem since their elevation in his court and their ensuing exemplary service, now evaporated like a crust of snow at noonday. Their flawless administration over the years, and even-tempered, congenial personalities, had gradually endeared them to the king. However, his sense of amicability was being scoured away by the fires of pride that were presently inflaming his anger.

"Meshach. Is it true?" he asked menacingly, his tone imbued with no hint of the usual friendliness upon their decidedly pleasant meetings and regular consultations over provincial affairs. "Is it true that you will not serve my gods, nor worship the golden image which I have set up?"

There was no doubt that the king had interpreted their secretly reported abstinence from the worship on the plain as a sudden betrayal of the trust he had placed in them. *"Is it true?"*

Miysha-El's eyes flickered to Nergal-Sharezer who stood with the parade of governors, a smug smile creasing his hard mouth. *This brood of adders*, Miysha-El thought. *Poison to the kingdom.* The king's fury flowed from the dais like a dense, writhing vapor that coalesced with the sullen loathing of the Order masters to form a palpable cover of hatred that lay over the three, oppressive and pregnant with malice. It rested upon them like an imposed burden upon a colt. Miysha-El recognized its weight and rolled it off onto his Lord.

"Defend us," he whispered again softly.

Word of their remonstrance had spread like a sore on a leper. For three days the palace halls had hummed with their supposed malfeasance until at last the king had been told, the whispers of his servants priming his curiosity and exposing him like prey to the insidious gossip. The revelation of his servants' actions had released a storm within him, such that he had reeled with its force. Ashpenaz, prince of the eunuchs, had warned them of the impending cataclysm which would descend mercilessly upon them. He told of a private audience that had been requested by the king's chief advisers. The account was garnered by a servant who had been polishing the king's bracelets in an inner chamber when the audience had been called. The words of the virulent discussion between Nergal-Sharezer, the king, and several other princes, was siphoned to Ashpenaz, who, for the love he bore the young Hebrews, had divulged to them the nature of the clandestine exchange within the hour after the encounter. Nebuchadnezzar had gone to his throne room before calling upon the three to attend him there in the presence of their accusers. Acid glares cast from the rows of courtiers sought to bite into their flesh, but were rebuffed by the calm that now sheathed these Children of Judah in a cocoon of peace. Many faces looked back in puzzlement, baffled by the calm expressions of the accused, their eyes reflecting a poise that went beyond a superficial veneer. The disapproving stares were of no consequence to Miysha-El, nor his brethren, for beyond the presence of their Lord, the hand placed the seal upon the writ was the only one that ultimately mattered within these walls.

The drone of displeasure emanating from the assembled nobles reminded Miysha-El of the hornets that swarmed the blossoms of the fields before harvest-time, scattering man and beast alike from their path. However, he did not regard their trivial jealousies that bred increasing disharmony among the ranks of masters. The dissension caused each to lose sight of his call to service, spawning instead a destructive rulership. The governors seized every opportunity to exploit the king's authority to the advancement of their private causes. There was much power to be gained, whether by vested authority or mischievous contrivance. Nergal-Sharezer had become adept at recognizing those selfish traits ingrained in the king that could be used to the advantage of the Order.

Miysha-El exhaled slowly. No. Little could be achieved by soliciting the king's good grace, for it had long been sacrificed on the altar of treachery. It would be rare for Nebuchadnezzar to relent. Furthermore, experience had taught that the king, in his pride and arrogance, oft foreswore clemency, for it intimated deference toward the wishes of another and somehow ate at his image of preeminence. In this den of adders, each allowance he granted would be targeted as a weakness, and plans would assuredly be made to sink their fangs into the heart of his absolute power. Nebuchadnezzar's continued strength lay in his unchallengeable dominion. Would their king even consider capitulation? The king normally allowed not even a hair's breadth for a usurper to slither through. Could today be any different?

Miysha-El shook his head. It was unlikely. *Nebuchadnezzar may not be prepared to relent, but neither are the Children of Judah!*

Nebuchadnezzar watched the three approach his throne at a measured pace that bespoke a peculiar confidence. *What have these traitors to be confident about?* A roiling fire churned in his chest, searing a scorching path up his throat. It was his wrath. He knew and yet he could not restrain its vile anger. His vision was hazed with crimson and he could see no-one other than the men who now stood before him with an air of impenitence. *Had they indeed refused his command? Surely not these three!* Nebuchadnezzar fought to suppress the writhing flames that clawed to consume him for their destructive purpose. He had subdued enemies, crushed nations and exterminated rivals at his whim. Was he then to be defied by slaves? *A misunderstanding perhaps?*

Nebuchadnezzar struggled to control the fury, which threatened to erupt, subsuming his will in its path. Each battle that he waged within himself against these onslaughts of rage became more and more difficult to contain. When an army stood before him, he could unleash himself into the all-consuming virulence of war. Now he was here, with these once loyal servants before him, and he could scarcely contain the force of its vehemence. It seemed unconscionable that these men would have gainsaid his order in so monumental a fashion. *Had not the penalty been spread abroad by the city criers and heralds by the score? Had not scrolls been erected in the meeting places? How then could they not have obeyed? No man would risk his life for such a simple matter! Would he?*

Nebuchadnezzar peered at the stoic faces being escorted toward him by the armed phalanx. Perhaps they had been challenged by Nergal-Sharezer, for it was no secret that the advisor was disliked by most, and often stood opposed in his court. Nebuchadnezzar inhaled a slow, deliberate breath, allowing the cool draught to bathe him. His anger did not abate, but he was no longer perched on the edge of the chasm that yawned beneath the shaky platform of his emotions, willing him to surrender himself to its rapacious maw. He could feel a presence emanating within —terrible, yet enticing. Before his spate of conquests it had been easier to resist the pressing urge to submit to its raw force, but now, after the harshness of war and the gouts of blood that were spewed alongside rivers of broken, subjugated peoples he could no longer quell the seduction to violence at will. Sometimes it took him as it bid, and he too was washed away amidst the fiery scourge. Today his will had not been claimed completely by the ravening darkness, for these men he faced were among his most trusted counselors, and he would deign to stay his hand until he knew the truth. Their answer would come shortly, and then . . . .

The men finally reached the dais that was the glory of the long hall. Presented now by rough hands they did not cower. They were princely in stature, these men of Judah. What misfortune if the allegation brought against them was verified by their lips. At one time Nebuchadnezzar was certain that he would have gained the truth, for prevarication was an anathema to these counselors whose measure of faithfulness seemed only to be exceeded by that of their kinsman Daniy-El. Many within the court coveted the skill of the four in matters of counsel and governance. They were unmatched in the affairs of the kingdom. Yet there was this overriding accusation of treachery!

Nevertheless, there was a surer way to determine the verity of the claim. The king signaled tersely to a small group of men huddled hesitantly in the corner of the hall. Eyes that had been riveted on the dais turned as the summoned musicians shuffled forward, instruments in hand and gazes lowered. The king gestured impatiently for them to draw closer, eager to have done with this escapade. He glowered, annoyed by their tentative approach. They moved with greater alacrity as he waved them forward to stand beside his throne.

"Is it true?" the king bellowed without preamble, shattering the suffocating silence that had been draped over the assembly as Shadrach, Meshach and Abed-Nego attained the petitioner's vantage. "Do you not serve my gods, nor worship the image of gold that I have set up?" He forged on without awaiting an answer to the charge. "If you are ready," he said, leaning forward, his voice becoming dangerously low, "when you hear the sound of the instruments, to fall and worship the image I have made . . . Well . . . ." The king spread his hands magnanimously, his face breaking suddenly into an generous smile that overflowed with providential grace. He took in the congregated officials some of whom chuckled. A few, more wary of the king's shifting moods, waited with lips folded and eyes narrowed as they gauged the king's suddenly expansive mood. Nebuchadnezzar was oft known to be capricious in the execution of his judgment and the axe may as easily fall on the neck of any attendee who displeased him. The wise took care not to unveil their opinions too freely in his presence.

"But if," he continued, his tone acquiring a razor sharp edge, "you do not worship . . ." The king shrugged then let his hands flop to his sides in a decisive condemnation. "You will be cast this *same* hour into a burning furnace!" He descended the dais wiggling a cautionary finger as he held Miysha-El's gaze. "This same hour," he warned, standing a span from the accused whose eyes did not waver in regard of his king. The expression that was carved on Miysha-El's brow was one of resignation, and sorrow. "And who is that God that shall deliver you out of my hands?" Nebuchadnezzar asked quietly, his voice sneering. He continued to stare into Miysha-El's eyes, which radiated an unearthly calm that discomfited the king. *Did they believe, perhaps, that they would be saved by this omnipotent God of whom he heard whispers?* He pursed his lips, turning away with a sudden frown as his thoughts churned. He shook his head firmly and sniffed. *It does not matter.* He stomped back to his throne, taking time to settle his robes about him, hoping to return a measure of the discomfort that he now felt in their presence. The sentence would remain in abeyance until his word was given. He had heard much of their God. Some God he was, to abandon them to their enemy. *Even the God of the Hebrews admits that I, Nebuchadnezzar, am the greatest king throughout the nations.* Here, it was the king's will that was sacrosanct. He gave a crisp nod and the musicians struck up a loud cacophony of sound, the coronet shrill above the clanging tabrets. Only a few dissonant notes had escaped into the air before Miysha-El extended his hand toward the king, requesting leave to speak. The king's eyebrows climbed in surprise. *He aims to make a plea? What speech could the counselor hope to make that would dissuade me in this?* He paused briefly before offering a perfunctory flip of his hand in acquiescence. *Very well.* The sounds that fractured the air ceased as abruptly as they had begun.

"Nebuchadnezzar." Miysha-El addressed him with a respectful bow. The corners of the king's mouth quirked as he ventured that some display would be forthcoming. He leaned closer, listening intently. "Abed-Nego, Shadrach, and myself, we do not need to consider how we should answer you for there can be no discussion on a matter such as this."

Of course, Nebuchadnezzar reflected. *It was always prudent for officials to present a show of unity before submitting to his hand. It was necessary to capitulate diplomatically lest their authority be completely eroded as dust around their sandals. One must salvage one's pride if one can,* he acceded. This was as it should be. He did not relish stripping a man totally of his honor, as long as he demonstrated proper obeisance and sought not to elevate anyone above the king's supreme station. He gave a wan smile. *Contrary to the pervasive belief of his ultimate cruelty, he was not an unmerciful king. On occasion he could be*—the king made a mental search for an apt description—*munificent. Yes. Munificent.* Today would be further proof of his kingship. He flipped his fingers casually, signaling that Miysha-El should go on.

"If it be so," Miysha-El affirmed, his voice echoing in the still chamber, "Our God whom we serve is able to deliver us from the furnace, and will deliver us out of thy hand, O King." At Miysha-El's declaration, a resonant gasp rippled throughout the hall. This was not the capitulation that all had expected. All that is, except Nergal-Sharezer who looked strangely smug. Rage pulsed beneath the king's skin, clamoring to be released. He struggled for control but knew already that he was fighting a losing battle for the force flared inexorably across his chest.

"But if not, be it known to thee, O king, that we will *not* serve thy gods, nor worship the image of gold which you have set up." Miysha-El concluded placidly. His brethren both shook their heads, showing solidarity and negating the possibility of misconstrued intent amongst themselves. The writhing fury cascaded into a roaring pit in the king's stomach before erupting within his limbs. A crimson haze eclipsed his vision as he surged to his feet, eyes wild with instantaneous hatred. No hint of the benevolent hope remained to fetter his wrath. Inflamed beyond his slim tolerance, he screamed for the royal guardsmen, whose muscled bulk descended on the dais within moments. Bracelet-encrusted arms closed around their captives, whose cries were muffled by sword-calloused hands. Arms tightened viciously about the limbs of their helpless victims who were trussed with ropes and herded from the audience hall like cattle to the slaughter post.

Nebuchadnezzar put a hand to his sweat-beaded brow and stumbled to his seat. His head throbbed agonizingly. *It will pass. It will pass.* He rubbed his temples but the searing heat within his bosom did not abate. It would be several hours before he could assuage the fiery beast that demanded recompense for its power. Was it the Children of Judah, or himself, who had received the penalty of the damned? A few more hours, then he would escape his own private inferno.

6

The Damned

O Lord God, to whom vengeance belongeth;
O God to whom vengeance belongeth, show thyself!

- King David

Oil-drenched wood popped and spat, adding to the malice of the building conflagration. Arioch grieved for the Children of Judah. *Have they been spared the blade, only to be condemned to this?* Where indeed was the God that they so revered and cherished? Why would such men be wasted to the fire? How many more would be sacrificed to the king's insatiable pride? Nebuchadnezzar would never relent now. His passion for vengeance ran hotter than these flames that licked the walls of the kiln, hungry to devour all that they touched. As the bite of the heat gnawed at his skin, Arioch moved back hastily. Despite his formidable reputation in the guard, he was not strong enough to defy the king and to be abandoned to a fate such as this —a living sacrifice. *No.* The fumes from the curling wood stifled the air of the yard, as great gouts of oily smoke spewed from the depths of the blazing chamber. Today the offal and leavings from the royal kitchens would need to be burnt elsewhere. A more vile purpose was now assigned to the deadly hearth.

Arioch covered his nose, yet the disgorged billows grated at his nostrils, burning his lungs with the distasteful odor of charred cedar timbers. He shielded his eyes from the intense glare.

Is this necessary? he immediately wondered.

The king had ordered the fires to be made higher. Already the clawing beasts of flame climbed eagerly above the wall of their confinement. Armed soldiers now hauled two more carts of denser firewood toward the furnace. *Hopefully their deaths will be the quicker for it.* He did not desire them to suffer. He wished fervently that he could devise a way of escape for the Hebrews, but none came to him. It was not that he was a coward, but he was a shrewd man who rather valued his life. Hence he preferred not to draw the king's attention beyond the realm of his duties.

Hungry tongues licked skyward, tasting the air and gaining strength. Arioch glanced to the low parapet where the king stood watching. An explosive burst from the core threw up ash-laden smoke, and Nebuchadnezzar nodded in grim satisfaction. The king looked directly at him, waving his approval, before moving away from the roof's edge. Arioch gladly broke his gaze and moved to instruct the soldiers who were piling stray tinder on the loading carts. As the task neared completion, the king reappeared in an alcove opposite the portal to the furnace. Several governors trooped in his wake, chattering excitedly like children gawking at the court games.

"Scavengers," Arioch snarled. He despised the conniving lot, but they cowered under the king's ambit, taking advantage of his protective shield.

"Proceed," Nebuchadnezzar shouted to his Chief of the Executioners.

Arioch responded unhurriedly, hoping nevertheless that the king may offer some miraculous dispensation of mercy. However, Nebuchadnezzar stood with his arms crossed resolutely before him. After a slow exhalation, Arioch withdrew to summon the prison guard who had cloistered their captives in a small chamber west of the royal kitchens. The brawny guardsman was compelled to bend his neck to enter the low doorway. He motioned to the sentries outside and closed the door fractionally.

"Miysha-El," he implored, palms upturned in despair mixed with frustration.

"I cannot shield you from this. Will you not have a change of heart? It would be a small matter . . . and your God, if he is so bountiful, would surely forgive." His eyes beseeched a change of heart. "What can be done at this hour? Will you not bow to the king's wishes? No-one can redeem you from the king's hand otherwise. I even approached Nergal-Sharezer, but he gave me no hearing. I am sorry, Miysha-El. Truly, I . . . ." He broke off, crestfallen.

"Arioch," Miysha-El said gently. "We have made this choice, not the king."

"But why?" he said through gritted teeth, glancing backward to the hall outside the door. He lowered his voice further. "There is no need!" Arioch insisted, somewhat angrily.

"There *is* a need, Arioch. A man cannot feign friendship with a viper. If you eat its meat, and follow in its tracks, all the while crawling upon your belly, what will separate you? Who then remains to oppose the fear of its tyranny, or to crush the viperous head under his heel? A man must stand against the works of evil while standing for that which is righteous, or else what measure is there of his mettle? He will not be blameless before God."

Arioch's eyes fell to the floor. "What can I say Miysha-El? This is the life that we know. What use would your God be to any of us at the last if we must all die . . . . Especially like that." His eyes flickered in the direction of the yard where the Hebrew's fate awaited.

"'Tis a pity, Arioch. You miss the best part of life—to know the faithfulness of a sovereign who suffers not from the frailties and pettiness of mortal men, nor is deaf, as are the images of wood and stone. Whatever the outcome, Arioch, we go not to receive a sentence of death, but to embrace true *Life!*"

Arioch shook his head. "Your manner of reasoning baffles me, friend. It is unfathomable. These things . . . . This . . . this *life* that you speak of . . . ." His eyes wandered skyward as if searching for answers. -Such things are beyond my reckoning. Nevertheless, your wisdom has proven infallible these many seasons, and so I shall trust that you have chosen according to the ways of your people."

Miysha-El nodded, giving Arioch a smile of reassurance, but it did nothing to ease the wrenching pain in his chest. A brawny soldier ducked through the doorway into the dim light of the room.

"The king awaits," he urged Arioch, who searched Miysha-El's eyes for the last time. He looked also to Hananyah and Azaryah but saw no glimmer of hesitancy in either of them.

"So be it," he said finally, motioning for the guard to usher the Children of Judah into the harsh light of the courtyard beyond. The three paused for a moment, blinking to adjust to the light's intensity and the acrid stench from the oily smoke that now pervaded the air.

"Go on!" a soldier said, pushing the small group along.

"Move. *Move!*"

Fearful of the king's displeasure should they be tardy in answering his summons, the soldiers jostled them forward. One prodded Azaryah forcefully. He tumbled the fettered Hebrew into the dust, and then aimed a kick of aggravation when he realized that his charge had fallen.

Arioch barked an order. "Nebuzaradan, desist". The captain could at times be similarly ruthless with his enemies, but these were not such.

The grouping resumed its ill-fated walk. They rounded the corner of the protruding out buildings that were banked against the wall to the yard. The mound that encased the blazing kiln rose ominously before them, its centre still belching ash and dense smoke as the last of the clay jars of camphor that sat within exploded angrily. Sweat burst from temples only to be blasted to vapor by the searing wind off the fires.

Arioch paused, casting his eyes up the fateful rise. It seemed now that the king had bid them fashion his own 'fire-mountain' akin to those in distant lands that spewed streams of molten fire and consumed all flesh within their path.

Arioch shook his head slowly, and then bit his lip before calling for two more guards. He was compelled to shout in order to be heard over the roar of the flames. Seething embers cracked to reveal radiant centers—deadly, yet wondrous in their intensity. Some spilled through the lone opening on one side of the pit as though seeking escape from the hell of their own making. The group of men stood amazed, for at more than sixty paces away the heat was nearly unbearable. Dry, hot wind churned around the banked walls, raising a glimmering mirage roundabout. The guardsmen cast about in uncertainty, and several awkward moments passed as they deliberated the peculiar predicament. It was evident to all in the grouping that to carry out the king's dictate could well mean death for the soldiers involved.

Arioch felt a surge of hope. He crossed the court to address the king.

"My lord," he greeted with a bow.

"Why is everyone standing around?" the king questioned in annoyance.

"Arioch cleared his throat. "The fire, my lord. It is too hot and—"

"Of course it is too hot!" Nebuchadnezzar exclaimed, growing further enraged. "It is a *furnace*!" The king stared at Arioch, seeming to find the delay incredulous.

Nevertheless Arioch persevered. "Yes, truly my lord. But the heat! My lord, no-one is able to draw nigh unto it. Even now the fire sears your flesh. I would lose good men in the attempt, my lord." He paused, looking back toward the kiln. "Meshach, Shadrach, and Abed-Nego, my lord—they will not simply walk into the fire." Arioch fought to maintain an impassionate flatness to his voice.

The king's eyes bulged, exasperation contorting his features. "You *will* throw them in!" Nebuchadnezzar growled through clenched teeth, his chest heaving. The king glared at Arioch who remained immobile. Arioch's jaw clenched, and then unclenched. The king continued to hold his gaze that now sparked with defiance. His will, however, could not surpass the dominant power wielded by his liege. He bowed and spun on his heels, and then walked stiffly back to the cone of heat.

"The king *orders* us to proceed." Arioch said, his tone gravelly with distress. "We are commanded to throw the prisoners in," he added, unable, at first, to meet Miysha-El's eyes. Assigning men to hoist each of the three fettered Hebrews aloft, he moved closer to Miysha-El. "May your God receive you," he said quietly. Miysha-El did not reply, but nodded slightly as he was heaved off his feet by muscular arms. Now, the king's order was not only for three men to be consigned to the fire, but potentially another six in the execution of their duty.

Nebuzaradan took stock of the task delegated to his troop. He motioned for the sixth guardsman, a soldier with scarcely a growth of beard, to step back into the rank. The young man protested in defense of his duty.

"Stand aside, son. I can bear this one alone," he said, indicating Azaryah, who was of smaller stature than his brethren. "We may yet make it," he said with a burst of optimism that injected a glimmer of hope in the men. "After a lifetime of battles together we shall not balk at the last. We serve our king. Come men. On my count we shall go. At nine paces up the mound, we shall cast them in. Fall back at once—if you can."

The guardsmen braced themselves upon Nebuzaradan's mark to make the surge forward. Within moments they charged away at a run, pausing mere instants to complete the lunge that hurled the men of Judah into the cauldron. Even as the Hebrews plunged into the seething wall of fire, the soldiers stumbled backward on the rise, wheeling away from the blaze. Arioch's prayer for their survival was crushed abruptly as a hand of flame snaked out from the core, wrapping wrathful, red-gold fingers about his men. The malice of the fire incinerated flesh and bone. Charred bodies grappled for life, but no-one could be swift enough to draw them to safety away from the torment that consumed them in a twinkling. The young soldier stared in horror as smoky tendrils wove skyward from his companions' broad backs, as leather and armor peeled and cracked. The stench of their cauterized flesh made him retch.

"They almost made it," Arioch ground out, angry at the sudden turn of fate that had snatched the soldiers so maliciously. From the corner of his vision, Arioch glimpsed Nebuchadnezzar as he watched impassively from his safe vantage— the king's face matched the stoniness of the hills beyond Borsippa. Five men had just died, and toward what end? Arioch suppressed a wave of indignation, returning his gaze to the burnt sacrifices that were made up of human lives, each a galling testament to a king's callousness and pride. What good would it do to take umbrage against his king? A soldier could too easily be eaten up by resentment and bitterness, should he allow the harshness of life to overwhelm him, and Arioch would rather not be consumed by empty hatred. Sufficient were the trials of each hour keeping his men in line. Arioch retreated several paces from the terrible heat as his mind turned, of necessity, to delegating replacements for the guards who now lay dead. He had lost able men, yet the king would need protection, lest Nebuchadnezzar's willful pique be exchanged for the scheming evil of the likes of Nergal-Sharezer. Tomorrow he would need to—

Arioch was jolted from his contemplation by an intense cry of fear. He spun, weapon in hand, searching for the source of the panicked shout. To his astonishment, the king was bolting toward him, gesturing frantically at the kiln. The king's words were at first indistinguishable. Arioch cast about in incomprehension, seeking to discern the cause of the king's agitation, but he saw nothing to alarm him. The king gained his side, still shouting. Two of his closest advisors followed closely upon his heels. Many of the others stayed back from the heat, including Nergal-Sharezer.

"Did we not throw three men into the fire?" he questioned, his voice trembling in agitation as he stared wide-eyed into the blaze.

"True, O king," chorused the counselors at his side.

Arioch stood aside, perplexed. *What deed could have drawn his sovereign's ire now?*

The king ignored the voices about him that murmured in confusion. He moved closer to the furnace, straining to distinguish some movement within the portal. However, he quickly stepped back as the heat flicked at his robes, warping the silk brocade and causing him to wince. Arioch regarded him with bewilderment, before turning to see where the king was pointing. "How then can this be?"

As the guardsman apprehended the king's revelation, his jaw dropped. The sword fell from his limp fingers and clattered noisily on the stones. His heart sang with joy, melting away any vestige of resentment yet cowering within his heart. *The God of the Hebrews be praised!*

"What is it, Sarsechim-Nebo?" Nergal-Sharezer demanded of the king's cupbearer. "What so interests the king? What could he possibly be pointing at?"

"How can I say, Nergal? Who ever knows what ails the king?" the cupbearer responded. "The fire is too bright for me to make anything out. Why do you not go inquire of him?" he quipped. "Why ask of me? If the king is agitated, it is the magicians' duty to placate him is it not? Go risk your own head," Sarsechim snorted.

Nergal-Sharezer gave him an annoyed look, and then focused his attention once again on Nebuchadnezzar, who continued an animated exchange with the Captain of the Guard. He sniffed in derision as he watched, thoughts churning all the while in his head. The foolish fellow had even come seeking him to petition the king for the lives of the Children of Judah. He had turned the guardsman away summarily. *Fool! A fool too, the king, for ever giving those Hebrews such power. Still, the king was finally exposed to their treachery for himself, and he had acted fittingly, for once. Those men certainly had no rightful place amidst rulers and true Chaldean nobility. No, not slaves. Furthermore, it was an insult to the Order, to have appointed the dream-reader Daniy-El to such a supreme post —* Chief of Governors. Nergal-Sharezer spat. Look what had become of the king's trust. Perhaps they had used some magic of their own to coerce the king. Yet Nergal-Sharezer could detect none of the usual powers at work. The astrologers had assured him of the day, and he had gently swayed Nebuchadnezzar into place as true as the stars alignment. And everything had gone so well, until now.

"The guardsman comes," Sarsechim-Nebo announced brightly.

"I can see that for myself," Nergal-Sharezer huffed. "The man looks too smug for my liking," he observed, eyes narrowing. *Indeed. What has Arioch to be smug about?*

After Arioch had approached, he bowed stiffly. He looked squarely at the magician and smiled broadly. "The king bids you all to approach," Arioch declared, his tone surprisingly merry, considering the events of the last hour. He moved aside deftly as the impatient grouping bustled eagerly toward the king. Nergal-Sharezer hurried to the fore of the gathering. Though leery of the scorching air swirling roundabout, none turned aside for the sake of appearances.

"Do you see?" Nebuchadnezzar asked animatedly, not waiting for the rulers to settle beside him.

Nergal-Sharezer mopped his brow and then squinted toward the opening in the furnace. His throat constricted, squelching a gasp that fought to be released. *Apparitions, surely? It must be. It was not unknown for those consigned to oblivion by the god Bel-Merodach to reappear. But*—He stared again at the four shapes traversing the raging conflagration, heedless of its power. *Four men? And the fourth was splendidly radiant! How could it be? Unless*—He placed a shaking hand over his mouth, his mind racing to comprehend the vision. The stunned silence of the assembly was broken only by the crackle of the flames.

"Do you see? *Do you see?*" Nebuchadnezzar repeated in excitement, his arms waving.

"Shadrach, Meshach, Abed-Nego—you servants of the Most High God, come out!" the king called loudly.

Nergal-Sharezer wrung his hands, fearing to see whether any would appear in the broad door. His disquiet infected the other governors beside him, and they fidgeted in apprehension. None wished to contemplate the outcome of the events unfolding. Nergal-Sharezer backed away as figures emerged from the blaze. As the unfulfilled flames slid back to release the shielded prey that they could not devour, Nergal-Sharezer pushed through his comrades and rushed from the courtyard. His blood ran cold, for he knew the heart of his king—and when the aftermath of the day had subsided, *the king would not be pleased.*

Miysha-El, Azaryah and Hananyah emerged from the smoke with broad smiles of relief. They put a distance of several dozen cubits between themselves and the fiery enclave before coming to stand before the king. Nebuchadnezzar hurried forward as they escaped the reach of the spitting flames. He touched Azaryah cloak reverently, gathering a fold of cloth and rubbing it softly between his thumb and forefinger. There was no unusual warmth to weave. A gust of wind threw combusted ash skyward, reminding the onlookers that the ferocity of the inferno had not been subdued. Oblivious to the oddity of his actions, the king leaned in to sniff the edge of Azaryah's garment. He recoiled with amazement, then leaned in again, incredulity forcing his brows to rise once more. No hint of smoke yet clung to the patterned fiber. The king reached out to touch the young man's hair, shaking his head in wonder—not a strand had been singed in the blaze. The ropes that had bound their hands were burnt away, and though red welts from the lashed cords yet marred their wrists, there was no evidence of blisters upon their otherwise flawless skin.

Princes and counselors crowded in behind the king, faces showing the pall of disbelief. Some muttered curses, appalled by the salvation of the men of Judah. Nebuchadnezzar noted their growing consternation at the irrefutable evidence of a Supreme Hand at work. The king clasped his hands, still nodding as he drew conclusions from the vindication wrought on behalf of the steadfast servants of their one God.—*"If it be so, our God will deliver us,"* they had said.

"How did you know?" the king asked, shifting his rapt attention now to Miysha-El.

"We did not, my lord," Miysha-El corrected.

"Nor would it have mattered to us," Hananyah rejoined, giving a matter-of-fact shrug.

The king twirled suddenly to face his palace officials. He threw his hands elatedly into the air. "Blessed be the God of Shadrach, Meshach, and Abed-

Nego," he hailed vociferously, "who sent his angels and delivered His servants that trusted in Him and have thus changed my mind."

The king touched his lips, looking toward the ground in thought. When he raised his head his eyes were as resolute as a preying lion's.

"I make a decree," he declared, searching the faces of the rulers before him. He noticed Nergal-Sharezer's conspicuous absence and sniffed. He needed to silence their insidious plotting. Even now, some cast anxious glances about for the king's proclamations were always sealed in blood. A red veil swarmed before his eyes as he contemplated any defiance from those who now hung back, nervously awaiting his words. "Every race, nation, and language, which speaks anything amiss, against the God of Shadrach, Meshach and Abed-Nego, shall be cut in pieces!" The king slashed savagely with a rigid hand. "And their houses shall be transformed into dunghills, because there is no other God that can deliver like this." He extended his hands to the men of Judah. "None!"

"I should not have doubted you," Arioch said, grinning sheepishly.

Miysha-El returned an easy smile. "Nevertheless, the outcome was not in our hands, my friend."

"Still," Arioch said, undeterred. "Whenever have you known the king to reverse a decision that he has made? When?"

"The statutes cannot be reversed. One may still be called upon to bow before the statue, as long as you say nothing against Yahweh. You Chaldeans serve many gods. Our God may yet be as important as another tassel to fringe the king's elaborate cloak."

"Ah! Indeed one may worship, but only if the proscribed instruments call for it—and have you heard any sweet chords from a dulcimer of late. The musicians do not stray without the palace walls, and the king has given no order for them to do so. Who will gainsay the king's order? The statue remains in place, but it no longer has power."

Miysha-El did not appear to be convinced that the king had forsaken his desire to be exalted.

"And besides, the king is scarcely dull of wit. The venom has been drained from Nergal-Sharezer's fangs."

"Hrmph! For but a moment," Hananyah quipped. "He hides himself from the king's face, but only until his brood empowers him again with their cunning words and foul sorceries. They take great advantage of Nebuchadnezzar's temper to fuel their contrivances."

"Much has changed since our arrival," Miysha-El affirmed, seating himself next to the south window overlooking the granary. We have been raised above the station of most rulers, yet these corridors harbor unseen doctrinal pits in which many have fallen to their deaths. The counselors and princes will not defer to the king's whim so easily. They know that he can be swayed, and they have powers other than his to appease with their foul workings. No. We will yet be cautious in this place even though we have been placed at an improved vantage. The reach of the Order is still long. We will be on our guard as always."

Arioch move to the door. "Speaking of being on guard, I must attend to my duties in the king's parlor." He nodded respectfully and turned to depart. At the doorway he paused, his hand upon the frame. He looked directly at Miysha-El. "You have given me much to ponder this day, my friend." He drummed his fingers thoughtfully, and then moved down the corridor.

Much indeed.

7

Machinations

They all lie in wait for blood;
They hunt every man his brother with a net.

- The Prophet Micah

"What do we do now, Strobos?" Nergal-Sharezer fumed. "This plan of yours has caused more trouble for us than—"

"Are you so easily discouraged?" Strobos ground out, allowing his disdain for the old man to drip slowly over the edges of his tabled deference. "You are the one who swore to expel them at any cost."

"Don't be snide, Strobos. Whatever our goals, it would not be wise to have *our* throats cut in the process." He gave his comrade a cold stare, emphasizing their shared complicity. "Now that the king is dispensing providence to the Judahites as though he is sowing seed, we shall be under greater scrutiny. These men from Israel are defended by some sorcery of their own. I have not unraveled the source, but when I do, I will sunder their shield of protection, and they shall then be subject to us entirely."

"We need more than sorcery and interminable incantations to achieve our aims, Nergal-Sharezer. What has your wizardry gained you against the Hebrews, hmm? Tell me! No. What we require is other hands to serve us in our cause, and for that I shall need silver to maintain our eyes and ears within the palace."

Nergal-Sharezer grunted irritably. He crossed the room to a crate that lay bundled beneath two stacks of scrolls. He opened the heavy lid slowly. Its carefully oiled hinges made no sound. Nergal-Sharezer retrieved a rough-spun sack and tossed it to Strobos. "This shall be your last," he warned with a raised finger.

Strobos released a snort of laughter. "Tallying your coffers now, Nergal? What? Has your access to the king's treasure house been restricted too?" His voice grew suddenly frosty. "What is this worth to you? Are you willing to spend your remaining years cleaning the king's sandals? There are other ways you know."

Nergal-Sharezer harrumphed and bent to replace the scrolls in a neater array atop the chest. He inspected his packing then nodded in satisfaction. He shuffled to a large oak desk it the corner where he sat gingerly, as though his back ached. Throwing his head back he rubbed his eyes slowly before returning his attention to the younger man. "Just do as you are bid and there will be no need for such *unpleasantries*."

"Very well. I shall speak to the eunuchs, and I will keep you informed." Strobos moved to leave, but halted at the threshold. "But hear me well, Nergal-Sharezer."

The master magician looked up sharply and Strobos held his gaze without flinching from the cold that had coalesced behind them. "Make no mistake! I will receive the reward you have promised, or else I shall—"

Nergal-Sharezer surged to his feet, his ache apparently forgotten. "Do not provoke me Strobos." His eyes narrowed. "I have chosen your aid for my own purpose but, contrary to your seeming disbelief, I am hardly without power and I shall not be bent like a reed before an emerging sapling. No-one's feet shall tread on my back, young man. Neither the Hebrews's, *nor yours*," he finished, pulling back his sleeves in a reminder of the forces that at times he could wield.

"Tread carefully, young one," he finished threateningly.

Strobos remained with his hand on the latch a moment longer. He pursed his lips, and then he left, closing the door without saying more. He stood outside the portal, considering the way forward. He had enough silver stored to bribe whomever he wished. It would be an easy matter to remove Nergal-Sharezer, for in his arrogance, the magician accepted no protection from the guard. However, none other could deliver the prize of which Strobos dreamed. He would be forced to endure the fission between himself and the old man for a while longer.

Mutual benefit, he reminded himself. *I do not need to like the braggart, only tolerate his condescension to my own gain.*

For now, he would find another way to get the old crone what he wanted. Before the tenth month, the Hebrews would be gone.

Sitting alone in a domed room off the treasury store, Daniy-El scrutinized the provincial tallies for the third time that morning. He had hoped that his original assessment had been an error, but the recalculations returned the same result each time. Nine of the provinces had submitted supply reports of grain and other cargo traded by merchants within their provinces. The majority of the tallies reflected the ample profits of a fruitful season but a few scattered randomly amidst the others offered atypically low returns to the treasury. Had the neighboring agricultural zones been equally meager, it would not have garnered even a moment's notice from the Chief Governor, however, there was no shortage of irrigation channels in the south where access to the flow of the Euphrates was practically guaranteed. Hence, the poor harvests were an enigma. The chief overseers had reported no pestilence, and it was evident that the yield had changed substantially since the years prior to his appointment as chief official over the princes. Daniy-El brooded over the numbers. Whose provinces were these few? None of the governors had complained of insufficiency. Daniy-El retrieved a roll of parchment from a tall, fluted cupboard in the corner. He spent much of his time now in the crowded space that was stacked with stone tablets and papyrus scrolls without number. The ever-present clutter on the old record repulsed most of the governors who relied on verbal reports from their own satraps before assessing the written records stashed in the vault. Much of the work there was completed by the scribes who endured long hours in the confines of the dusty chamber. The volumes of scrolls that had been compiled from the length and breadth of Shinar filled many such rooms as this.

During the evening meal of ground pulse, Daniy-El questioned Hananyah about the faltering crops in these isolated southern regions.

"This province is in your jurisdiction, is it not?" Daniy-El questioned.

Hananyah chewed a morsel of flatbread, then cleared his palate with a draught of water.

"It is. Is there a problem? The harvests have produced well and—"

"Well, you say?"

"Yes. The dues and taxes were collected, as is the custom, and carted to the storehouse for the tallies that I have followed for the past few months. Why?"

Daniy-El shrugged. "Something is peculiar about the records. None of the years before our tenure fared even reasonably well in these zones. The king has received a mere pittance in tribute where there was any profit recorded at all. Have you changed the crops, perhaps? Or the time of harvest?

"No. All is as it was before we were given authority to manage the lands beyond the plains. You would need to seek Rabsaris for the answers. I replaced him as governor."

"I shall do so," Daniy-El said, chewing deliberately. This discrepancy was only one of several inaccuracies in the records. Hananyah's aid would make it easier to unravel their origins. *It will become clear in time*, he thought, settling back to his meal. *In time.*

Hananyah threw aside his quill in exasperation. "The irregularities continue to mount. One nest of adders breeds another."

"I spoke of the discrepancies with Rabsaris. Since he manages the treasuries, I believed he should have been the first to know. However, I received a very gruff dismissal. I thought also to review them with the governors, but most likewise gave me the cold shoulder. It may be the influence of several officers, or simply one, but at least any attempts at deception will be curtailed." Daniy-El sighed, rubbing his eyes. "We have been at this long enough to see that this will be no simple task. At least in the provinces within our jurisdiction we shall be able to initiate a proper order. Then I shall extend my hand further to restore the balance. Jeremiah has rightly titled this place Merathaim—Land of Rebels. Shoa and Koa. . . .Captains and rulers all. They are the greatest of lords, yet lacking in virtue. Discipline is not well-received here where freedoms abound."

"Agreed. From the reactions that I have thus seen, it is certain that we shall be opposed in restoring the king's absolute authority," Hananyah commented sadly.

"Already we have faced death. What more can be threatened against us? We shall serve nevertheless. Our lives are under the hand of Yahweh. Within these walls that confine us *He* will be our strong tower."

"We shall renew the battle tomorrow then," Hananyah said yawning. He stretched his aching muscles that had cramped while sitting at the desk poring over a host of tablets and scrolls selected from the provinces across Shinar.

"Yes, tomorrow." Daniy-El agreed.

He bid Hananyah goodnight and extinguished the small lantern. As he knelt to pray a familiar sensation washed over him—it was His peace, as gentle as a mother cradling a newborn. All thoughts of the last few hours were displaced by His Presence, washing away his disappointments and struggles in a flood of serenity. The shadow of captivity cast an ever-present pall on the days, but the love of Yahweh erased the haze and mire.

"Thank you, Lord," Daniel whispered, consoled. "There is none above your name."

Hananyah completed his calculations with a flourish, having risen early to resume his task. "That's it," he announced triumphantly. Leaning across the broad worktable, he pushed the scrolls and tablets over to Daniy-El who perused the first with interest.

"Is that what you need?"

"It is. Though I had hoped to have been proven wrong at the last," he sighed. "At least it's not as severe as it could have been."

"Nevertheless it is no surprise, wouldn't you say?" Hananyah gestured broadly. "This is certainly no enclave of holy men as we have found. Circles within circles. The life of the court thrives on treachery, bribery, fear. . . . Duty-bound prefects redirecting taxes, servants paid handsomely to betray their masters who in turn cover each indiscretion with further misdirection and promises of reward." He held his head. "The words of the prophets are amazing to behold in this place that seeks to defile ones spirit with its unrelenting whoredom. Who could have believed that we, having so little, dispossessed and subdued, would yet not suffer ourselves to be possessed by their temptations nor shamed into capitulation to their way of life?"

"Aahhh," Daniy-El agreed. "We praise Yahweh for being our strength these many seasons. He has been faithful, can we be any less so. A remnant, the prophets promised. Jerusalem will rejoice when its sons and daughters finally return home. This place will not hold the Children of God forever."

"Nevertheless, it is disconcerting to watch as servants shuffle behind draperies when we pass, or peer from behind vases when we are about our duties, or scrub the floors the more diligently awaiting some errant word from our lips to rehearse to their masters to inveigle a reward. . . ."

"Indeed," Daniy-El laughed without humor. "If there was something to find they would surely find it." He moved to look out the narrow window at the lowering sun. "We are still slaves. Their efforts would be better spent seeking the true source of life, instead of shadowing servants such as they. Sometimes it wearies me Hananyah, but I am sustained by the vision that I beheld." He shook his head in amazement as he relived the dream that had played so vividly within his mind. "He will come, Hananyah, Our Lord. He *will* come! The kingdoms of the earth shall scatter before His majesty. The great Babylon is not the beginning, nor will it be the end, praise be to Yahweh. Our Lord will triumph and this sham will crumble."

Daniy-El looked around at the vast columns and thick beams that bore the many buildings of the palace, then shook his head and closed his eyes, remembering snatches of what had been revealed to him. "All the artfulness of man will fall to His might. This age will fly in a twinkling, and His throne will be established." Suddenly he clenched his fists. "Victory, Hananyah. Victory *will* come! Oh Hananyah, it will be glorious. *Glorious!*" The light of his smile lit up his eyes, and his emblazoned joy transferred to his friend who laughed with equal exuberance.

"Let us put away these tallies, my friend. We have seen enough and it is not a grave enough matter to broach with the king, as long as there are no more occurrences."

"We shall see." Hananyah replaced his tablets atop one of many stacks, as Daniy-El returned the scrolls to the inventory. He tucked one scroll bearing his many calculations under his arm. "Come Daniy-El. Miysha-El and Azaryah are awaiting us in the libraries."

As the friends joined in light-hearted banter on the way to the libraries, a thin figure slid noiselessly from the rear of a freestanding rack of shelves that were laden high with parchments. She tucked her cleaning cloths into the waistband of her skirt and hustled to the desk at which the men had sat. She had not understood all the words that the men had spoken in Aramaic, for few amongst the Chaldeans shared company with the Hebrew slaves. However, she had sensed the importance of the clay tablets and the scrolls that the two men had perused so diligently. Retracing their movements, she retrieved two of the records, turning the clay pieces over in her palms. She squinted intently, but she was unable to discern any meaning in the markings. Still, they must be of some value. She folded her apron deftly into a deep pocket and laid them carefully within the concealment of the fold. Searching quickly she retrieved one tightly rolled parchment from the repository where she had watched the Chief Governor place his documents, and secreted it atop her treasures, praying that her master would be pleased this time. The woman slipped into the corridor and took several stairways leading to the eastern quarter of the palace where she entered an empty room. Unpacking her bounty with shaking hands, she laid them out on the broad windowsill, and settled to wait, knowing that he would soon come.

The elaborately robed courtier inspected the scroll carefully. He scowled as he checked the tablets.

"Rabsaris," he muttered angrily. "He's the only one fool enough to steal from his own province, and be so blatant about it."

"Are they of value then?" the woman asked hopefully, biting her lower lip.

"Not to me," he said wistfully, "and hence, my dear, not to you either. Sorry." The servant's mouth upturned sullenly but she said nothing.

The bejeweled man collected the plaques under his arm and fished the scroll into his yawning sleeves. "Keep looking," he said brusquely, dismissing the woman who departed with her head hung dejectedly having expected a more prosperous result from her evening's work.

The man watched until she had ascended the last flight beyond the grand tapestries of battles and bloodshed before drawing the scroll. This time the meeting had not been a complete disappointment. The previous one had shown promise, though he had garnered information that he already knew of the Hebrews. If the trend continued, he would soon have what he needed. Four doors over he rapped softly and entered as a gruff voice bid him enter.

"Your old friend in the treasury seems to have developed a hearty appetite for silver," he greeted without preamble. The lone occupant of the room pushed aside his inkpot and looked up from his writing. "He must. How else would he be able to siphon the magi enough coin to supply your fine tastes and boundless adventuring, eh Strobos?"

"His source for my payment is no concern of mine," Strobos grunted. If he wishes results, there must, of course, be some sacrifice."

"Take my advice Strobos. Be careful, or your scheming may end with a knife in your gut." He looked back to his writing, inspecting the delicate script. "What drives you?" he asked without taking his eyes off the parchment. "You must have enough by now to build a small palace of your own."

"A palace is nothing without the power to go with it."

"What? Will you be king then?" the older man said, laughing.

Strobos shrugged. "Not I, but another."

"Surely you don't mean Nergal-Sharezer."

Strobos snorted and shook his head. "No. He is but a means to an end."

"I thought you were *his* means. Who is leading whom around by the nose, eh?" the man sniffed. "Games, games, games. . . . So many games you choose to play, Strobos."

"This is no idle sport," Strobos corrected. "I can be patient, if I must, but he makes plans with no urgency whatsoever. I have set my sights elsewhere."

"Nergal-Sharezer has survived the rise and fall of nations. He is a clever magician. Do not underestimate him."

"He is no more clever than you."

His compliment elicited a small smile, but the eyes grew immediately cold.

"Do not flatter one such as me. Keep to your skills, Strobos."

"Of late I tire of the shadows. My hand should already be lifted up! Furthermore—"

"The light of day is just as dangerous, boy! When the eye of the king roves, he sees those who shine brightest and he can pinch them out whenever he wishes. Did you not take a lesson from those Hebrews? The king honors them one day and then throws them in a kiln on the next. A king's favor is fickle. Do not place your trust in it. Provoking the king's displeasure too often proves fatal."

Strobos stood erect, his broad shoulders thrown back. "I am no lowly Hebrew. The Greeks have a respected lineage."

"Respect? Hrmph! In Babylon, it is only strength of arm that ultimately commands respect. You will find yourself milled under along with so many others if you persist in this."

"It is always so wonderful to talk to you, old man. You have always been so—*encouraging*," Strobos said stiffly. He turned as if to go but his the man tapped the desk insistently to call him back.

"Don't go sour on me now, boy. I speak the truth. Come, sit down." The old man gestured to a chair. Strobos sank down reluctantly and scraped the chair forward to draw closer to the table.

"Nothing is going as I had hoped," he said rubbing his temples. "The king sits immovable upon the throne. Now these Hebrews serve him to the letter, and we can do nothing to extricate them for they seem to be blessed by the gods. Still the Order clamors to regain authority over the provinces that the foreign slaves currently rule. If I can aid Nergal-Sharezer in his goal, I will have the position and further influence that I need in order that I may court Cyrus—or Darius. Already the process has begun."

"You stalk a bear, trifle with a wolf, and woo lions! Beware, Strobos. Your head rests between too many rows of teeth. These Persians and Medes . . . They are no friends of ours. Your bloodline will count for nothing. Do not be deceived. They are wedded to conquest and you will find them no easier task-masters than the Chaldeans."

"I will cast my lot as I see fit. I have much more to accomplish here," Strobos asserted, rising suddenly to his feet.

"Very well," the old man said tiredly. "I had your passion for power once. For dominion over the souls of men. We serve the same master, you and I. But now. . . ." He brushed off his thoughts with a wave. "Now it no longer matters. . . . *I* no longer matter. Our ambitions are for naught, Strobos." He looked drained. "My soul aches for you Strobos, on this road to destruction that you have set yourself on. I have walked it before and I wish—"

"Let it not trouble you. Rest easy. We will talk of this on some other occasion."

Strobos was answered by a shaky nod as the old man eased his bent frame towards a pallet in the corner. The young fellow exited quietly. This forgotten shell of a being whom he sought on occasion for his deft knowledge had naught else remaining to sustain him beside the unholy spark of cunning that yet remained.

During a more glorious season, this man had relished his days within the hierarchy, twisting vain, greedy men to his will. However, an unexpected turn of events had aged him swiftly, plunging him from grace and filling his days with drudgery in this dim, forgotten room where the light of his power was now diminished beyond redemption. He had truly become a creature of the dark, only to be replaced by one of more vitality, and a greater hunger to serve the indwelling need that pulled him onward, forcing him to commit deeds that had warped his original hopes beyond his recall.

I will not have an end such as his, Strobos swore to himself. *I have received the promise of too much to allow myself to fail.* Even now the voice that had first found him pressed upon his mind, urging him to greater purposes and directing his course. He closed the door behind him softly.

Either the king, or the Hebrews, will need to go. Either will serve my ultimate purpose just as well. I will yet find a way. I must!

Deep within a citadel across the eastern desert, a young ruler hunched determinedly over a host of parchments, some of which were showing signs of decay along tattered edges. He remained convinced that the solution he sought lay buried within the tumble of maps and etchings that were strewn before him. His officers drew in close, discussing the possibilities available to them. Thus far they had proposed a fleet of options, but few offered any real prospect of success.

Cyrus banged suddenly on the table. "There must be something!" He glared at his men in annoyance. The conquest that he had hoped would crown his triumphs remained a mere dream.

One of the officers pursed his lips, then pulled a fresh parchment from a side table and reached for an ink jar. He drew animatedly. "Perhaps we could try this route . . ." he said hopefully, pushing the sketch toward his lord.

Cyrus surged to his feet. "That strategy will see us all killed and spitted!" the young ruler bellowed, throwing his hands into the air. He snorted with disgust and shoved the crudely drawn map back toward the army commander. The officer slumped dejectedly.

"By the time a third of our men are over the walls, the other half would have either drowned in the river or been skewered by a fleet of *hitz*. Given the height of their walls such arrows may even pierce our armor! You have seen the lay of the land and examined the fortifications. Can you propose nothing better?" he shouted, eyes bulging.

The captains returned downcast looks. During the tense silence several fidgeted with their scrolls that on which were scribed a multitude of plans and potential routes into the city. However, none bore the mark of genius that would see their men safely into the fortress that straddled the Euphrates.

"Well?" Cyrus pressed. "Is there no way to gain entrance to this stronghold? Are we to be content with spitting at his walls? Nebuchadnezzar will mock us from the battlements all the while." The king struck the arm of his chair in annoyance. He pushed the chair back, the heavy timber scraping loudly on the stone floor. He rubbed his chin then leaned, straight-armed, on the back of the chair.

"It is not so much the walls as it is the river," he lamented, rubbing the back of his neck. He knew that the task he had given his men was nigh impossible. He too had travailed over the maps, seeking any weakness that may have lain hidden from sight—and nothing. Babylon would rebuff the greatest army he could build.

The commander grunted his agreement. "Our spy has fed us chaff thus far. The head of the guard will not be bribed, and our grip on the provinces is tenuous at best. It is reported that the newly appointed chief of governors is likely to be as resistant to our advances. Efforts to dispatch them without suspicion have failed terribly. We need to seek an alternate recourse."

The king exhaled loudly. "Very well. We shall convene again in three months. Meanwhile I shall confer with Darius. If there is yet no fit strategy by year's end, we shall abandon the war for another summer. A long siege will strip our kingdom bare. We must find something. . . ." He pounded the table, startling his men briefly. "Know this," he asserted, tapping the table definitively with a stout forefinger, "However long it takes," he said, holding rapt their gazes with an unflinching glare, "How ever long! I *will* make Babylon my footstool!"

8

Changed

Let a beast's heart be given unto him. . .

- The Prophet Daniel

"Again?" Nergal-Sharezer exclaimed, striking the table. "Dreams, dreams, and more dreams. . . Will we have no end of the king's obscure imaginings?" Nergal-Sharezer leaned way back in his chair, wearied by the ill-begotten news. He strove to regain his composure. "Has he deigned to say, this time, what has befallen him?"

Sarsechim-Nebo shrugged. "He spoke of it to some of the counselors, my lord, but it is as much a riddle as the last."

"Which reminds me, have any of the Men of Wisdom discovered what pertained to the first dream? I have asked the sorcerers and soothsayers, but none can advise me in depth. The king rants about his supremacy, but his words are still a mystery. Since that peculiar meeting with the slave Daniy-El in his chamber the king has been veiled toward us."

"Nebuchadnezzar has never spoken of that sending again, my lord. I have pried, quite gently, but he dances quite nimbly around my probes, and he questions me with even more riddles. He mocks me I think. He spoke with Belteshazzar only. Then he made an end of it."

"If so, then so be it. As long as he is content to let matters lie," Nergal-

Sharezer consoled himself. He disliked being in any way ignorant of the king's affairs. As Rab-Mag he had earned the privilege of close confidence with the sovereign of all Assyria, and he had relished it, until now.

"Belteshazzar has the king's ear, thus we must be cautious. These Hebrews have limited our reach in many things, but we yet have sufficient authority to flourish throughout the kingdom."

"Certainly so," Nergal-Sharezer agreed. "Should Nebuchadnezzar wish the Jew to continue as chief over us, we shall find other means to influence the realm, never fear. I have given our friend further freedom to rid us of this Hebrew *oracle*."

"There is yet the interpretation of this latest dream. The king requires an answer of us."

"I shall perform a reading tonight. The *power* will surely tell us what we need to know."

"For this I hope, Nergal. I truly do," he said with a cynical twist of the lips.

"Not you also. What thinketh thou? That the Order has somehow lost its dominion?" the magi rumbled, his face growing dark.

Sarsechim-Nebo raised a placating hand. "This I have not said, Nergal. Be at peace. Let us see what comes with the morn." He hurried to the door, eager not to inflame the magician further. "Goodnight, my friend."

"Goodnight," Nergal-Sharezer replied crustily. Perhaps the morning would indeed bring happier tidings.

To his dismay, the light of the morning did not bow to Nergal-Sharezer's desires. The king's summons soured his stomach as he broke his fast. He stood before Nebuchadnezzar along with the senior officers of the Order. He strove to conceal his chagrin as the king berated the grim-faced assembly.

"I told you all and yet you answered me nothing. What of this dream? Have you nothing to offer your king—no balm for me?"

Nergal-Sharezer spoke slowly, hoping that the king's bubbling temper would subside. "We simply need more time, my lord. The Order toils unceasingly in your service. We shall—"

"I tire of this, Nergal-Sharezer. You have always been dependable before this. Must you force my hand? Must I continually resort to threats, and the ministering of slaves for succor! What has become of your touted mastery, eh Nergal?" he turned his ire on the astrologers. "And what of you lot? Have the stars fallen from the skies. Does the sun not rove the heavens as before? Does my future hold no good-fortune?" he accused.

The grouping gave no reply. They had all seen the king in this mood before, and they wished to offer no fuel for his fire that had begun to rage.

Facing Nergal-Sharezer again, he raised his finger slowly. "If you keep this up I may need to spend more time in the slave quarters seeking counsel." He waved his hand to dismiss the congregated advisors. "Leave me. Get out." He shooed them vigorously. *"Out!"*

Red-faced, the men filed though the broad doors that were flung wide by the guards. Nebuchadnezzar shook his head, watching them go. "Guard," he bellowed. "Send for Belteshazzar, master of the magicians. I need an honest man before me. His word I can trust."

Nergal-Sharezer's ears burned as the words carried on the air to the departing group. The slight by his king in titling the Hebrew master of magicians was like gall upon a fine palate.

I will see an end to this, he vowed, angrier than he had been in many a season. *I will search as long as it takes.*

Daniy-El knew, and yet he hesitated. When the king had described his vision moments before, images had flooded his mind. On this, he wished fervently that there was another way, but still the meaning pulsed within him, as alive as the blood that coursed through his veins. Once more, the certainty of the reading made him weak with its import. There was, however, no associated surge of joy to propel him forward. He stood before the king, but no words came. He opened his mouth briefly, but closed it again as he sought a way to convey the Lord's directions.

Raising his left hand, the king gestured reassuringly, as though to salve the distress that swarmed about Daniy-El, as thick as a cloud of gnats. The misery was stifling his willingness to speak.

"Do not let the dream, nor its interpretation trouble you," Nebuchadnezzar said soothingly, as though it were Daniy-El, and not he, who was the subject of the dream's intent.

Daniy-El fidgeted with his robe. Finally, he pressed his fist to his lips, gathering his resolve. *I must say,* he decided. *There is no gain in delaying further.* He had agonized long enough., and now he could think of only one remedy.

"My lord," he said softly. "The dream will benefit those who hate you! It's interpretation will please your enemies." Daniy-El drew a short breath and chose his words. "The tree that you saw, that reached to the heaven, and succored all below it—it is you, my king, who has become strong, with dominion throughout the earth."

The king continued to focus on his advisor without comment, but leaned in to close the gap between himself and the younger man. He waited to hear more.

"The watcher that descended and commanded that the tree be hewed down, leaving a stump amidst the beasts of the field, came to warn you that you will be cast out as king and made like an animal until you acknowledge that God rules in the kingdom of men and that he will give power to whomever He decides. The stump signifies that you shall not completely lose Babylon, but you will be as a beast, an ox, feeding on grass."

Daniy-El drew nearer the king, his eyes imploring. "My king, let my counsel be acceptable to you, and change your sins for righteousness, and your iniquities by showing mercy to the poor; in the event that it may lengthen your peace."

Daniy-El followed the king's gaze to a jewel-encrusted effigy of a minor deity that stood in an adjacent chamber. It bespoke the flaw in the king's reign—he placed his ultimate trust, not in the God that Daniy-El knew, but in the marvelous creations of his own hands. Nebuchadnezzar did not outwardly challenge the rebuke in Daniy-El's tone. He bit his lip in thought, and then slumped backward on his throne. For several moments he sat, silently staring through the large window that framed the azure sky. Golden rays of light poured in, but Daniy-El did not feel their warmth. A cloud of condemnation settled in the silence. After a long while with no response from the king, Daniy-El withdrew. If only the king could sunder the bonds of pride that had set like iron fetters about his soul. However, the deadly shackles offered a seductive veneer of power that few could escape.

Choose, my king. Choose freedom!

"We must encourage the king," Daniy-El urged Sheshbazzar, who served as high-commander in the kingdom. "Perchance he may lend an ear."

"To what end, Belteshazzar?" The king has never demonstrated even a vestige of loving-kindness toward his servants. His heart yearns openly for riches. He—"

"Nevertheless," Daniy-El interrupted with a strange urgency, "he may yet be blessed with a new heart." The counselor placed his hand upon his breast. "I may not speak of my reasons, but please, honor my appeal. Any guidance that the king may receive toward righteousness will stand him in good stead, lest he fall into the chasm that he has cleaved with his own hands. The king had been given an opportunity that many men are not afforded—to stand on the cusp of judgment, and yet be allowed to turn again from the path whereupon one avoids the severest of penalties. We shall see whether he accedes. He may choose to accept the grace offered, or he may not. If he holds to a stubborn course, his enemies will rejoice. The implications are grave. That much I can say. For that cause, I shall give my utmost to prevent such a tragedy, for those below the king do not have his fortitude. The kingdom will be in severe danger if he is brought low."

The older man patted his shoulder. "Be at peace, my friend. The king will listen. He is apt to take good counsel. If the penalty is as harsh as you suggest, then he shall relent. "

Daniy-El clasped Sheshbazzar's hand, and then embraced him warmly. "I dearly hope that he does. We shall all be hard-pressed otherwise."

Sheshbazzar nodded. "Your request is honorable, and more than the king deserves. I shall offer my support in this cause and pray that the king shrugs off the mantle of pride that binds of him."

"Thank you," Daniy-El said smiling. "Thank you."

Nebuchadnezzar roamed the familiar halls of the palace, the words of the Jewish counselor fading with the turning of the seasons. Many months had passed since Belteshazzar's admonition, and he was still hale. He ran his hand over a masterpiece of artistry that adorned the wall, soaring to meet the grand cornice overhead. The carvings and etched stone were a great marvel. Perhaps the God of Gods delighted in showing him mercy. His chief governor had been so certain! But so too had others in the past. Perhaps the source of the counselor's power had waned. Whatever the implication, there was naught amiss. On Belteshazzar's advice, he had given some consideration to the more impoverished servants within the provinces, lowering tributes and taxes. Perhaps Belteshazzar had hoped that he would offer some boon to the enslaved Jews. It seemed possible, for Sheshbazzar too had added his voice.

"*There is no harm in doing good,*" Sheshbazzar had supplied, seeking to persuaded him. "*And the measure you give out may be returned tenfold or even one-hundred fold. Who can say?*"

These are worthy men who sought not their own aggrandizement, as do many in the Order, the king surmised. Moreover, the treasury had not suffered substantially for the reduced burdens. He had allowed the poor to purchase more corn to sustain them in the winter, and fewer had perished from hunger in the fields. As a result, the crop yields had been bountiful and the kingdom continued to prosper, especially with the increasing goodwill of the people.

Nebuchadnezzar rested his hands on the balcony wall, surveying the throngs of merchants that bustled below in the main court. It had taken him a lifetime, but his boyish dreams had coalesced into reality. Some had opposed him on this journey toward the seat of power, but he had persevered, undaunted. *Is this not great Babylon that I have built as the centre of the kingdom by the might of my power, and for the honor of my majesty?* he exulted, throwing his arms out as though to embrace the wonder of the city. The great Hanging Gardens that he had fashioned were the envy of nations. Water gushed off the manmade terraces that rose like a mountain. Swollen streams cascaded down to a pool that lay amidst dense groves. Massive arches supported the garden, which towered above the ornate Ishtar Gate that was entered from the main thoroughfare. The gate itself was decorated with the signs of Babylon's wealth. Ninus and Semiramis were immortalized along with grand hunting scenes that wreathed the walls. The promenade to the palace was flanked by massive animals and people captured in frozen celebration; splendid ornamentation and glazed reliefs depicted annals of the city's emergence. Its unparalleled treasures included a hundred gates of bronze, kiln-baked bricks cemented with bitumen for the houses constructed within the city, two hundred and fifty towers that loomed skyward, and the Temple of Bel-Merodach. The whole of his creation inspired awe from all who viewed their wonder. Located astride primary trade routes, the city thrived off the great waters of the Euphrates that flowed south through their borders. The city itself was the dais suited for his majesty. The fortress adjoined the main citadel of governors. Triple walls rose in tiers above the deep, navigable canals. A tunnel below the river joined the two palaces on either side into one. The bridge itself measured more than fifteen hundred cubits. Under his hand, this city that spanned the river had grown in prosperity and tremendous power. Moats protected the inner palace wall and the magnificent ziggurat—the Temple of the Seven Spheres, towered within, its levels colored separately in black, orange, red, gold, yellow, blue and finally silver. An ark covered most of the upper platform, crowning the shrine in the glory of the gods.

The might of Chaldea had claimed what others had failed to conquer. He had defeated the Scythians and Cimmerians before turning west to Syria. Finally, Jerusalem and all its resources had been subsumed into the great dynasty of Babylon. In addition, he had rebuffed the nations of the north. They feared his prowess, these Medes and Persians. Now he was certain that while he yet lived they would not overtake him. The God of Daniy-El had spoken it. "With all this, who could gainsay my supremacy?" Nebuchadnezzar rejoiced.

Thunder overlaid his final words, splitting the heavens, which remained a cloudless blue. A second Voice, awesome in power, rolled on the back of the booming rumble that shook the earth. "KING NEBUCHADNEZZAR, TO YOU IT IS SPOKEN. THE KINGDOM IS DEPARTED FROM YOU!"

The silence that followed was almost as deafening as the Voice that had uttered it fearsome pronouncement instants before.

Nebuchadnezzar recoiled. Legs wavering, he reached for the wall to steady himself but it eluded his grasp and he fell. His thoughts rolled into panic. Strange images swam before in his mind, dispelling his celebration with the swiftness of a sandstorm. Noises clamored to gain his attention. He looked up and faces foreign to him peered down . . . faces disturbed with alarm, and . . . confusion. *Who are they? This is my home—my palace—I am—king!* He shouted for the guards but a growl escaped his throat in place of his cry. He continued to shout as the faces backed away in undisguised horror.

The chief steward rushed to retrieve the king's cloak that was laid out upon a cedar table. Moving forward cautiously, he draped it about him. Oblivious to their efforts, Nebuchadnezzar curled into a ball against the east wall of the balcony, still scratching at the elaborate tiles. He shivered uncontrollably as dementia wrested his clarity askew, batting aside his feeble attempts to secure his sanity. His clutching fingers lost hold of their very reason for existence as the fragile threads that wove his memories together frayed, then unraveled speedily as an unseen hand drew them away from his grasp. Panicked now, he groped wildly, fighting against the darkness that claimed him.

I am Nebuchad—. . . Nebu—? I am . . . I. . .

The servants moved aside to allow, Ashpenaz, the prince of the eunuchs, to Nebuchadnezzar's side. Except for the royal steward, the servants had all fled as the king scrabbled frantically at the stone floor, seemingly unable to find his footing. A prolonged howl of anguish tore from his throat. It ripped through the citadel, bringing the life of the palace to an abrupt halt. Prefects, guards, servants and slaves emptied into the halls, each seeking to discern the source of the wounded cry. Many leaned from their windows, throwing questions to similarly befuddled occupants of other quarters. Some searched the sky for the origin of the Voice of power that had shaken the brick walls of the fortress instants before. A whirlwind of alarm shred the calm that had previously enveloped the home of the king, as news of his affliction spread.

'It is the king."

"His mind has been taken by spirits."

"He grovels and spits like an animal."

"Send for the chief magi. Fetch Nergal-Sharezer. He will aid the master."

"No, send for the astrologers. If the voice came from the sky it is the stars doing."

"No he can do nothing against this."

"Send for this son," Ashpenaz decided. He spoke urgently to the chief servant. "Some curse or manner of madness has come upon him. If aught befalls the king, Evil-Merodach will likely accept command. The decision should be his."

The servants stood aside, wringing their hands. "You may leave now," Ashpenaz instructed. "Speak no word of this on your lives," he warned, knowing inwardly that the instruction was fruitless, for the lips of servants were as free as the winged storks that sat amidst the reeds by the river, scattering to the winds at the first hint of disturbance. He could trust them to fly to the nearest noble in search of silver for their salacious tidbits of information. Gossip would probably be on the street before Evil-Merodach could reach the king's door.

Ashpenaz shook his head in dismay. He could already envision the strife that this event would spawn. By the evening, some ambitious Babylonian aristocrat would have hatched a means to steal some grain of power without the piercing eye of the king to watch them. Ashpenaz looked up from his ministrations over the king as the young lord entered. He seemed irritated by the urgent summons by the eunuch.

"What is it that requires such haste, Ashpenaz? I was sitting at meat when you disturbed me. Let this not be trivial." He looked along the hall, puzzled. "Where is the king? I was told that you summoned me on his behalf. Where is he then?" Evil-Merodach gestured to the ornate doors that led to Nebuchadnezzar's chamber. Thick curtains masked the interior of the room. "Does he wait within?"

Ashpenaz moved aside and extended his hand toward the bundled figure cowering upon the floor, eyes wild and vacant of understanding. In a sudden fit of agony the king tore at his clothes, his teeth chattering uncontrollably.

Eyes wide, Evil-Merodach swallowed hard, and then drew back over the threshold to the portico. His hand flew to his mouth. "But—but he was—he was well at half-light? What manner of sorcery is this? Is this the work of the magi?" he stammered.

"Don't speak foolishly, Evil-Merodach," came a voice from within the bedchamber that was hidden by flowing drapes." The heavy cloth parted as a slim figure emerged onto the balcony.

"N—Nergal-Sharezer!" The young lord stuttered, still discombobulated by Nebuchadnezzar's incomprehensible sickness. "I did not mean to imply—"

"Of course you didn't," Nergal-Sharezer sniffed. He stepped past the prince who remained in the doorway, his bulky frame quivering. "It's unlikely to be catching, my lord," the magi said. "You need not stand aside." Nevertheless, the prince stayed rooted on the threshold. Nergal-Sharezer's mouth quirked sardonically and he moved toward his king who shuttled backward a pace. "It was so sudden," Nergal-Sharezer observed to himself in a low whisper. "Is his cup-bearer well?" he asked of Ashpenaz, whose attention was turned to contemplations of his own.

"Hmm? Oh—yes. He is indeed. The king's food has been tasted. None of the food-tasters has succumbed to any ailment such as the king has."

At the mention of poison, Evil-Merodach clutched his ample middle with a grunt. He released a warbling moan that brought stares from his companions.

"If so, some other power has crippled him thus. I will seek a remedy amongst the Men of Wisdom."

"Is it within your power to restore him, then," Ashpenaz said hopefully.

Nergal-Sharezer pursed his lips briefly. "We shall do our utmost," he assured. "These remedies are often difficult to concoct. The stars may also not favor his restoration at this time. We may simply need to let the effect run its course."

Hearing this, Ashpenaz frowned. He regarded the magi doubtfully.

Evil-Merodach raised a tremulous hand. "I entrust him to your care, Ashpenaz. Nergal-Sharezer, should you discover a cure, you have my blessing to proceed. Use your good judgment. Ashpenaz will see to his comforts meanwhile. If he should recover in any way you must send for me at once." Evil-Merodach tumbled out his instructions before departing hurriedly.

To drown himself in wine, no doubt, Ashpenaz surmised. *He is aptly named— Merodach's fool.*

To the eunuch's surprise, the magi gave one final look at Nebuchadnezzar's shaking form and then followed quickly in the prince's wake.

He has assayed nothing at all to restore his king, Ashpenaz thought in dismay at the magi's peremptory departure. Troubled, the Chief of Eunuchs made a solemn decision, then clapped his hands to summon the servants back in.

"Send for Belteshazzar and have thick woolen blankets sent from the store. Also, have varied fare sent to the king's chamber, perchance he grows hungry. This stupor may yet dissipate before the morrow. I shall coax him to his bed if I can. Hurry now." Ashpenaz gave three sharp claps to disperse them to their duties.

I pray you are able to grant an answer, Belteshazzar, for I can see only ill coming of this. Only ill.

"Did you say seven?" Ashpenaz exclaimed, immediately beginning to pace. "That will be too long a duration. The kingdom will not last."

"It will be seven," Daniy-El confirmed. "The sign of the times is clear. Until then, the king's mind will be fettered. He seemed to have turned aside from his transgressions and I was hopeful that. . . ." Daniy-El shook his head, and then drew a slow breath. "Never mind. It is as Yahweh has ordained, and we will need to bear the weight until the king is granted freedom from this bondage that tears his mind asunder. He was offered the opportunity to forestall this, but the heart of man is desperately wicked, and we are often our own worst enemy. We must simply endure until the season proscribed by the Lord has ended. He is given to extending His mercies, but in a time of His choosing. In His wisdom he will not hasten the judgment. I pray that Nebuchadnezzar heeds the chastisement—though men may see it as harsh. We must abide nevertheless. Yahweh's hand is sure."

"What shall we do for leadership in that time? This will be impossible!"

"The counselors shall advise the prince should the need arise."

"He is not ready," Ashpenaz insisted. "He is painfully weak."

"I agree. It is not yet his time, though he may learn something in the interim to prepare him for rule. It will be possible, if we keep our hands on the reins. The Lord has ordained that the kingdom will stand, and stand it shall. We need only guide Evil-Merodach, and I, and my brethren, will keep the reins steady. There is sure to be some initial tumult, but in a little while, it shall cease as fears wane."

"I guess," Ashpenaz said, yielding a small measure of his own fear to Daniy-El's confidence.

"Please inform Evil-Merodach that he may be called upon. Also, Rabsaris will need to be advised promptly, in order that the tributes owing may be secured. I will inform the governors. All will be well. Worry not," Daniy-El said, forcing a smile for the eunuch's sake.

"I suppose," Ashpenaz said, his response non-committal and devoid of enthusiasm. "May it be according to your words, else we are lost."

The prince of the eunuchs watched the younger man, who had once been his charge take his leave. Daniy-El, now titled Belteshazzar, had been the most promising of the young men drawn from the palaces and courts of Jerusalem. Captivity and servitude had not broken him, as it had so many others. Rather, his faith and servant hood had placed him in the highest seat of Babylon, save the king's. Ashpenaz had expected the young lad and his companions to have ailed within the first month on their meager diet of pulse, but what a surprise. He smiled. He was glad, for he favored the young man highly above the others, enough to have acceded to the atypical request that could have brought him trouble from his sovereign, had the boy been stricken by some illness as a result of hunger. The boy was blessed with a humble spirit, and it became his strength. *I pray he is proved right yet again. I must trust in his word.* However, faith was difficult to maintain when falsity pressed in close like an accursed specter everywhere one turned in the palace. *Still, I must trust him,* Ashpenaz reasoned again. *What else is there that I can do?*

Ashpenaz left the lodgings set aside for the palace eunuchs, still muttering to himself. He crossed a myriad of passageways on his way toward the residences of the high officials of Nebuchadnezzar's governance—halls of majesty, their beauty now lost on a king whose eyes regarded only a dark void. Again, he considered all he had learnt from Belteshazzar—all of the glory, even of a king, counted for naught at the days end, when shadows fell and one's light was near extinguished. Who, or what, could draw one back from death's door, or from insanity such as plagued Nebuchadnezzar? And all the while he was surrounded by liberal comforts. Neither his crown, nor his vaunted deeds held sway. Now, none could extract his mind from the skeins that had smothered his reason and snared his will in webs of madness. With equal dread, Ashpenaz was loathe to have the Order take hold of the throne and weave their subtle manipulations about the affairs of the empire, but what alternatives were open to the realm? Belteshazzar could not manage the entire kingdom without the aid of the officials. The accompanying posturing and interference he could do without, though.

Turning a sharp corner along a dim passageway Ashpenaz collided with a tall man, his face hidden by a grey cowl. The fellow mumbled an apology and hurried away. The prince of the eunuchs peered at the form that disappeared into a perpendicular corridor. His eyes narrowed. *Strobos.*

Ashpenaz turned again and looked closely at the lone door that lay ahead at the end of the dead end corridor from which the young lord had emerged. It was the abode of Sarsechim-Nebo. The chamber door closed quietly on its well-oiled hinges. Ashpenaz advanced toward it, curious about the occupants whose voices echoed beyond the timbers. There was yet another visitor, or visitors. He hesitated then moved back down the corridor to a deep alcove— the storage bay held dusty carpets and wall hangings awaiting replacements. Ashpenaz bent his broad back and squeezed his large form farther into the depths of the confined space, draping his robe over his nose to stifle a sneeze. The voices rose louder, their words heated, but still indistinct from his hiding place. Ashpenaz could feel his legs cramping within the confined nook. He bowed his head so that he could raise his body a fraction. He felt a familiar tingle as blood moved slowly into his lower limbs. He considered leaving, but his curiosity overrode his discomfort. After a long while he decided that he would send a servant back to formally announce his coming to Rabsaris, lest he be an unwelcome interruption in whatever meeting had been convened in the treasurer's private quarters.

He was beginning to rise when the latch clicked open and the door thudded back. Ashpenaz did not attempt to peer out for his discovery, he knew, could be perilous. Eavesdropping was a dangerous pursuit, but often proved a necessary aid to safeguarding one's hide.

A heavily-embroidered cloak swept past the opening of the alcove, its purple and silver trim unmistakable. *Nergal-Sharezer.* Another moved by in quick succession. *Sarsechim-Nebo? What is the royal cupbearer doing in the company of these men?* The unlikely association of the four men caused him grave concern. With the king disabled by the unknown malady, such alliances did not bode well, and justified the trepidation that he had felt earlier. *And Strobos?* The young man caused him the greatest disquiet, for he oft disappeared on odd occasions from the court with no trace of his departure until he had re-entered the gates with the merchants. The man had no true friends that the eunuch could discern, though, Ashpenaz had long known of the youth's association with the old man who now resided in seclusion in the east quadrant of the palace—the senior lord was one of many whose governance had run afoul of Nebuchadnezzar. The king's tolerance for ambitious satraps, and even princes, went only so far. Officials who survived their stations could count themselves fortunate, for many a lord has seen his prospects for power curtailed by the gaoler's axe.

Strobos himself fulfilled diverse roles in the court, engaging frequently with the royal scribes.

It was not these simple facts that troubled Ashpenaz the most, but rather the circle of spies that the man had managed to established in his short time in the court; they crawled like venomous spiders through every crack in the palace walls. Strobos, he knew, fed his garnered tidbits to whichever official offered the highest price. He laced the news with untruths and spiked them with vitriol, causing dissension and hatreds to spring up amongst the governors and princes.

These four—together in counsel? It worried him greatly. Again, he was powerless to intervene. There were many eyes throughout the palace but his were the most keen for he could see beyond the flowery phrases and coy smiles that shielded malfeasance. The disguises of the court were countless, and caution precluded a multitude of hidden dangers.

Ashpenaz straightened from the cranny where he was bunched alike the discarded piles of hangings and rolled his aching shoulders. His limbs popped at the joints as he locked into his full height. He crooked his neck to loosen the last of the knots and moved to the door, knocking loudly.

"Who calls?" a gruff voice said curtly.

"Ashpenaz, Master of the Eunuchs." He was left outside to wait an inordinate duration before the door opened a crack.

"Yes?"

"You have heard," Ashpenaz stated.

"Heard what?" the man snapped.

"Of the king's predicament."

"I have heard. What of it?"

The man's obtrusive manner did not dissuade the eunuch. He was accustomed to such arrogance. "It seems that the king will be indisposed for a longer season than anticipated."

"Who has told you this?"

"The dream-reader, Belteshazzar. He has suggested that the king knew of this potential ill, but did not act to prevent it."

Sarsechim-Nebo sniffed. "Nergal-Sharezer shall aid the king. We do not need the services of your *dream-reader!*"

"Very well." Ashpenaz conceded. "But you do need his services as *Chief Governor,*" Ashpenaz added lightly. "And the Chief Governor has instructed that the counselors and governors aid the prince in maintaining the balance until Nebuchadnezzar's recovery whence he shall retake the throne."

"We know what we must do, *eunuch*!"

Ashpenaz stepped back just as the door slammed before him. He smiled. The man's malice was a thin veneer that masked a trembling interior—Sarsechim-Nebo was nervous. His acerbic words and brusque manner were aimed at concealing the fine tremor that had made its way into his hands. Though muffled, his had clearly been the loudest, most agitated voice that had warbled through the door while Ashpenaz had waited, listening. Whatever bog Sarsechim-Nebo had sunk into with this lot, it had obviously began to creep up toward his chin. Ashpenaz sighed. *Ultimately, as with all these things, it shall shortly cover his head.* Men of power seldom learnt to tame their lusts, resorting then to schemes and ill-advised alliances to fulfill desires that danced beyond their grasp. The offices of too many counselors, governors and princes had been cut short by a sharp blade in the night hours. The servants often discovered the bloody results when repeated knocks received no answer and entry was gained after several days of wondering whether the occupant fasted or was abed within the chamber. It did not go well for servants who had entered prematurely and few would dare venture forth now without the permission from the head servant and the presence of the Mater of Eunuchs. Within these halls, many practiced dark arts, or found perverse activity to entertain their senses. As such, days could pass without seeing someone emerge. If Sarsechim-Nebo wished to indulge the company of dangerous allies, then so be it. The reckoning of such men was often swift, and without mercy. Babylon was like a viperous core that leached its venom throughout the Empire, snaking trails that disappeared across the borders of Shinar. Like the leprous unfortunates that begged merchants for alms along the road, there was neither salve nor cure for the festering ailments of his nation.

Ashpenaz guffawed. Sarsechim-Nebo was wily, but decades of survival in the court had taught Ashpenaz that there was always one who was the more clever. After he found himself sinking into a mire of his own making, Sarsechim-Nebo had likely taken hold of some proffered hand, thinking it to be the source of his deliverance, and then found the beast to be rabid. In all his life, Ashpenaz had never encountered a source of deliverance as powerful as Belteshazzar's God was. Could all that the young man had spoken of this God then be true?

It was good that the dream-reader had given him hope. The time would be long, but Belteshazzar had assured that it would end. Though the king could be callous, he alone who stood between the realms of power and the reaching claws of predators that lurked in the shadows. Deliverance could come none too soon.

The king fought within to gather his senses but could not. He snarled, seeking some escape from the darkness that befuddled his thoughts. . . .

Searching. . . .

Darkness. . . .

Cold. . . .

Darkness . . . .

Only darkness . . . .

Reach. . . . *farther* . . .

Search. . . *!*

Only . . .

Darkness. . . .

From a parallel window, Daniy-El observed the frenetic movements of his sovereign. He and Miysha-El were keeping Arioch appraised of the tiny shreds that had begun to appear in the fabric of the realm. Daniy-El's insight was indispensable to the maintenance of the efficient governance of the kingdom whilst Nebuchadnezzar was *indisposed*. The glitches in the provincial system became more apparent as the unscrupulous techniques of the palace officials became more familiar to the four friends whose own small alliance garnered many critical bits of information that, individually, would have been a pittance against the forces of the Babylonian administrative monster, but collectively, exceeded the typical deviance of wayward governors. Ashpenaz supported the collaborative efforts of the five men. Moreover, an unseen hand, whose purposes could not be changed, aided them. The rulership itself was plagued by disunity and it was necessary to diffuse the effects of the destructive plots by having opposing instigators nullify each others plans. Throughout the period of abeyance of Nebuchadnezzar's rule, the governors and princes watched each other with hawkish intensity, determined that none should gain the upper hand. Hence many plots were betrayed without the group needing to lift a finger. Sheshbazzar, a prince of Judah, lent his intimate knowledge of the treasuries. This precluded much of the pilfering that may have occurred without the ability to monitor individual provinces on a daily basis. The officials had become cautious of their inquiries into the affairs of each province, lest they divulge some plot of their own.

Only a few more days, Daniy-El thought, *until the season is fulfilled and the king is freed from his cage of torment.* Daniy-El prayed that Nebuchadnezzar would be released into a new life, devoid of the frivolities and trappings of grandeur that had previously fastened him to an unforgiving yoke. The king was needed, for though the tides of disturbance were temporarily quelled, the roiling mass that was Babylon continued to heave against the bonds that constrained it until Nebuchadnezzar's return.

Arioch had placed a guard about the meadow where the king sojourned. No curious eyes were allowed to trespass, except at a distance. Those close enough to the king to be trusted, had watched in mortification as Nebuchadnezzar's nails had grown into curved talons with which he foraged, scraping at the earth as he sought the tender shoots that pushed aloft from the grassy pasture. His hair emerged as thick as eagles' feathers, obscuring the once pampered skin. The stench of the field overlaid him, his clothes rotting upon his skin.

Some of his subjects claimed his madness to be retribution by the gods for the levies he had instituted on the poor. The passing days offered less and less hope of recovery to those who could not apprehend the source of the affliction. Nergal-Sharezer had withdrawn into silence, having arrived at the field on several occasions casting spells that had made no impact on the king's animalistic raving. The malady defied the most favorable predictions foretold by the soothsayers and astrologers. The sorcerers too discovered no true remedy in their exotic potions mixed with ingredients collected from across the nations. Even less effective were the emoluments that they assayed to administer. Adorned in soft cloaks and finery, some scampered unabashedly back to the safety of the palace, as the king's bestiality was unleashed.

The visits soon ceased when they at last determined that their treatments were useless against the might of this God. It was this God whose providence had set Daniy-El on the seat below the king, where he could be ready in such a time as this. His title as Chief Governor sat with its full weight upon his shoulders. There was much to account for while Babylon stood. Daniy-El had been elevated in order that he might serve, and he was determined to serve as best he could.

Those who understood the penalty of the seven times duration that had been imposed on the king, and cared aught for their sovereign's well-being, would be eager for the coming days to pass swiftly. They need not abide much longer. The time was fast nearing and end, but whatever the outcome, nothing within the empire would be the same as before. Daniy-El considered the trials of the full season that the king had endured. *For better or for ill, the king will be changed.*

The gloom was falling, and Ashpenaz searched the shadows for any sign of the Captain of the Guard whose indulgence he had begged for several nights now. He was out there, Ashpenaz was sure. His unease lessened as he uttered a prayer to shield the guardsman and his king. *Be safe, Arioch.* His eyes made a final scan of the wood before he turned away from the window. He could not be certain of incident but with the time drawing nigh, carelessness was the watchword of a fool, whereas caution could save one from a pit that yawned in the night. The usual conspirators had renewed their conniving ways and, though he hated to be suspicious of anyone, their activity had inspired his concern and watchfulness. He was still Master of the Eunuchs, and despite the abhorrent circumstances, he dared not neglect any aspect of his king's care. Nebuchadnezzar slept in a field and ate grass, but he was their lord, and Ashpenaz saw to his duties with utmost care. He would not slacken his responsibilities as many had sought to do while the king was unable to oversee their intimate affairs. Soon the king would be home, but first, he would need to survive the coming nights.

It was the fourth night that Arioch crouched amidst the dense grove of cycads that populated a small knoll. Already he had been there for hours and his second watch was now beginning. He was restless and, perhaps, the fresh air would be a balm to his soul. The night sounds began again, his presence no longer causing alarm to the nocturnal creatures within the glade. Despite having the appointed guardsmen, he had come personally on the eunuch's urging. Though reluctant, Arioch had agreed to stay a while, for tonight he was oblivious to the seductive call of his warm bed. Even as the dew settled gently on the back of his neck, he did not budge. He carried no defense save his breastplate and *chereb*—a light short-sword, for venturing out in full armor would have been foolish. He would stiffen within an hour. Now, the sword lay unsheathed at his side but within easy reach of his fingertips. He could see little, but his keen ears searched the dark for any sound that was amiss. Ashpenaz was wary that someone other than a friend could potentially visit the king, who deserved the best protection that the two could devise on behalf of the realm. Arioch had decided to be the king's shield for the last, rather than trusting his security solely to his officers.

Arioch sighed softly. In men's hands power begat a cauldron of evil. After a time, its enticements perverted wholesome desires, and twisted noble causes askew. A pity, for much good could otherwise be achieved. Belteshazzar was the first ruler he had encountered who had completely rejected the corrupting lure of the lofty title that too often warped men's honor. Not so, Belteshazzar. His mounting accolades served only to instill further humility.

A muffled scraping jarred Arioch from his reverie. Without hesitation the guardsman surged from his concealment, his short-sword cleaving an arc through the night. He was rewarded with a gurgling cry that was cut short by his second thrust. A rustle of leaves to his right warned that the aggressor had not ventured out alone. *How had they known where he was lodged?* Arioch dropped to his left, barely evading a cut from a *cidon* that severed the strap of his breastplate. He lashed out forcefully at the source of the attack, his foot connecting with the hard flesh of the man's arm, wrenching the javelin from his grasp. The man shuttled backward to avoid a lunging kick and Arioch bulled forward, catching the attacker off-balance. Realizing that the man wore no armor he delivered a blow to his midsection. The man rocked from his feet with a grunt. Arioch's fist thudded heavily against the man's jugular, and his opponent stilled.

Arioch rose to his feet and moved over to where the king lay asleep. Throughout the scuffle, he had not roused from his deep slumber. Arioch retrieved a lantern from a low limb where he had hung it before commencing his vigil. He struck the flint and the lantern glowed to life after several moments. Moving toward the prostrate figures, Arioch extended his lamp, expecting to discover the visage of an enemy, but as the light bathed familiar features Arioch recoiled in disbelief. The lamp swayed precariously in his hand as the startling revelation of two of his own guard seared his mind. *No!* The two were regularly posted on watch together at the south gate. He was glad, now, that guarding the king was not part of their regimen. Whether they were after the king, or on their way to complete some other foul business within the palace it was not clear. It could also have been a personal attack, for the guardsman knew that he had made several enemies within the court over the years. They were probably waiting—biding their time as they sought the moment when his watch was lax. Arioch's gut tightened as he realized that, again, he had come close to death. His jaw clenched as his eyes darted to the huddled figure of the king. All in all, Arioch was thankful to have intercepted them afore some tragic outcome from their mal-intentioned alliance. There were many hours yet remaining until morning, and the assailants would not be rising.

Had I not been here . . . ? Arioch did not wish to contemplate the possibilities, for he would not know now what their objective had been. He would remain until the daybreak, at which hour the watch would be changed. If Belteshazzar's reading proved true, sanity would be returned to their king within the fortnight. *Would that it comes with greater wisdom!* Arioch prayed. The realm was in dire need of restitution, and a true king was needed again.

Strobos saw the flickering light and knew it had all gone awry. His men would not expose themselves to view. He struck the sill in anger and pushed away. He rubbed his temples vigorously. It was taking too long to complete the tasks he had set. So many clandestine allegiances still held him bound—wheels were spinning within wheels and he was getting nowhere. He longed to move on to the path that lead upward and away from this brood of small-minded officials, who each grasped for miniscule rewards and piddling titles.

Their paltry ambitions raise them to be no more than glorified servants, he realized. *No! True power lies in headship, and there were few positions accessible below that of king.* He was no fool to covet supreme kingship, though it was clear to him that had his birth been one level higher, the possibility, though remote, would not have been utterly unthinkable. Even now, there remained a vein of royal blood that he could tap, its power leaching its way down the imperial arteries toward his proffered cup.

Strobos strode to a small cupboard in the wall and felt along the back for a small catch that released a slender panel. He removed a scroll with delicately written letters. The fine script seemed to mock him with a hidden answer to all his problems. The text recorded an intricate network of routes and palace schedules. The daily regimen of dozens of key prefects danced across the scroll, taunting him to decipher their use. His fingers traced caravan routes, names of camel traders, suppliers of horses and mules, wheat allowances and yields. . . . The list drifted down the rolled page, guarding its secret close. A map of the city had been drawn painstakingly on the reverse side that curved into view. He turned the scroll over. The king's fortress stood its ground, impregnable and forbidding, like a giant astride the swirling Euphrates. He shook his head. He had dredged this stagnant pool of Chaldeans for whatever information coin could by. Still, he could find no way in that would not be detected by the guard within the same hour that a siege was launched.

Then his assignment had been complicated even more so by the king's decision to set aside his former Chief Governor, placing the Hebrew in his stead. Now the Child of Judah was also acclaimed as Master of the Magicians. Nergal-Sharezer was greatly displeased by this grave turn of events. This Belteshazzar caused him many sleepless nights, for the man did not fit the mold of his predecessor and had placed obstacles in the way of the usual court processes by his mere presence. The Judean was resolute about administering justice and adhering to some personal standard of morality—two distinct wedges in an otherwise unprincipled system. Strobos preferred the latter, for he was afforded more latitude to plan. He sat at his table in the glow of a lamp that was now low on olive oil. He trimmed the wick of flax, deciding to retire after the disappointing day. From Egypt to Assyria, majestic carvings and statues immortalized the greatness he so admired—men who had changed nations or bent them to their will. He had labored his entire lifetime to be more than common men seemed to become in their waning years—disused and forgotten by those they served. What use was loyal service to most men? He bundled the pillow beneath his head and lay staring at the darkness of the room. The dawn would bring new opportunities, he was sure, for it was his destiny—a destiny which the gods would not deny him.

Flashes of sensation and impulse pervaded the king's mind. They were interrupted by bouts of darkness.

Grass. . . .

Heat. . . .

Water. . . .

Grass . . . .

Eat. . . .

Water . . . .

Light . . . ?

Light . . . .

Light . . .!

"Your own men?"

"Yes, my friend. A discomfiting circumstance. Nevertheless, these skirmishes happen on occasion. The men may brawl and harbor grudges after being disciplined for some infraction. Otherwise, a pouch of silver can persuade the most staunch loyalist, it would seem. The two kept to themselves and were often stationed together. They showed no disgruntlement or displeasure with their service. The men in the king's guard I trust explicitly. When the king is once again hale the palace guard will resume their duties and—"

A soft knock came at the door. Daniy-El raised his hand to beg a moment's forbearance. A young eunuch stood at the portal.

"My master bids you come. He wishes you to know that the king has arisen."

Relief spilled across Daniy-El's features. He glanced at Arioch who motioned for him to go. Daniy-El hastened to the border of the field where the king had lain. Many officials had already converged at the edge of the glade, unsure how to proceed. Nebuchadnezzar knelt several paces away, with his arms raised to the sky, his skin restored. Ashpenaz had brought him a woolen cloak to cover himself.

The prince of the eunuchs beckoned Daniy-El forward.

"The king has asked for you," he whispered.

Still Daniy-El hung back for the king, eyes closed to the surrounding furor, continued to shout praises to the Lord. Daniy-El too lifted his face toward the heavens and marveled before the God who had given him new life—his might was not his own but rather, that of an omnipotent, all-seeing God who had granted him grace.

For a while yet, Babylon would have a new king.

Strobos's blood boiled. He had received a transcript of a decree that Nebuchadnezzar had dictated that same morning to the Chief Scribe:

"Nebuchadnezzar the king, unto all people, nations, and languages, that dwell in the earth; peace be unto you. I thought it good to show the signs and wonders that the high God hath wrought toward me. How great are the signs! And how mighty are the wonders! His kingdom is an everlasting kingdom, and His dominion is from generation to generation. . . . "

As he read the full text of the proclamation his jaw dropped. He clenched them shut to prevent his teeth from grinding as he read on. Strobos's anger escalated as the words of the king rang terribly familiar, their tone echoing that of the Hebrew, Daniy-El. This preoccupation with a *Most High God*—it was unconscionable? It was not so much the proclamation that infuriated him as much as the upheaval that it foretold. Could the king possibly expect them to adhere to the dictates of this Hebrew God? He concluded the final words of the lengthy script in annoyance:

"Now I Nebuchadnezzar extol and honor the King of Heaven, all whose works are truth, and His ways judgment; and those that walk in pride He is able to abase."

Strobos crumpled the scroll in disgust. He had built his aspirations on a dependable network of sedition, but already the amendments that Belteshazzar had made to the palace under the king's authority had hewn great cracks in the fortress of deception that he had so carefully erected. Now, for the king himself to also be influenced! The storm of change would shift his foundation like the desert sands and he would be compelled to begin again. If Nebuchadnezzar vested even more authority in this Hebrew who had gained his confidence, Strobos's hope would disintegrate like sandstone beneath the paw of a leviathan.

Since his appointment, the Chief Governor had inadvertently opened the doors to many of the cages binding men and women whom Strobos had manage to entrap with their greed. Strobos wondered if it were a simple coincidence that the majority of the counselors who had been indebted to him had been relocated to alternate provinces. The young man's brow wrinkled in frustration.

How can I be certain? I must bide my time. Yet a little while, and greed shall win out again.

Strobos had made leagues with men who did not easily brook failure. The magi did not concern him overly so, but the Medes. . . . Therein lay the key to his aspirations. Still, there was hope, for these men of like ambition prized Babylon above all other trophies. *They will wait,* he concluded. *They can do nothing but wait, for these towering walls of stone defy them. Nevertheless, Nebuchadnezzar will soon grow old, and soft,* he encouraged himself. *His strongest years are now far behind him, and Evil-Merodach will be easy prey.*

"The day is not done, my king," he growled. "We need only wait."

He ground the wadded scroll vehemently beneath his leather sandal. "Babylon shall be taken, one way or another!"

9

Transitions

And he spoke kindly to him, and set his throne above the throne of the kings that were with him in Babylon. . . .

- *The Prophet Jeremiah*

Evil-Merodach was certain that most would think him a fool, but he was determined to follow the leading of his heart. It had been thirty-seven years since his father had taken the son of the king of Judah captive in revenge for the fateful alliance that the Hebrew sovereign, Jehoiakim, had made with Egypt. Nebuchadnezzar, ruthless and determined, had refused to forgive the boy, the king's complicity in the affair. It was a turbulent time, and Evil-Merodach knew what it was like to be the son of a stubborn king. Most saw the pomp and the glory, and hence envied their princely stature, but the callous yoke that accompanied the status was a significant burden. The boy Jehoiachin, whom some in the prison also called Coniah, had been eighteen when Nebuchadnezzar had taken him, along with the other slaves such as Belteshazzar, into his court. They had paid the price of all royalty who stood on the captor's end of a violent war. The Judean prince was the last in the lineage of Jewish kings descending from King Solomon, who all Assyria had grown to know. Coniah was innocent of all except his lineage. Unfortunately, his birthright had been enmeshed in cords of death, owing to the recalcitrance of his father. Nebuchadnezzar had deigned to leave behind a remnant of these subsumed peoples, feeble and poor. Now, Nebuchadnezzar had gone to the bosom of his fathers and, half of a lifetime after the deed, Evil-Merodach wished to end the cycle that his father had instigated. He had been forced to endure it as a son, but no longer, for he was king in his father's stead. He could not reverse the decades of pain that had fomented during his father's reign, but he could bring peace to the two houses.

The guards returned from the dungeons, their faces grim. Between them shuffled a bedraggled figure, who drooped like a half-empty sack of grain. Evil-Merodach felt a surge of pity, for it was only by the mercies of heaven that their positions were not reversed. The ways of war were perilous for the progeny of a king. It was as though the greater the blessing, the greater the expectation placed upon them, and the harsher the penalties for failure in one's charge. The boy had surrendered himself to the Chaldeans, knowing that death was the likely course, but instead, had been forced to endure the degradation of dark imprisonment. Evil-Merodach extended his hand, speaking kindly to the middle-aged man whose bearing was that of a grandfather, bent by the weight of harsh years.

"Your imprisonment is ended, Jehoiachin, son of Jehoiakim, king of Judah."

The man's head raised slowly at the sounding of his royal title. His eyes struggled to gain focus and he stared weakly at the man whose visage he would not know. Evil-Merodach continued his formal address. He was prepared to right the seemingly unjust acts perpetrated by his father as far as he was able. And this man had reaped beside a bitter pool. Yes, there were other kings who languished in the depths of the prison, placed into captivity by his father throughout a long spate of conquests. But the stories of none of the others endeared themselves to him as had that of Jehoiachin.

"Your prison garments shall this day be changed, and I shall restore your liberty and your honor. Accordingly, you will be given a seat in my house and you shall be given a continual allowance from the king's treasuries."

The prince turned king—though a king deprived of a kingdom—still regarded him with eyes that nestled in sallow cheeks, his body and soul having been starved of such charity for two-thirds of his life span. Upon his declaration, Evil-Merodach was rewarded with a spark of hope that he knew would restore the man's mind and body were he to be shielded in the king's care. *So it will be*, he decided. Jehoiachin could do little more than close his eyes in acknowledgement.

"Melzar." He waited for the chief steward to approach. "Melzar, have his garments replaced with those of a prince. He shall abide in the palace. Prepare quarters for him within the palace, for he shall eat bread before me all the days of his life."

"It shall be as you command, my king."

With the disgrace of Jehoiachin's confinement ended, a part of Evil-Merodach's own spirit was unfettered—a part that had never been allowed free reign, until now. With the new sovereign, the kingdom, along with the Jews within Babylon, felt renewed hope.

A wave of excitement coursed through the Jewish quarter, breathing new life into heart-sick souls—it was a glimmer that lit a flaring spark, which in turn shed light into the darkness of a long captivity.

"This is a good thing," Hananyah commented regarding the establishment of Jehoiachin in the court of the king.

Daniy-El nodded his agreement. "We were spared the straits of imprisonment, but God's wrath was nevertheless poured out on us all."

Differing levels of imprisonment had been imposed on the Hebrews, whereby each strata of the Jewish royal court was sentenced to varying degrees of misery, and for the prince it had been the worst. Had Nebuchadnezzar not visited upon his own son a stint in the same prisons as purported instruction against the mismanagement of rule, Evil-Merodach may have remained oblivious to the plight of the son of King Jehoiakim.

However, the Babylonian prince had thus become intimately aware of the cruelties of the prison house, and determined not to suffer Coniah the fate of the others.

"It is a true blessing that Yahweh has chosen to show mercy to the prince in his affliction. Providence indeed smiles upon him. He sups with the king, and they converse together."

With the grace of God, his seasons would be long in the king's favor.

"Do you think that Evil-Merodach will be strong enough to withstand the captains and governors?" Miysha-El wondered aloud. "They press him daily, hoping to influence him toward their desires."

"It is clear that Nergal-Sharezer angles for power at every turn. His dissatisfaction and animosity toward Evil-Merodach bloats to bursting. Even the tenets of the Order will not contain him for much longer!"

"We shall see. It is difficult to remove the head of a snake once it is curled in the master's bosom."

"You speak truly, Daniy-El. Evil-Merodach will need to show wisdom in governing these men, otherwise . . ." Hananyah shrugged his shoulders. He did not wish to contemplate the course that was being set.

"Yahweh will decide. The way will be paved as He chooses. We will serve as we always have," Daniy-El said finally. "We can but be good stewards in the meanwhile. The judgment of Babylon will occur in His time."

The people of Judah, God's children, had paid the penalty of rebellion in blood, and it was likely that Babylon would suffer no less. Yahweh could neither defend the sheep that repeatedly refused the shelter of his sheepfold and far less the wolves that that had torn it apart.

For two years Nergal-Sharezer seethed. Having stood by Nebuchadnezzar's side through the fires of conquest, the magician could scarcely contain his ire as Evil-Merodach slowly altered the structure of the realm. During the winter months, the governors grew restless and pressed Nergal-Sharezer to intervene.

The magi's own discontent slowly melded with their disgruntlement, until, at last, the cauldron of vehemence bubbled over.

"He dines with our enemies as though they passed from the same loins," he complained to Strobos. "I suspect that he may also have little use of us if he continues to give ear to those Jewish advisors. The realm will not tolerate his feeble reign, and the great Babylon will hardly survive long at this pace. It is enough," he swore, sitting forward to the meeting table. "Strobos, the time has come."

"You have waited long enough to come to your decision," Strobos replied languidly. "I was beginning to think that you too were growing feeble."

"Do not test me, Strobos," Nergal-Sharezer growled. He leaned back in his chair, his face breaking into a smile that was both smug and conniving. "See to it, and you may finally claim somewhat of your desire."

"And you must not test *me!*" Strobos countered. "I shall hold you to your word."

"Oh hush," Nergal-Sharezer said with a flick of his hand. "Your reward will come. You keep to your promises, and I shall keep to my word. It's that simple."

"Done."

True to the ways of traitorous men, the murder of Evil-Merodach brought no glory to Strobos's doorstep. The kingdom mourned under a new taskmaster who sucked hungrily at the cup that promised untold power. After a year of rule, Nergal-Sharezer was growing comfortable. The reins of power tugged against his grip, but he was determined to hold them tightly. He would not be weak, as Evil-Merodach had been. The glory of Nebuchadnezzar would soon return to Babylon, and none would dare challenge his authority then. He had even sent to remove a thorn that yet ached in his side. There were so many threads woven into a life of power, that disentangling just one would be decidedly difficult. He had thus determined to sever the thread cleanly.

The magi entered his chambers, plump from supping upon lusts that most men could only crave. He removed his ornate robe, relieved to be alone with his thoughts for the morrow. As he sat upon the bed that was a symbol befitting the grandeur of his improved station, he was startled as a dark shape emerged from the shadows of the plush window hangings. Nergal-Sharezer recoiled, perceiving in the man's eyes the malevolence that had crouched in wait of his return.

Noooo! He had only just begun. Yet he sounded no cry as the man approached, for he knew that he would be unable to escape this foe. The man held open his cloak and withdrew a *chereb* as sharp as a shard of flint.

"Nergal-Sharezer, *my king*, an old friend sends his greetings. He bids you salute Evil-Merodach in his stead."

The sudden elevation of prince Nabonidus to the throne surprised many within the palace who thought Nergal-Sharezer to have finally secured his position. The prince soon elevated Bel-Shazzar, his son, to the throne at his side. Both shared the title of regent, though Bel-Shazzar would soon claim pre-eminence over his father. In many ways, the youth was like his grandfather Nebuchadnezzar—willful and proud; would that Bel-Shazzar could have learnt from his forefather's errors. However, with the turmoil of the past seasons subsiding, Daniy-El's close relationship with the king quietly died, his advice no longer sought after by the new sovereign. Many of his friends and compatriots within the royal court had similarly passed into anonymity, or had gone the way of the earth. *New chiefs, new captains and governors . . . yet the same old ambitions reign,* Daniy-El observed as rivalries blossomed afresh.

Still, Daniy-El was more at ease now. He spent many of his hours in obscurity. Nevertheless, the peace of the times did not make Daniy-El complacent. His Lord was at ever at work toward a purpose far greater than even this massive empire could encompass. He therefore undertook his tasks with an equal diligence to that he had shown the young ruler's grandfather. He would fulfill his part, however small, and pray that the will of Yahweh would come to pass.

10

Beasts

. . . And there was written therein
lamentations and mourning and woe.

- The Prophet Ezekiel

It had been a while since he had been here, yet he recognized the unmistakable shift in the air, as images began to coalesce within his inner sight. They brought with them a familiar reverence and strength, but overlaid with foreboding. In the realm of his spiritual shelter, Daniy-El was transplanted to beyond Babylon, to a desolate place within the reaches of the great oceans. Winds ripped at the surface, and great gouts of water tore the air, clawing as though they strove to overcome some unseen barrier that restrained the limit of their boundaries. Yet they could not breach them indefinitely.

Daniy-El shuddered. The instinct of a man would lead him to huddle against the bluster of the enmeshed winds that ripped the salty expanse, seeming to reach at some thing that lurked within the watery depths. And so it was, that in a span of unknown time, an unearthly creature ventured from the roiling deep, a lion that shifted upon eagle's wings to become—a man! The otherworldly figure gave way to another—a bear-like being that was imbued with a fearsome command to devour all flesh. It too was supplanted, and in its place stood a winged leopard, which, despite its great power, was forced to cede authority to a yet more terrible beast—horned and vicious, and of exceeding strength. Wherever it tread, it brought destruction. Within the horn were eyes—the eyes of a man—and a mouth that spoke great things. One smaller horn transcended the others, tearing them asunder from their roots. However, their dominion did not last, for each throne was cast down, eclipsed by an ancient whose garment and hair were pure white, as he sat his throne that pulsed with streams of fire that blazoned outward. A multitude ministered to Him, whilst some stood before Him as judgments were cast. Daniy-El observed as a man, radiant in glory, was brought to the Ancient, His supremacy unchallenged and infinite as the horned beast was slain, its body consumed in flame.

In the midst of it, Daniy-El was assailed by an inexplicable grief that welled within his breast. He was compelled to seek an answer to the flood of alarming images from one of those found standing by. The answer came simply: "These great beasts, which are four, are four kings, which shall arise out of the earth. But the saints of the Most High God shall take the kingdom and possess the kingdom for ever, even for ever and ever!"

"And that fourth beast?" Daniy-El had been troubled as the beast, which bore no resemblance to the others, made war against God's people, and prevailed until the Ancient of days came to end its reign of terror.

"It is the fourth kingdom," the watcher pronounced. "It shall consume the earth with destruction. It shall even challenge the Most High and weary His people who shall suffer under its rule, but not forever. After this time, all dominions shall serve the Most High, and that shall be the end of the matter."

No further revelation was offered Daniy-El, who now wrestled with all he had seen. How could he convey to anyone the scale of what he had perceived? Entire nations would be enmeshed in a purpose that transcended petty wars over lands and supremacy. Such was the extent of the human mind—finite goals birthed by finite minds with self-centered desires, whereas Yahweh was infinite and all-consuming. He would not permit His enemy to prosper indefinitely. The final battle line would eventually be drawn. There would be no middle ground, no truce, no bargains made, and no quarter given. How many would hear Yahweh's call? How many would give heed to the blast of the *shofar* in this spiritual wilderness? Even his children, Israel, had rebelled. There would be some who gave heed to the truth, for the vision had shown thousands revering the Master. Hundreds of thousands, and thousands upon thousands had embraced false gods and false hopes, suffering needlessly in fleshly houses, feeling the pain of separation from a loving God, yet belligerent and stubborn, determined to ignore the source that beckoned them to life. *Yahweh! YHWH!* Daniel cried inside. So many throughout this age and the next would perish in ignorance. *So many . . . . Too many! Man will have his day in the sun, but when Yahweh withdraws the protective hand that shields us from the brunt of the enemy's malice, the reckoning for man's arrogant self-reliance will be severe. Our pride will be our undoing, Lord. Dear God, may we learn before it is too late.*

Troubled but silent, Daniy-El bore the knowledge of this vision without divulging it to anyone, but a reoccurrence two years later left him shaken and weak. He was transported to Shushan, the capital of Elam. This place, populated by the descendants of Shem, stretched along the banks of the Ulai river. As the vision unfolded, a ram with two magnificent horns arose to subdue the earth, but soon its conquests were surpassed by a goat with a horn of 'sight'. The emerging conqueror charged the ram in the fury of its power, breaking the ram's horns and stamping it into the ground, and none could deliver the ram. Victorious, the goat grew four horns toward the four winds of the heaven and waxed great. Out of one horn grew another, even as Daniy-El had seen before, and it caused the same destruction, bringing challenge even to the Prince of the host of heaven. Its evil endured, and it committed transgressions in the holy sanctuary. *An indignation! How long shall the sanctuary and the host be trodden underfoot?* the saints wondered. The reply was given in thousands of days, and as Daniy-El sought to make clear the vision, a man's voice called and said, "Gabriy-El , make this man to understand the vision."

Faced with the presence of the angel of the Lord, Daniy-El could not keep his feet. He fell upon his face. A deep sleep overcame him as he laid still, his face to the ground. Moving to his side, the angel touched him and he could then stand.

"The ram which thou saw having two horns are the kings of Media and Persia, and the rough goat is the King of Grecia, and the great horn that is between his eyes is the first king." The messenger of Yahweh patiently explained the destructive power that would reign before the Prince of princes again took preeminence.

Having heard all, Daniy-El was bidden to keep what he had seen—a great burden for one man alone to carry. Over the years there had been more and more that he was called to shield within his breast. Overcome by the shock of the vision, Daniy-El slumped into a faint. Unable to rise to do the king's business, he languished for a number of days, receiving several concerned calls at his door. However, no-one could comprehend the enormity of what had suddenly befallen him. They could not see what he had seen, nor endure the distress that it spawned.

"They would never understand!" Daniy-El said softly as he gained his feet days later. *How can they?* The vision had been given to him alone, for the time being, and it would be his burden to bear.

11

Chest of Silver

For out of the north cometh up a nation . . .

- The Prophet Jeremiah

Fear coursed before him and destruction flowed in his wake. He redeemed those peoples that he could, for an angry slave was more dangerous than a dragon. He had exhausted many of his options for conquest. His empire was thriving, yet the lust for more power pulsed in his veins. He was a conqueror more than he was a leader—his soul required much more than a victor's seat, languishing in a throne room, imbibing the heady wine of praise. Something drew him on, nation after nation, until he had set his sights on the most coveted prize that remained: Babylon. Its renown for rebuffing armies exceeded his own growing fame in battle, but not for long. Since his triumph in a revolt against his overlord, Cyrus could envision greater and greater victories ahead. He had grown strong and resilient amidst the changing thrones of Persian dominion; his mother was daughter to Astyages, king of the Medes, whose hand had rested on the scepter for a wealth of seasons. Now Cyrus, having secured dominion over Croesus, king of Lydia, and consolidating his rule in the Ionian Greek cities that lay on the coast of the Aegean sea, had this summit yet before him, drawing him on. Its pinnacle of achievement still lay outside of his possession, but not his reach. Had not Jerusalem, once thought to be unassailable atop its perch, already fallen to Nebuchadnezzar? The victory over Croesus had afforded him untold riches. Enough to see him through many a campaign. He had also gained precious experience that would serve him well in his future conquests.

I will carve a vast domain, and my son Cambyses shall possess it in power, he vowed, watching proudly as his men marched in step, intent upon the goal that their king had set them. The promise of glory infused each with a greater collective purpose—much more than one man alone could conceive. Babylon would fall to Persia, and the legacy would be passed on.

The whinnying of horses pierced the air. Across the plain, he could see the source of their excitement. *Water.* Stretching into the distance, the Gyndes tributary wound deliberately toward the Tigris, where the massing waters would converge.

Cyrus signaled for the regiments to move ahead as he circled to the right, taking in the breadth of the river. He halted his white mare on a knoll, resting the reins before him. It was the first he had seen of the watery expanse. With a soft click and a gentle thrust, he urged the horse into a slow trot. The mounted battalion slid into formation at his heels, followed by the crisp ranks of soldiers. They spread out as the terrain opened up across the floodplain, allowing for easier movement of each group.

Dismounting close to the bank, Cyrus exhaled then folded his lips in thought. *The far bank is within reach of the horses, but the current is swift.* He had not anticipated the rains that had swollen the river ahead of the season of plenty. It was those same rains, though, that afforded his soldiers supplies off the land and fodder for the horses once encampments were set.

Cyrus stooped and plucked at the lush riverside grass. He rubbed his chin. *If we tarry, the season will change, and we shall be trapped by more than this river.* There would be insufficient supplies in this sun-blistered land after the rains passed and the winter crept in. The army was vast and its sustenance was his priority. Without them, his might was lost and his journey to the walls of Babylon would prove futile in the end. The men would need to press on hard while strength prevailed. Cyrus struck the ground in frustration at the unforeseen setback. His horse shied backward, its hoof dislodging a sizable boulder that lay beside a clump of brambles. The horse suddenly reared, its nostrils flaring as the rock bed rippled with a nest of slithering adders. The writhing mass slid from the depression, hissing menacingly. Eyes wild with fright, the mare bolted, its panic-stricken flight causing Cyrus immediate alarm. The horse stumbled on the mucky riverbank but, heedless of her master's frantic shouts, it plunged into the swirling river. The mare clawed for purchase on the muddy river bottom but there was none to be found, and despite her powerful lunges, the horse slipped farther into the embrace of the deadly currents. Her white mane tossed briefly before the churning deep closed over her head. The mount reared up, whinnying in distress and pushing her nose skyward in an attempt to draw breath before she sank once again. The current quickly pushed her farther downstream whilst she continued to struggle to regain the bank. Cyrus raced alongside the horse that had been his main companion on the grueling march south. He called desperately as he crashed through the reeds, but the waters swept the mare farther away with each moment. His commanders pursued feverishly but there was no nearby bend in the river where they could attempt a rescue, and they were forced to watch as the mare disappeared into the distance, still fighting valiantly for its life. After a while, the intermittent flashes of white merged altogether into the murky river. The horse was lost.

Cyrus slowed to a walk, realizing the futility of the chase. He clenched his fists and bellowed at the tumbling water whose eddies continued to swirl, oblivious to his boiling rage. One of his army commanders pulled alongside, clambering down beside his sovereign. He stood aside for a long moment as his lord fumed, his chest still heaving from exertion mixed with unvisited anger. As his master calmed, he held the reins out. Cyrus hung his head and closed his eyes for one last moment before taking the proffered leathers and swinging himself astride the man's dusky brown mount.

"That was one of my best," he said, shaking his head.

"I know," the high commander replied.

"When we leave this place any man will be able to cross without wetting his knees!" Cyrus swore with bitter determination. "This river will be broken," he growled. He glared at the river before turning the young stallion into a canter. *I will have it be so!* he declared.

The Persian Lord surveyed the three hundred and sixty angled channels that thousands of his men had assiduously dug over the ensuing weeks. They stretched away from the river like the legs of a gargantuan centipede. He nodded in satisfaction, and then gave the order for the makeshift dams to be broken and the successive levees flattened as the intermediate canals filled. Dry trenches churned with the life of the Gyndes as the first curious rivulets danced along arrow-straight furrows, the first waters being drunk by the thirsty ground. The process repeated along the length of the river that mellowed into subdued ripples as its strength was leeched into the plain. Over the course of several days the water ebbed away and the river bed became exposed along its edges. The soldiers muscled bodies had toiled at their king's behest to both satisfy his anger, and to provide their companies an easy way across the deadly tide.

Cyrus had been loathe to be delayed from his conquest yet he acknowledged that the deferred march would regain time, having benefited from a crossing that did not require his men's lives to be sacrificed as had his mare's. With nations at his command, it seemed that the loss of his horse was a theft by the river, and a man such as he could not suffer the challenge, even by nature itself. Variance within his domain always met with swift judgment, and he never balked at administering a penalty. In like manner, he felt himself equally justified in dispensing ample rewards where merited. Hence his men were loyal, and vigorous, in implementing his will. In addition, there was much other than wealth to be gained in these foreign lands for those who stood with the conqueror. His origins tempted his bloodlust for dominion.

In addition, Cyrus's fascination for the wonder of distant civilizations urged him on to new lands. He never shirked the call for battle. It was necessary to his ambitions. It was by grace that his strategies had gone uncontested thus far. His newest quarry was larger than he was, but had grown fat off complacency and unopposed dominance. *Not for much longer, however.* Persia and Media would be the beneficiaries of Babylon's lengthy stupor. The lion had come to seek its prey. He, Cyrus, would reap the fatness of the land, whilst Chaldea wallowed beside the lake of self-aggrandizement that it had filled ponderously over the decades with the blood of enslaved nations. Babylon, its capital city, was likened to the ancient bulls of Bashan, of which tales had been told over the centuries; strong and terrible, they ripped the earth. Yet their might had been culled by a smaller foe—the Jews, who themselves were now over-run and enslaved. It was a mystery throughout the lands, for Israel was long known to be invincible, their God going before them into battle and consuming their enemies like a violent blaze. Perhaps they had lost favor in His eyes or angered Him in some way. Once outside a Master's mantle of protection, a servant's back was then laid bare and susceptible to a new taskmaster's scourge. Israel, it was told, had fallen to such a course. Whatever the cause, they would be part of his realm once he took the great city. He would be as a calf wrestling against the horns of the mighty Babylon. Yet he had tested his strength on other enemies and had vanquished them through unsurpassed cunning.

Cyrus smiled, relishing the contest that lay ahead. He had secured an alliance with the Medes and thus increased his advantage over the Chaldeans. He was certain that the combined guile and prowess of their two armies could subdue the war beast that Babylon had once groomed meticulously, but now left to welter in idleness. Its bloated carcass would soon be his stomping ground. They would flounder through their own encumbrances—titled generals who had not fought the scale of war that would camp at their doorstep; administrators who had grown complacent in their power; a figurehead leader who gloried in his own reflected pride. The merged forces would harry the recalcitrant bull until a weakness was discovered and they would claim their victory.

His first course would be to draw them out of the city. Their king's ego would press him to attack the seemingly smaller force, thinking to mangle them on the banks, but Darius' contingents would be held in abeyance until the Chaldean foray was extended beyond the security of the city perimeter. Then, Darius would deploy his fleetest soldiers to the Chaldean flanks, capturing their quarry in their vice-like jaws. Bel-Shazzar would assuredly take the bait. His pride would demand it, for the man was reportedly arrogant enough to be tempted into folly. On this he could depend. It was a solidly devised plan, and still. . . . Cyrus scrubbed at his beard in momentary indecision. His troops would be as plenteous as the river, yet the foul waters still barricaded him from his prize. He would defeat their initial force and reduce their strength but it would not cripple the Chaldean monster. He would be compelled to remain outside the walls whilst the gates within the river-way were barred to him. Each gate was lowered several measures below the surface of the river but did not extend into the riverbed. When fully lowered, his men would need to swim unarmed to pass below the gated teeth, for the weight of their weapons would hamper their efforts. If the Gyndes had been the Euphrates he would have rejoiced. Unfortunately, diversion of the tremendous waters of the Euphrates would require them to dredge hundreds more canals than he had at the Gyndes, by which time Bel-Shazzar would have deduced his intent and made provisions to secure the portals by some other means. No. The water needed to be lowered—and lowered fast! However, despite overcoming his trial with the Gyndes, Cyrus could still devise no way to do so. He sighed, his thoughts straying again to the walls of the city, the inner one of which was surrounded by a yawning moat. Outside the moat lay another wall, two hundred royal cubits high and fifty cubits thick. Some traveling merchants spun tales that it was wide enough to turn a four-horse chariot, and even though he knew this to be an exaggeration, the truth was no less staggering. The outer wall was protected along its eleven mile length by two hundred and fifty towers. Even if he could employ siege engines to pierce the fortifications, his armies would stall at the inner moat. Meanwhile, his engines would be beset by fire arrows.

A sharp twinge between his eyes reminded Cyrus that he had been striving all day for a viable solution. Each plan for an incursion would prove to be equally disastrous. He would need something more if he meant to mount a successful assault. Although no sure course had yet been determined to breach the well-defended city, he was trusting in divine insight to reveal the opening. *If it is there, I will find it!*

12

Viceroy

Bel-Shazzar snorted derisively as he surveyed the army that was amassed beyond the broad reaches of the Euphrates River. Two years after the trumpets had first sounded the battle blast, the northern invaders yet sat watching their walls. *Admirable show of patience, Cyrus, but it will avail you nothing.* With twenty years of supplies in the city stores, Cyrus would be graying and feeble before he could claim his prize. Ridiculous though it had seemed at the hour of the report, the scouts had indeed spoken truthfully. More enemy battalions were approaching from the northwest. Bel-Shazzar's military training gainsaid the strategy being employed by the Persian. The Babylonian king observed with initial curiosity and concern. His unease was soon tempered by escalating incredulity.

What manner of ill advice from the gods could Cyrus be following? What would prompt a man of his renown to act so foolishly—to assail Babylon? Then, to mass even more troops without dependable rations? Bel-Shazzar pondered.

Cyrus would need to take the city or be eaten up by the wasteland that would be created by such a large force. What ruse could Cyrus intend perhaps? A costly one, no matter the intent. Surely he did not plan to encamp thousands of foot-soldiers beyond a river that was as effective as a moat, since the gates all opened onto the river. The viceroy could not sail boats across the desert sands, and siege engines were useless here where the walls were thick as houses. In addition to this, the narrow banks would not support the cumbersome devices. The walls of the city dwarfed them like ants before a behemoth. His spies had been unable to discern the strategy of the Persian offensive, but they did confirm that the Medes had joined their forces to their new ally. It was known that the warriors with their shining battle armor had converged upon the greatest trophy north of the mountains in expectation of victory.

Word had flooded along the river of an approaching army, but the rumors had initially appeared to be the ramblings of lunatics. *Will they assault the soaring walls with arrows? Will they throw stones at the battlements and seek to set alight the fire-hardened brick fortifications?* Bel-Shazzar was as perplexed as his advisors. Each proposal seemed as preposterous as the next, but there they were, as bold as hunting lions. Cyrus himself, it was told, was leading his army into the fray.

It will be along a road to slow starvation if the Persian does not relent and take his men back north, Bel-Shazzar surmised. He sniffed at the thought. Yes, there was ample water to drain from the Euphrates but food would need to be trekked across the scorching expanse that stretched between himself and his enemy whose homeland lay scores of moons away.

The king leaned over the parapet. He squinted into the distance where chariots careened through the rearward ranks. Trumpets cleaved the air with three forceful blasts. *Cyrus!* Bel-Shazzar straightened determinedly. *I will not be cowed by an idle show of pomp.* The trumpets were an insolent gesture to goad them perhaps into some rash action. *Well, I am no simpleton to be twice lured, to my detriment, beyond the safety of my fortress. Let them prattle and dance with halberds at the reeds edge.* He planned to answer their taunts in a way that would show his disdain for their empty posturing. *Buzzing horseflies*, he sneered, turning away. Let them plant seeds of fear elsewhere. Babylon was his to command now. His reign had just started to take root, and he would let nothing mar his success. The anniversary of his coronation neared, and he would toast his great city and show himself to his lords. They would bask in his glory and the majesty of his presence. Many would even tremble at the honor. He would show that he did not fear Cyrus's pitiful display of might set out below. He threw his hand off, dismissing the nuisance war. Let Cyrus skulk around with the river rats. Merriment awaited, and the lords would not be denied the company of their king.

The gates . . . the gates . . . the gates . . . Cyrus repeated to himself, pacing in his tent. *Our men will be cut down before they set a foot on the ramps*, he admitted grudgingly. *We need the water gates open. . . . Or two at least. With two we could make it. Otherwise, it will be suicide for the men in armor.* The Persian king rubbed his temples vigorously and sat, hoping to ease away the pulsing ache that had clambered from the base of his spine to squat upon his shoulders before straining upward to hammer upon his temples. It caused a throbbing pain to spread across his forehead. The Median and Persian armies had reached the plains of Shinar and marched on Babylon with still no final recourse for taking the city. Their first offensive had been thoroughly successful. Bel-Shazzar had sent his army out to meet the invasion, and the Medes and Persians had trounced the Babylonian companies, cutting off the bulk of the Chaldeans from retreat within city walls. Now there they sat. Not even his gleaming parades could taunt the Babylonian king into a second attack, and with each day that passed, his men grew more restless for a battle. Without a purpose for their bloodlust, they would soon start squabbles and brawls in order to relieve the tension of waiting.

The king's vision strayed upward toward the roof of the black goat's hair tent. Through straps at the fore pole, he glimpsed a star as it streaked by, and then winked out of existence. *O that I could snuff out the Chaldeans as swiftly. The walls are too thick. The river is too deep. . . . I can neither ford the river nor batter the gates. The banks are a bog of reeds and my men dispirited.* He squeezed the bridge of his nose and expelled a huff of air just as Darius entered.

"You cannot sleep either," the Median lord commented.

"How can I sleep whilst we waste away mere paces from our goal?"

"I have considered the land before us and their defenses. The most skilled of our companies could advance with leather breastplates and short-swords alone. The long march is over. They would need no sandals within the city. If we set the secondary ranks to besiege to the walls on the south and east away from the gates, we will have a chance to get enough of these men in. The decoy is likely to find success."

"Indeed!" Cyrus raised his head sharply then winced as pain lanced behind his eyes. He savored the thought of a night's rest before returning to the matter at hand. The proposal paralleled his conceptions for the siege; however, would it be enough? The idea, though, inspired him. "Our best strategy will be to pose a night attack after wearying them during the course of several days. "The feat is possible, but what we need desperately is some aid from inside the walls. Is your young Mede within the walls still with us?"

"He is."

Cyrus drew in a slow breath, and then sat back heavily. "That is good. That is very good. We may need him least we be sucked into a pit of death fighting these Babylonians through the winter. Any information at all could save us a grim fate and a humbling defeat. Would that we could wish away this river that stands between us and this plump fruit that is ripe for the picking."

Darius sat silent a moment, drumming his fingers on the low oak table between them. The Mede pursed his lips.

Cyrus perked up at the light that suddenly sparked in his friend's eyes. "What are you thinking, Darius?" Cyrus asked slowly, his eyes narrowing as he recognized the telltale cue that his companion was devising a war strategy. "What remedy, Darius? Do not keep me waiting. Tell me."

His companion smiled slyly. "Did not our spy send word of an upcoming feast for the princes and high officials of Babylon?" he asked, grinning broadly.

"Yes. Bel-Shazzar mocks us from his wall." Cyrus balled his fists together. "Would that I could—" He stopped short as a pain lanced across his forehead. He buckled his lips, determined to drive away the menacing headache. The effort of devising a successful plan was draining his mental and physical reserves hour by hour.

"Perhaps you can after all," Darius interjected, leaning forward.

"How, my friend? How?" Cyrus exclaimed in fresh excitement, a glow returning to his visage.

"If we drain the river, then—"

"I thought of that already. It will not work," Cyrus said, slouching in renewed frustration. "It would take far too long and—"

"No. Patience, Cyrus. Patience. Attend to my words. On our way in, did not the scouts report a low marsh not far east of here. It stretches for perhaps a mile."

"Yes. This is so," Cyrus acknowledged, still puzzled. "I can't see how that can be of a help, but what of it?"

"You are slower than I am at sixty-two, Cyrus,' Darius joked. "I thought you would have caught on by now. Out of curiosity, I questioned our advisors on the history of the city. From what I can piece together, one of the rulers of old, Queen Nitocris, I believe her name was, dug a channel for the same purpose of draining the river in order that she could build that monstrous bridge that stretches between the palaces on either side of the river. While the river was diverted she laid the great stones for the foundations and the vast columns before releasing the waters again."

Cyrus clapped his hands like a gleeful child, finally comprehending the scope of Darius's revelation. "And we needed hundreds of channels at the Gyndes, but with the marsh and sink already existing, we shall have a ready catchment for the flow. We need only throw all our forces into carving one or two channels the short distance to the depression. We can be finished within the week and—"

"In time for the feast of feasts!" Darius finished, nodding along with the Persian sovereign. "The river flows south. If the channel starts far enough upstream then curves toward the marsh we shall go undetected until it will be too late for them. I shall assign continuous shifts of two-thousand men. The task will be completed swiftly, and the men will not tire before the battle."

"The Chaldeans will be blissfully drowning themselves in vats of wine or frolicking on the beds of their concubines whilst we slip in!" Cyrus exulted. He stood, revitalized by the sudden change in prospects. *At last, a plan worthy of execution!* "You have merited the greys in your crown, Darius. You leave no stone unturned in your wisdom." He walked over to slap the Mede on his back then went to the flap of his tent. Torches burned in the distance, casting shimmering reflections off the river. The dappled glow could be seen all along the guarded perimeter.

Cyrus shook his fist toward Babylon. *We are coming, Bel-Shazzar. Feast while you can, for we are coming!*

Strobos watched the dim shapes emerge from the enfolding gloom. There was no need for the revealing glow of a lantern. Each knew whom he would meet on these soggy banks, where the cloying stench of dead reed fish assailed one's nostrils. Many had been trapped in shallow pools with no escape. It was unfortunate that he had been forced to sink to these deplorable depths, but to his chagrin, circumstances had evolved such that he was left with no further options that appealed to his ambitions. Once the night was over, he would regain his footing enough to claim the stature that he craved. He had not been amongst the lords who toasted the royal splendor with riotous merriment, but he would sip the victor's cup before long. Muffled voices drew closer to the agreed meeting ground.

"It is not low enough yet, I say. We poled it just before half-night, and the men could scarcely breathe without choking on these stinking reeds. We need another hour at least before attempting it."

The men halted a few cubits from his shielded position.

"We know you are there, Strobos. Save your skulking for the Babylonian fools and their drunken stupors. Come out I say!"

Strobos raised himself slowly. "Good to see you again, Ugbaru."

"High Commander Ugbaru, pup! Have you a way to secure the gates for us? Six cubits is all we may need. Your men must raise the two gates nearest to the south section, but only enough to just about break the water. We do not need the creaking of iron to betray us prematurely. Shall they be ready to do your bidding?"

"They shall, my lord. In fact—"

"They'd better. I will not have my men skewered in the palace yard like rats. With your aid, we can avoid much bloodshed. The others will be waiting to cross the bridge when the signal is given. Take heed Strobos. Do not fail us," he grated.

"I shall not. I guarantee you, my lord."

The commander harrumphed. "No you will not, will you?" He turned to his companion who handed him a small but weighty sack. Ugbaru hefted the bundle in his large palm, and then tossed it to their accomplice. Strobos caught the bag and exhaled in a *whoof* as it struck his midriff. He silenced the chink of coins against his thick robe.

"You have never missed an opportunity for riches, have you, Strobos?" The commander chuckled low, but with little amusement in his tone. "You should have garnered sufficient *darics* for you to woo a queen. Be gone now. There is much to be completed. We have few hours before dawn to meet Cyrus's appointed time. Watch for the torch. It will not be bright, so keep those hawk eyes of yours trained on the plain."

Strobos extended his hand in which he grasped a small scroll and the third man came forward to retrieve it before returning to his commander's side. Ugbaru nodded in satisfaction. He slapped the other man on the arm. "Let us depart." He turned away without looking at Strobos. The night would soon be warped by violence.

Strobos felt the weight of the sack. Such affairs were not as lucrative as many supposed. He needed most of this simply to bribe the guardsmen at the palace gates and two at the water gates who had allowed him to pass. He would keep the silver but the *darics* would be useless, unless their ploy was successful. The coins would serve, but there was a greater reward offered for his concupiscence—a position of power where tributes were counted in souls and measured in blood. The promise of a high office lured him on. He would answer the call that beckoned him farther. His name could yet be etched upon the bricks of Babylon along with those such as Nergal-Sharezer, who stood amongst the few who were truly counted in these realms of power.

13

The Last King

Thus saith the Lord, write this man childless,

a man that shall not prosper in his days.

- Jeremiah - Prophet of Israel

"To the king!" A resounding cheer crested as a toast was raised from some unknown quarter within the Hall of Feasts. It echoed into the courts beyond the great doors. At last the decree had gone forth. The reign of Nebuchadnezzar had officially been passed to the prince, Bel-Shazzar, after the culmination of two brief spans of power by aspirers to the throne. However, they could not hold sway over the throne for very long and their tenuous grip would shortly fail Nebuchadnezzar's crown now sat atop the glistening brow of the portly prince, Bel-Shazzar, who stood proud before the feasting assembly that now toasted his rise to power.

"It is a good day," he laughed heartily. "Let us dine and be glad." He spread his hands magnanimously, and then sat heavily on the elaborately decorated cushions that received his bulk with a whoosh of air. Bel-Shazzar's advisors had urged him to dedicate his feast to the gods. Already the celebrants had emptied dozens of vats of wine stored in the royal cellars, and the pitchers continued to be filled. The effect of their hearty consumption was evidenced in their too-loud voices and spontaneous laughter. He had waited a long time for the endowment of this accolade in addition to the endorsement of the Men of Wisdom. The brusque dismissal by the Order had stung him on many occasions while Nebuchadnezzar had yet reigned. After the old king's passing the power was open to be taken—it was useful to have made allies. It was more useful to have had the resources to make it a reality. His nation was mighty, his lands extensive. At last, the wealth of the kingdom was his to command.

King! The word tasted more delicious upon his tongue than the sweet, sun-ripened melons from the fields of Duroc. Bel-Shazzar reclined, taking in the expanse of the gathering. He wished that he could present some unique spectacle to delight this grand assembly, but what marvel had these men of power not yet seen? Nebuchadnezzar had provided a gamut of sensations to dazzle the most auspicious visitor to his court. A stroll through the Hanging Gardens was a delight in itself.

He had summoned his wives and numerous concubines such that all could envy him in his splendor, but he needed more lest the tenor of his celebration wane. *Hmmmm. . . . What is there to present that would evoke their passion for rarity?* A small tray of savory meats and curious delicacies were proffered at the king's table. The worked gold edge of the platter glittered in the candlelight. Disregarding the sumptuous fare untouched upon his plate, Bel-Shazzar made another selection absentmindedly. The sliver of lamb joined the other forgotten delicacies as he watched the spangling light weave its way toward an adjacent table at which were seated several princes of the kingdom. As he watched, the scintillations danced alongside a row of lords as the tray was rapidly emptied. Bel-Shazzar's drained cup slipped absentmindedly from his fingers as a nugget of an idea formed suddenly within his mind. *But dare I remove them?* he thought with a tremor. They were stored in the dim vaults of the Temple of Bel-Merodach. He had seen them once, these objects of Jewish glory, and they were beyond the imagining. Bel-Shazzar righted his overturned chalice with a self-assured smile. *I am king am I not? In this, I shall demonstrate my sovereignty—an unchallengeable fact.* His eyes lit as brightly as the shimmer that had sparked his inspiration. *It will be but for a short while and then they shall be returned.* Surely there can be no harm!

"Rabsaris!" Bel-Shazzar called excitedly to the adjacent grouping. "Send to the Temple! There are riches ensconced there whose radiance has not seen the light of day in decades. Is that not regrettable? Go. Bring them hither that all may share in their splendour."

"Your majesty?" Rabsaris asked, perplexed by the peculiar instruction. He arose from his comfortable seat and came to stand beside his master.

"Bel-Shazzar leaned in to draw the officer into his confidence. "The vessels, Rabsaris. Have them sent from the Temple."

"Vessels, my lord?"

Bel-Shazzar rolled his eyes and extended his hand to grasp the sleeve of the man's cloak. "The Hebrew vessels, Rabsaris. In fact. I do not blame you for forgetting. They have been stored for so many years that they will easily have passed from men's memories. Go, retrieve them for my pleasure."

"The holy vessels of the Jews, my Lord? But Nebuchadnezzar—"

"And Nebuchadnezzar is dead. Of course you know those of which I speak! Surely you do not fear, Rabsaris. Not you who have held Jerusalem in contempt for so long!"

The high official's face blanched at the rebuff. Bel-Shazzar's face grew hard as he fingered a thread of his newly bestowed power. "Do as I command."

Rabsaris bowed. "As you desire, my king." His clipped tone betrayed his affront, yet he moved away with alacrity.

Bel-Shazzar sniffed. The Order, these lords, these princes that huddled below his wing—they would gainsay him if he gave them the smallest of opportunities, he knew. All in all, he was determined not to grant them that. They would contrive methods through which they could ingratiate themselves to him, for the glory resided with him now. He rested back on the down-filled pillows. The items he had requested were breathtaking to behold. When he had been invited to view them after Nebuchadnezzar's victory over the Jews, they had been placed for safekeeping within the dim recesses of the vaults. Here, in the radiance of the lantern-light filling room, their magnificence would shake the foundation of the gathering, which prized such wealth above all. His heart pumped fast with anticipation of the wonder he would see on the faces of those about him when they beheld his riches.

As Bel-Shazzar held out his cup to be refilled and took a draught of the sweet brew, he scanned the crowded hall. Pleasure already wreathed the faces of his guests like silken cocoons. This memorable night was destined to be spoken of beyond the borders of Shinar, as the envy of the invited princes made indelible etchings on their souls. Each would carry tales of the evening's splendor back to their far-reaching provinces.

At last, the doors were flung back to admit a streaming procession of slaves bearing gilded trays by the score. Each held burnished goblets that gleamed like trapped tongues of fire as they reflected the blazing lamplight. Porters arrived with an unwieldy crate which they rested heavily onto the glazed marble floor. The slaves moved back from the large object and the king nodded his acquiescence. There ropes holding the walls were drawn through the brass loops and the timbers fell. The braziers encircling the room were fed once again and the renewed flare made the feasting attendants gasp with awe. They beheld for the first time the wondrously molded chargers that had sat in the temple of the Jewish God; their superior craftsmanship surpassed that of the king's finest furnishings. A hush fell over the stunned assembly as they witnessed the untold beauty that once had been for the eyes of only the Levite priests that had tended the house built for the God of the Hebrews. Bel-Shazzar had been very young when the war had been launched against Israel and he had cared little for its distant outcome then, but now its legacy would serve him well.

Gold and silver goblets were handed to the concubines who laughed as gaily as the king who was enjoying the impact of his tribute. Bel-Shazzar stroked his beard as he noticed the delighted expressions flooding the faces of the guests who pressed forward with rapt attention, as more treasures were unveiled. At the king's word, the palace slaves came forward. The hum of admiring voices now rose to a crescendo as jeweled pieces were distributed to the royalty and governing officials who vied to hold the finest pieces. Holy vessels that had once borne the blood of the sacrifices to God were soon brimming with wine or sundry spiced treats. The laughter of the guests became even more boisterous as the show of the king's bounty did not wane until all the tables were resplendent with the glory that had once graced the Temple in Jerusalem.

"Such artistry! You have outdone yourself this once," a swaying prince cheered the king. "To Bel-Merodach," he said, raising his goblet.

"There will be more to come yet," Bel-Shazzar rejoined enthusiastically. "To Bel-Merodach!" Bel-Shazzar shouted, and a lusty cheer was raised. He was pleased to have won the people's approval and relished the promise of more. One of his wives crooned in pleasure as she traced the artwork and embroidered gold tracings that enhanced a bejeweled cup. As she placed it gently to her painted lips, her sultry eyes suddenly bulged incongruously and the large cup tumbled unceremoniously to the ground, spilling dark wine over her soft garments. The runnels pooled around her delicate cloth slippers, staining them the red of blood. She grew pale and slumped sideways beside him, her lids still parted.

Poison? Bel-Shazzar shrunk back, fearing that his wife had been gripped by the initial spasm that accompanied the first pangs of ingesting a deadly brew. On occasion he had witnessed the effects of the vicious practice the oft stole the life from an unsuspecting officer of the court. *The brew might have been meant for me. But how could it be?* The wine-taster yet stood at his post, awaiting the king's usual beckoning nod. *What manner of sorcery is this then?* The king was stupefied. His eyes darted across the Hall of Feasts, searching for the Rab-Mag.

"She's fainted!" someone shrieked, jarring the king away from his befuddled thoughts.

Bel-Shazzar's brow furrowed as he realized that the woman's eyes continue to stare beyond him. Simultaneously a ripple of disturbance coursed from the king's table to the farther reaches of the Hall. The room became a sudden mill of dread as courtiers dashed to and fro, some toward the doors, others to aid friends who were pushed to the ground in the wild melee. Many stood in confusion, hoping to discern the cause of the abrupt dispersal of guests. Several pointed to the columns behind the king, shouting unintelligible words before turning to join the distressed rush away from the hall.

Look not behind! Run! Escape! Stay not! Despite this inner warning, Bel-Shazzar turned, slowly, fearfully, as he too sought to discover the root of the tumult, for the reactions of his normally stoic guests bespoke some grave calamity. The king was unprepared for the scene that was unfolding at his back. His legs failed and his bowels weakened as he beheld a disembodied hand, its finger extended as it hovered several feet above the heads of those in the room. Its slow passage across the soaring wall revealed a cryptic phase, the intent of which he could neither read nor understand. The etched words were being formed with uncanny patience that made Bel-Shazzar's blood run cold and loosed his loins. The hand made a final stroke that was imprinted upon the stone as easily as a quill upon parchment. The limb floated several moments, its fingers still extended as though toward him. Then, it simply faded.

Bel-Shazzar's heart pounded maniacally. He looked in desperation toward the Rab-Mag, one of the few in attendance who yet remained, hoping that the magician would diffuse his fear with a wave. However the turmoil that dominated the visage of the magi banished the king's hopes of relief from his own terror. The inexplicable apparition had seemingly evoked an equal horror in the practitioner of dark arts. The guests had flooded from the room like weasels fleeing a conflagration. Now he was alone save for a shockingly small number of his counselors and servants. Even as the deserting horde spilled out, rumors began to crisscross the palace like flaming arrows. His guardsmen had been powerless to defend him from the otherworldly intrusion on his sanctum.

Bel-Shazzar beckoned to Rab-Mag who plodded woodenly forward, his eyes yet fixed on the wall that bore the undecipherable message. As the counselor approached, Bel-Shazzar forced words past his lips, which he willed to cease their quivering.

"T—tell me—" the king choked out. He cleared his throat to suppress the croak that escaped unbidden. "Tell me. What does it mean?" the king pleaded.

The magi did not reply but continued to stare at the strange letters scripted boldly into the stone.

"Rab-Mag!" the king screamed, desperation interlacing his cry. "What does it mean?" He extended his hand toward the wraithlike script.

The counselor shook his head, his tone tinged with dismay. "I know not, my lord."

"You know not? How is that possible?" Bel-Shazzar screeched. His hands shook with a mixture of fear and anger. It was obvious to all that Bel-Shazzar was not as stoic as his grandfather was, but though his confidence and self-assurance had been whittled away by his present helplessness, it had not crumbled completely. "Confer with the council at once. I will have an answer this day!" he shouted. His voice quavered with distress. I shall await you here. Bid them all come that they may give some solace to their king. Go!"

The counselor nodded, bowed, and then backed away, his jaws clenched. He tore his eyes away from the wall. "You will have an answer, my king," he assured, before exiting swiftly. Most of the remaining Men of Wisdom trailed in his wake, still dazed.

Bel-Shazzar slumped back, covering his face with trembling hands. Still the vision loomed before him. He peered between shaking fingers at the words that flowed in an ill portent over the surface. The king instinctively knew that something had gone terribly wrong, and for all his power, he could do nothing in this, save wait. *Be quick, Rab-Mag,* he cried silently. *Be quick.*

The Chief Magician hustled through the long corridors, his thoughts aflutter with hieroglyphs and translations, but the symbols continued to merge incoherently in his mind. He could make no sense of the language that had been scribed on the wall in the Hall of Feasts.

Where can we start? What God had the king offended? The magi wondered, mystified.

If he had known, he may have been able to give the king an answer, but no dialect within his experience even vaguely resembled the writings that now hovered ominously above the king's table. His steps quickened along the hall. The Men of Wisdom, and the Order of magicians, had been placed in this predicament countless times before, yet each occurrence seemed more harrowing than the last, for a distraught king could be unpredictable and those closest to him oft suffered his wrath. Hence Bel-Shazzar's distress could not be overlooked. Rab-Mag had seen many kings cower under the shadow of terrible portents. Though the implications were familiar to him, he had come to realize that he was not impervious to a king's retribution.

Nebuchadnezzar had demonstrated his propensity for reprisal should his wishes be thwarted. Likewise, Bel-Shazzar, though less given to violence than his predecessor, was nevertheless willing to exert his power forcibly, should he suspect any deviance by those enacting his will. Bel-Shazzar was less apt than Nebuchadnezzar in weathering the burdens of power, least of all a spiritual matter. The repercussions of headship often rattled the staunchest nerves.

Rab-Mag halted abruptly outside the door to the counselor's hall. Taking a deep breath he pushed the heavy doors open. A cacophony of shouts rushed past the tall man who leaned back in surprise. He had expected to discover only a few of the senior Men of Wisdom, he was prepared to summon the others, yet every seat was filled.

"My good men—please!" Rab-Mag raised his hands for silence and the hubbub gradually ebbed. He closed the doors behind him and turned to face them as the final stains of discord died away and were replaced by solemnity.

"We are confronted with another challenge, as you are well aware by now. Most of you were in attendance at the king's banquet hall. I noticed several of your hasty departures," he commented with a wry twist of his mouth. A number of the men lowered their eyes abashedly. Rab-Mag huffed. "Nevertheless, we are faced with a severe problem. Most of you would have seen the inscription. . . . He turned to the sorcerers and astrologers who returned his incisive gaze with equal gravity. "A foreboding writ has been issued, I believe, against our king. The king desires our interpretation, and undoubtedly, it is urgent for us all to fulfill this task. I assume that I need not explain the potential consequences of denying our sovereign's command. Most of you will remember, or have been told, of the proclamations of death often imposed by kings at such times as these. It is therefore in our heartiest interest to unravel the peculiar notation to avoid any reoccurrence of the same. I assure you, the king is less than convivial at this moment. Whatever spirit it be that haunts him, we must give him succor lest we be blamed. The king will wait in the hall whence we have been commissioned to present an answer regarding this extraordinary event. He will depend on our counsel to dispel his fear." Rab-Mag did not relish the prospect of quelling the king's anger should they fail. Bel-Shazzar was not a vicious man by nature, yet the fear that had gripped the king's heart could drive him to some act of desperation. Rab-Mag too had tasted the terror that rose like bile in his innards, but he had striven to master himself. The reaction that had swept the feasting hall showed that no-one present had been oblivious to its effect. Rab-Mag had never before experienced a power that was felt so forcefully within his being. No wonder the king's knees smote against one another. The image of the hand replayed once again in his mind and he shivered.

"Is something amiss, my lord?" a voice probed tentatively.

Rab-Mag shook himself back to the present, momentarily disturbed by the return of the fearsome sensation. He did not wish to reveal his own unease and doubt to these men.

"We have not one, but *two* dangers besetting us. The threat outside our walls remains, and now we have seen one more insidious lurking within. Perhaps it would serve best if—"

"We have been discussing the matter amongst ourselves," the chief astrologer interjected. "It is clear to most of us that the sign holds no threat. It may be a simple communication by the gods to our master confirming his kingship. Would not a God of undeniable power do more than make markings on a wall? Would this God not show himself mighty and deliver a sign more terrible than a simple script?" Murmurs of assent bubbled from various corners of the assembly. "If this were indeed some deadly edict would we not have read its shadow in the stars? I speak for my brethren here." He threw his arms wide to include the grouping that sat close by. "In spite of the king's disquiet and the temerity of *others*, we believe that this demonstration need not be attributed to evil fortune."

A clamor arose at his words. A few of the sorcerers rose to their feet in obvious annoyance at the astrologer's slight. Rab-Mag rose along with them. He had been one of those standing closest to the king when the writing had appeared, and he was sure that this had been no whimsical portent or idle threat. He raised his hands once again to request a return to sobriety.

"Nevertheless, the king waits for our interpretation, not our vague impressions. Therefore, each order amongst us is asked to return to the hall after seeking an answer. We have been afforded no alternatives. Despite our varying dispositions, I advise due diligence, as lives may depend on it. The king has promised a reward to he who divulges the mystery. The title of Third Ruler in the kingdom, and a chain of gold." He smiled sardonically. "This may stimulate some of you to be that much more thorough! We shall practice our arts, then attend the king. Go, gather what you need and return."

After a time in frenetic conferral, the magicians shook their heads in despondence. The soothsayers and astrologers were equally perplexed having gained nothing from their steady communion. Seeing no alternative but to present themselves to the king, Rab-Mag led the forlorn assemblage back along the winding corridors to the main hall.

At the sight of the approaching procession, the guardsmen flanking the doors hastily bid them enter.

Bel-Shazzar looked up then extended a shaking hand. "You bring an answer?" he questioned eagerly.

Rab-Mag took in the small gathering that clustered about the king, offering whatever succor they could. The magician chose his words carefully, lest he inflame Bel-Shazzar with his speech.

"My king, we have spared no effort to bring you swift tidings. The practitioners of arts have applied the strongest of magic on your behalf and that of the kingdom. I assure you that their ministrations have been diligent and their conclusions astute. This we have appertained. We judged that the appearance of the writing may be wholly a device of the armies that lay outside our walls, some invocation by their foreign god—a basic device to strike fear in our hearts that they may snatch us unawares. I adjure you therefore not to fear, as we are held safe and secure in the bosom of Babylon. Here you are protected, my lord and—"

Bel-Shazzar's eyes bulged suddenly and he found his feet in a rush. "That protection avails me nothing if the Hand of God reaches out to pull me to the grave!" he shouted. "Give me a reading lest I be undone." He clutched at his robes, and, as his strength began to fail again he sat, still holding the fine raiment bunched in his fists as though, through the effort, he could hold himself together. "Rab-Mag," he said wearily, "my patience is drawn thin. What ails the Men of Wisdom? Have your arts deserted you? Is this God that shadows me more powerful than yours? Must I continue in terror whilst you whisper your secrets to each other?" Bel-Shazzar moaned, his voice trembling again.

Rab-Mag was compelled to silence. He extended his hands, beseeching the king to be calm, but as a tremor shook the king's entire body, he let his arms flop to his side. There was nothing that he could say to the king to dispel his fear. This Spirit was closed to their magic. In all his years as Rab-Mag, he had never seen such opposition to his remonstrations. Yet he must try.

"There are some other spells that may be cast, the times and the alignment of the stars are against us. If we but abide perhaps another week—."

"Have the soothsayers no advice at all?" Bel-Shazzar pleaded. "Why can no-one reveal this thing to me? O, I am perished indeed," he moaned woefully.

Rab-Mag flinched uncomfortably at the piteous display, and rued his inability to respond to the king's dire request.

"Leave me," the king said softly. "Leave me." His words were barely a whisper.

The magi ventured to frame a reply in consolation, but thought better of it as Bel-Shazzar's eyes fixed glassily on some unseen horror. He did not even notice their departure. He needed more than they could provide, and when he needed him most, the god Bel-Merodach had failed to answer.

Toward twilight swirling visions came, and Daniy-El pushed back against the crush of thoughts that converged out of the gathering night. It was dangerous to become complacent, for the enemy of his soul would snuff out the Light that gave him life at the first opportunity granted. Not every spiritual presence that sought him was his Lord's. He rejected those that clave to the dark, and instead sought his true Master, releasing himself into prayer. *Be ever watchful*, he reminded himself. He had not been given grace and extended seasons to no good end. Yahweh would have His reasons.

From its onset, the day had been stamped with a distinctive mark of providence. It had begun with a series of travesties by the king whose taste of power had cloaked his good judgment. A sense of foreboding seemed to accompany the new king of Babylon from the light of the dawn. The prince of the court was enthroned in pomp as successor to the throne whilst his father, Nabonidus, journeyed afar.

In the prior months, Bel-Shazzar had continued to spend more time in the banquet hall than was prudent for a king. His governance did not exhibit Nebuchadnezzar's awareness or foresight, and his delight in frivolity had been noised abroad since the inception of his reign. Few held confidence in his ability to maintain the strength of the kingdom. Having survived the brief reigns of two ambitious interlopers to the throne Daniy-El prayed that Babylon's newest king would grow in understanding and wisdom.

The first lapse in judgment had occurred with Bel-Shazzar's decision to proceed with the wanton display of wastage in spite of the siege that had continued outside the city walls for two years now since the first battle. Few officers now spoke of the complete rout that had occurred during the first weeks of the war. The Babylonians had been sent scampering to the safety of the city walls. Assured of twenty years supply in the storehouses, Bel-Shazzar had thumbed his nose at the Persians and Medes from atop the battlements, assuming that his longevity could not be threatened. However, there were greater forces at work than the mere will of a king, as Nebuchadnezzar had discovered. Moreover, as is wont to occur, the lessons of the past were lost at the advent of the new reign, and the results were currently being manifested. Most of the reeves who had remained throughout the roiling shifts in power had, by now, forgotten king Nebuchadnezzar's dream, but Daniy-El had not. The chest of silver was becoming a stark reality, and the present king was nonplussed—a wading bird oblivious to the stealthy creatures that stalked its footsteps. The banks of the river were a perilous place for a both man and beast, and Bel-Shazzar was treading carelessly about the lair of dragons, ignorant of the violence to come. At the time, Daniy-El had not been given knowledge of the timing of the impending offensive that would surely rip the kingdom from the kings of Babylon when Nebuchadnezzar's eyes were finally closed, but that it would come was indisputable. That much he had ascertained.

Now the reavers were waiting outside the gates, and they would be granted entrance by the God of Heaven. The river and the walls were sturdy assets, but had not Jericho fallen? Men continued to trust in strongholds built with hands, rather than fortifications that, by His Spirit, could guard the heart and soul from works of evil. Yahweh was the ultimate defender, and also the worst of enemies. Bel-Shazzar had culminated his folly by also thumbing his nose at the King of Heaven, polluting the holy things plundered from Yahweh's temple with his festive debaucheries—the lips of concubines and unwashed men supplanting the ministrations of the holy priests in deference to false gods and idols! Was the idol Bel-Merodach the one who wrought life, that he should be toasted above Yahweh? He certainly was not, and the blasphemous act would not be overlooked on this day.

As the visions closed Daniy-El chose not to speculate on what strategy the enemies of Babylon would use or when the shift would transpire. *Time will tell,* he thought. *It always does.*

Bel-Shazzar fought against the pall of dread that clutched at his throat. It was sure to overwhelm him. *Who can aid me? Who?* He looked about in desperation at the servants. He could send them to seek out aid, but where? The sorcerers had been his legs and arms for many a season after he had put aside many of the older officials of the court. Their counsel had sustained him well, until now.

Bel-Shazzar looked up hopefully as the large doors opened to admit an aging but erect form. Her steps were even and purposeful. She advanced toward his seat then paused as the newly drawn inscription confronted her in accusation against her son. She stared a long moment before continuing her procession to the low dais. Bel-Shazzar's face was now a deathly pallor as the strain leeched the self-assurance from his thick frame, rendering it a flaccid husk of doubt. He had placed his faith in sorcerer's arts, but they had failed him when he most needed wise counsel. Many princes and governors returned to the hall seeking fresh news regarding his dilemma.

'Mother?" Bel-Shazzar croaked. *Mother!* The Queen Mother walked the length of the hall, concern etched on her aging features. Her eyes drifted between his pallid face and the script overhead. Bel-Shazzar could discern from her intense scrutiny, that she was assessing his disposition before she spoke, for his whole body was visibly quaking now. It was clear that his circumstance was grave.

"My king," she started slowly, "I have heard of your plight. There is yet one to whom you may turn at this hour, should you be willing."

Bel-Shazzar raised his head a fraction. He had already consulted the enchanters. *Of whom does she speak?* He needed no physician, for his distress was not born of his body.

"There was one who aided your grandfather in such a time as this. This man resides in the king's service still. His is of those taken captive in the land of the Hebrews. His talent for the reading of dreams and the revealing of secrets was highly spoken of then, and he was made master over all the Men of Wisdom. Moreover, he was found more excellent than each within the king's court. The man's name is Belteshazzar. Perhaps he can unravel this mystery also, my king."

The room grew silent as all those within awaited the king's answer.

"Send for him," Bel-Shazzar commanded. He would consult this Jew. What could he lose thereby?

Daniy-El had noticed the tremor in the king's voice as he was summoned forward by the king to decipher the message that had been carved upon the plaster in the hall of feasts—some said by magic, but Daniy-El knew otherwise. Daniy-El read the Aramaic inscription on the large stones carefully, its words and import as clear to him as the breath that coursed within his frame. He had been summoned partially at the queen's behest. Seeing the king now, he understood the full extent of the terror that was afflicting him. Even without a translation of the writing, its warning was palpable. Bel-Shazzar could not define the source, yet he understood that he was at the centre of a flow of power that was directed against him, and the fact terrified him. Tragically, he had walked the road of a spiritually blind man, blithely ignorant of the guides laid down by his forefathers. Unfortunately, at the end of the road lay destruction.

Daniy-El read over the glyphic to himself. "*MENE, MENE. . . .*" He paused briefly before continuing to read. Nebuchadnezzar's dream had indeed come to sever the reign of his successor, and it would be a sentence of death. He looked directly at the king who stood weakly.

"I have heard of you," he said softly. "That you can make interpretations, and dissolve doubts. Now, if you can read the writing, and make known to me its meaning, I will clothe you in scarlet. A gold chain will be placed about your neck and you shall be made the third ruler in the kingdom."

Daniy-El shook his head vigorously and raised his hands before him. His gesture of refusal caused a stir amongst the attendants. "Let your gifts be to yourself, and give your rewards to another," Daniy-El said placidly and without a hint of malice. As it was from the first day that he had entered this illustrious court, he had no need of the king's beneficence that seemed only to be measured in costly objects, lofty titles, and grand declarations of power. These were futile clamourings of self-interest. Such bounty paled in comparison to an Almighty God.

"Yet I will read the writing unto you, and reveal its interpretation. The Most High God gave Nebuchadnezzar your grandfather a kingdom, and majesty, and glory, and honor; and for the majesty that He gave him, all people, nations, and languages, trembled and feared before him. Whom he would, Nebuchadnezzar slew, and whom he would, he kept alive. Whom the king would he set up, and whom he would, he put down. But when his heart was lifted up, and his mind hardened in pride, he was deposed from his kingly throne, and they took his glory from him; and he was driven from the sons of men; and his heart was made like the beasts; and his dwelling was with the wild asses; they fed him with grass like oxen, and his body was wet with the dew of heaven; till he knew that the Most High God ruled in the kingdom of men, and that He appoints over it whomsoever He will!" Daniy-El's voice rose higher as he strove to convey to the young man the magnitude of his recklessness.

"And you, his son, O Bel-Shazzar, hast not humbled your heart though you knew all this!" Bel-Shazzar stared back with liquid eyes full of guilt and a silent plea. *There may have been some excuse had he not known, but to know and yet to err in such a fashion,* Daniy-El ruminated, shaking his head again, this time in regret for the king on whom judgment would be passed by Yahweh.

"You have lifted up yourself against the Lord of heaven; and they brought vessels from His house before you, and you, and your lords, and your wives and your concubines drank wine in them! And you praised the gods of silver, and gold, and brass, and iron, and wood, and stone, which you cannot see, nor hear, nor know!" Daniy-El held a clenched fist out before him, his voice falling to a whisper, "And the God in whose hand your breath is, and whose are all your ways, Him you have not glorified." The old man let his hand fall to his side. "MENE; God has numbered your kingdom, and finished it. TEKEL; You have been weighed in the balances and have been found wanting. PERES; Your kingdom is divided, and given to the Medes and Persians."

Daniy-El recognized the moment that the finality of the pronouncement coalesced within the king's understanding, for within his spirit he did not doubt the truth of the words. Bel-Shazzar bit his lower lip and stood, no longer trembling. There was trespass, and there was consequence. He clapped his hands for the steward to come forward.

"Have the robe of scarlet brought, and a chain of gold. Also, have the chief scribe attend me that a proclamation may go forth. Let it be known that the one named Belteshazzar shall henceforth be honored as the third ruler in the kingdom after my father and I." The servant departed, the clip of his sandals echoing rapidly down a far corridor as he hurried to fulfill the king's order. A ripple of discontent swelled in the hall. It was obvious that the king intended to hold fast to his word. Two servants brought in the fine garments and jewelry. The objects, which lay in ornate, gold-encrusted boxes, were presented before the king.

"Bring them hither," Bel-Shazzar said. He came to stand before Belteshazzar. He would hear no protest. Taking first the robe, and then the chain, he laid them about the older man's shoulders. Daniy-El flinched as the cold metal was hung about his neck. Bel-Shazzar looked around expectantly and the gathered lords awakened from their haze of shock by the authoritative rap of the king's staff, bent into rigid bows before the slave who would again be master. Purple color flooded the faces of many as they straightened their backs once more. Given the prediction cast, they would have much more to fear than the appointment of a slave, but they, too, were blind to the import of what had been said. Daniy-El saw Bel-Shazzar shake his head, as he perceived their consternation. Mere hours ago had he not been as foolish and prideful as they? However, he could not save them, for at this hour the king could not even save himself.

The coveted honor was bestowed upon Belteshazzar, according him an even higher status than he had been granted during Nebuchadnezzar's reign. Princes, governors and lords marveled anew at the providence that had catapulted the Hebrew above their stations. Blotting out their whisperings, the king gathered his retinue, excused himself from the presence of the queen, and returned to his quarters to give rest to his soul.

The Hall of Feasts soon cleared but for a shadowy presence that lingered, its animosity renewed. Angry and bitter, it hissed at the accolade afforded its nemesis. Yet it gloated as it scuttled toward the dark recesses of the palace, for the day of reprisal had come, finally.

14

Vanquished

Behold a people shall come from the north, and a great nation . . . .

They are cruel, and will not shew mercy,

The king of Babylon hath heard report of them,

And his hands waxed feeble: anguish took hold of him,

And pangs as of a woman in travail.

- The Book of the Prophet Jeremiah

"They're inside!" the guardsman bellowed as he ploughed up the stair. The Captain of the Guard wheeled frantically at the foul news. Heedless of the king's request for undisturbed privacy until noon, he pummeled thrice upon the door of the bedchamber before rushing in.

"My king, hasten! *Hasten!*"

Bel-Shazzar stumbled groggily from his canopied bed. He appeared to be dazed, and moved slowly, oblivious to the exigency of the moment. Gaining his feet, he blanched as he saw the captain's taut face. Many had heard of the old dream-reader's pronouncement, but did not believe. They had all supposed that the king had simply chosen to humor the old man in his dotage. *Could it truly be that the night would not be ended before the terrible penance from the God of Belteshazzar was enacted?*

"So soon!" Bel-Shazzar whimpered, echoing the captain's thoughts.

"Hasten, my king. Hasten!" the captain pressed, batting a servant away as he sought to lay out garments for the king. "There is no time for that," he shouted urgently. "Fetch his cloak alone.

They are already within the palace. We must take the south corridor to the tunnel. Hurry, my lord! We —"

His insistent entreaty was cut short as the second captain barreled into the room with a small battalion, each man with his sword unsheathed. "The west guard defends their stair but others come. They will be upon us in a moment. The third battalion is upon the lower floor. They will defend the door if we but hasten. There may still be time to save the king." The captain swiftly assessed the worsening circumstance. "Bar the door," he screamed. "Get the king out to the south passage. Now!" he roared.

The guardsmen bustled Bel-Shazzar along a darkened corridor leading from the back of his bedchamber. Watching them go, the captain huffed in relief then he turned to relay orders to his commander. Perhaps the enemy had succeeded in scaling the wall. Their defenses may be sorely pressed at first, but the gates would hold, and the moat would offer added protection.

However, his reprieve proved to be short-lived, as the cordon returned in panicked flight.

"We are lost," the forerunner grated out in undisguised distress. "They approach even from the escape passage. The east retreat likewise. We are lost."

Bel-Shazzar slumped onto the floor, clutching at his stomach. The spirits of the men sagged as the captain rubbed a hand over his mouth. The seemingly impregnable walls that had once been their boasting were now a sure trap. He moved to a window and blinked in horror as he saw streams of torches ascending from the riverside gates. *How could they have breached the great river? He thought incredulously. The God of the heavens truly opposes us, for indeed, we are lost.*

Chaos erupted within the inner sanctum of the palace as princes and governors, counselors and captains came awake to swords held against their throats, some for the last time. Constricted cries echoed in sleeping chambers throughout the great stronghold on the east bank of the Euphrates, as the might of Persia and Media poured through unfamiliar halls on both sides of the river. The Persian captain was single-minded in his quest. In the dim glow of the lamps he was forced to mentally trace the map that would lead him to his goal. The hive of corridors taxed his memory, for he had been unable to study the small parchment provided by the Median spy for more than an hour before the assault was initiated. However, he could not fail in this. The men—his king—were depending on him. His company raced past chamberlains who backed against the walls in stunned disbelief as heavily armed soldiers bounded through the halls in close formation. They bludgeoned aside the random opposition from pockets of poorly organized guardsmen who raced to contain the enemy snaking through their midst. The small but incisive attacking force swept aside their resistance as easily as the dust in the chamberlains cleaning pans. The captain turned the final corner and stopped abruptly ahead of large ornamented doors, which were now shielded by a cordon of soldiers. The defenders stood with spears facing outward menacingly. The captain moved aside, giving way to a discrete group of his men who notched arrows to taut bows and took aim. At short range, their impact would be deadly. The Chaldean soldiers focused eyes wide in recognition. Save for small bucklers, they were unprepared to defend themselves against the barbed shafts in the confines of the palace where swords and spears were the anticipated weapons of attack. The trained men nevertheless threw themselves to the ground an instant before a shower of arrowheads thudded into the oiled wood at their backs. The men glanced upward to see a flurry of quills embedded at eye level. They scrambled desperately to evade the subsequent barrage. The twang of the bowstrings reverberated through the air, and even as the second flight was airborne, the captain barreled forward. His men surrounded him as one to rebuff the counter-attack launched by the king's men who regrouped quickly. He aimed to reach that chamber. The sally brought his company within reach of the portal and he lunged ahead eagerly, pushing at the massive doors that blocked him from the one he sought. The clash of swords rang around him yet he focused on his objective. He moved back, braced his feet and thrust his weight against them. Still they resisted him. He leaned back and heaved mightily, yet he was denied admittance. Two more came to aid him, but the leaves held fast. *Barred from the inside*, he surmised, gritting his teeth in vexation. *Within moments it will be too late!* He had been certain that with the stealth of the invasion, which had proceeded unhindered until now, the king could not have been carried to safety in advance of their foray to the royal chamber. Nevertheless, without a ram, his men could not reach their prize. Further, reinforcements from the king's guard would be alerted within the turn of a spindle. He himself would have two more companies within moments. He looked wildly along the adjacent corridors. The king was not to be sequestered in a dead end room, he reminded himself abruptly. The corridor branched in three directions. The closest disappeared at an unlit junction with another hallway. The captain's eyes narrowed. He had come along the first corridor only moments before. Nevertheless, he could leave nothing to chance. Two of his support companies emerged from the end of the farthest corridor, having broken through from the palace court. They bore flickering torches aloft that cast brilliant flares to dispel the gloom. The increased force repelled the king's guards who had battled on valiantly, but, now outnumbered, their beleaguered ranks scattered toward the darkness of the nearby hall.

"Second-captain! Pursue, but only until you find the door on the west side," he shouted as his men charged after the retreating guardsmen. "It is likely to be barred also. Nevertheless, station your men there until I send word."

The captain signaled urgently to the newly arrived commanders who approached at a run. "Split your men. You will find stairs at the end of each hall. Take the upper and lower floors in turn. Seek another route to the king's quarters. I will hold this position with ten from each rank. Go!" The men separated briskly, issuing crisp commands to the soldiers who fell in behind as they rushed in opposite directions to fulfill their commands. There would be few routes through which the king could flee, even should he bypass the vice formed by the commanders. He had already ordered the underground passages to the cellars cordoned. At that moment, seven ranks of soldiers would be ascending the passageways, fanning out along the corridors at each level. They would subsequently converge on the king's chamber, denying him a way out.

"You will not escape me, Belshazzar," the captain growled, clenching his fist on his sword. *No. Not on this night!* He spun as a large company of the Chaldean guardsmen surged from the corridor through which their companions had previously fled. His pursuing force was pushed back once more, and the fight resumed with renewed intensity. The captain willed his men onward as he traced the pounding steps that sounded overhead. He turned his sword outward and joined the fray. One way or another it would soon be over.

A scuffle sounded beyond the heavy timbers that cut off the captain's access to the royal chamber. Echoes of the fierce conflict bled through to the hall. The clash of weapons sang ominously along the hall as a battle was waged on the other side of the portal. The Chaldean soldiers cried out in alarm as the import of the deadly reverberation sunk home. They increased the ferocity of their defense, but as the doors were flung open and Persian soldiers poured out, the Chaldeans knew that their efforts were now in vain. The king was lost to them as the pride of Babylon was overtaken by death.

PART 2
The Second Kingdom

15

Change of the Guard

Surely I will no more give thy corn to be meat for thine enemies;
And the sons of the stranger shall not drink thy wine,
For which thou hast laboured.

- The Book of the Prophet Isaiah

The air above the gathering rippled with an unseen force as Cyrus strutted before his war council. The veiled whispers that had once questioned his wisdom in challenging the mighty Babylon were now forever silenced. The power of Babylon had been conferred upon him in majesty and splendor within a court that had witnessed a flurry of kings after the unmatched stability of Nebuchadnezzar's lengthy reign.

"My lords, hearken to me," Cyrus intoned, drawing silence about him. "We have been granted an unprecedented victory." There was no need to impress upon these men the enormity of the triumph. His eyes roved piercingly over the council. "The alliance between Media and Persia has borne magnificent fruit has it not?" Cyrus said, extending his hand to the man seated below and to his right. "Darius," he said, in an invitation for the commander to come to the dais, "Come, blood of my blood! This glory is both yours and mine. The kingdom is equally in your debt." Cyrus shifted a pace to allow his viceroy to stand at his side. His next words rang in the hubbub of the room.

"My lords and princes. I shall not grace these walls for much longer. I shall be moving my conquests to those lands that lay ripe for the picking in the valleys beyond the eastern mountains. I shall tarry but a few more seasons in Babylon, after which Darius and I have agreed that he will serve as king over these Chaldeans. The Medes and Persians have come far, and we shall go farther still. Our names have been etched in unison upon time itself, and thus it shall remain." Cyrus's bold stare swept aside the initial ripples of complaint that surfaced amongst those in the hall before him. Many had not anticipated that the older lord would be given rein over them. Darius was a subtle man and his favor would be less easily courted than that of his young counterpart. Plans had already gone afield and expectations were high for the honors that the king would bestow.

"Darius will choose the new princes of the land, and the duties of each will be made known to all. Until then, my lords," he concluded with a wide grin, "let us toast our victory."

"To victory," several voices cheered, lifting the temper of the assembly. A cry went up that resounded off the walls of the hall, heralding the advent of a Medo-Persian dominion of the coveted realm.

The watcher retreated to the heavens, satisfied that the transfer of power was complete. Soon a new king would be enthroned as scripted on the walls mere days before, but the same God would be watching, to note the deeds of kings to whom He gave power over men, for He was the King of kings.

Darius pored over the scrolls that had been brought out in a continuous stream from Babylon's court archives. The kingdom was vast, and it was ever-expanding. It would require more than one hand upon the reins to steady its thrust forward. After days of deliberation, he had decided that there would be three men chosen to preside over six score satraps. The latter would allow him to oversee the provinces, whilst the three presidents would prevent him from coming to harm through rebellion, thievery or plotting amidst the third ranking princes or the nation's people, whose cultures and languages were multitudinous. He must be certain of them, for they would be his primary shield against subversion. The responsibility of naming the princes and presidents for the new Babylon weighed heavily upon his shoulders. There were many amongst the Medes and Persians who had courted Cyrus and himself throughout the audacious campaign, yet discretion was the hallmark or a true leader and he could not dismiss the many vagaries of his countrymen in order to pander to their lusts. Several did indeed earn the acclaim that would be given them, but others were as vacant receptacles, full of pomp and bluster. Still others were vessels of deadly brews, which would poison his reign if he were not cautions. Three score years in the company of willful men such as these had taught him much. Any whom he chose would need to be strong in character for they would surely be compelled to withstand the corrosive efforts, both of their counterparts and any who felt they had been denied their due measure by not being selected for rule. If he chose the wrong leaders, he would jeopardize more than men's egos. Neither could he allow personal desires, or past loyalties, to overwhelm good reason. The Medes and Persians had come this far through the sacrifice of both riches and lives, and he needed trustworthy men to support him across this immense domain. Darius was adept at recognizing deviance in his own men, but he was yet to assess the full measure of the mixed following now awaiting his direction. Many of the names put forward were unfamiliar to him, but Cyrus had given his blessing on a select number whose reward was just. Cyrus had chosen to warn him of a few, who though useful in war, abhorred peace, and harbored a base propensity for evil. Such a one was Strobos, who seemed to have an uncanny delight in devious acts and quiet sedition. In Persia, the temple priests taught young men of Ormuzd and Ahriman, the dual sides of infinite power, one good and one evil. That one, a seemingly incarnate shade of Ahriman, he would need to be watchful of, for the man was already highly placed and even more hungry than the others were. Darius sighed and sat back from the table. *I am getting old. I will need to be more cunning than they are, if I wish to withstand their lusts.* It was a deadly game. Here, men with a taste for blood pounced at any hint of weakness, and their efforts, if combined, could founder even the most powerful combatant.

A servant spread the accounts of the region before Darius. Nebuchadnezzar had done well to hold the kingdom securely for so many decades. If it were not for his demise, and the eventual coronation of the weaker Bel-Shazzar, the Medes and Persians may not have made the journey to these great walls. It was the advent of a new era. Darius slowly traced one of the records, recognizing in the halting script a name that at first he had supposed to be the name of the deceased king Bel-Shazzar. But this one was mentioned early in Nebuchadnezzar's reign. Darius enunciated the Chaldean syllables.

"*Bel- te- shaz- zar.*"

He frowned suddenly. *Belteshazzar?* Had not that name been mentioned also in the reigns following Nebuchadnezzar's, even unto Bel-Shazzar's downfall? He bit his lip in concentration and sifted through a pile of tablets sitting at his feet. He found several that had been signed with the same inscription over the span of nearly seven decades. *He is a governor then, and former counselor to Nebuchadnezzar. This man will be very old by now,* the king gauged. He returned to one scroll, the last record of the court before the Persian invasion and nodded in satisfaction. Darius smiled to himself. This Belteshazzar was a slave, but obviously one of great repute. *To the last he told Bel-Shazzar the truth,* Darius marveled. It was no small matter for a slave to tell his sovereign that the kingdom would be ripped away and given to another. The accuracy of the prediction shocked Darius. He waded through another pile of scrolls, casting aside many until he found what he sought, a scroll with an elaborate gold seal. He broke the binding and stretched it upon the large trestle table. Alike many of the royal documents, Belteshazzar's name appeared on this one also. He read with interest. . . .

Nebuchadnezzar the king, unto all people, nations, and languages that dwell in all the earth; Peace be multiplied unto you. I thought it good to show the signs and wonders that the high God hat wrought toward me. How great are His signs! And how mighty are His wonders. His kingdom is an everlasting kingdom and His dominion is from generation to generation.

Darius paused. *An everlasting kingdom?* He read on, his curiosity aflame by the words of the renowned king. *Could this be a God greater than Ormuzd?* he considered. Was this God the God of Heaven of whom he heard tales upon the wind? Darius sat back, his eyes remaining fixed upon the words. *I must know,* he thought with bubbling curiosity.

I Nebuchadnezzar was at rest in my house, and flourishing in my palace: I saw a dream which made me afraid, and the thoughts upon my bed and the visions of my head troubled me. Therefore, I made a decree to bring in all the wise men of Babylon before me that they might make known unto me the interpretation of the dream. Then came in the magicians, the astrologers, the Chaldeans, and the soothsayers: and I told the dream before them; but they did not make known unto me the interpretation thereof. But at the last Daniy-El came in before me, whose name was Belteshazzar.

Daniy-El? That name too Darius had seen in many places in the records. *He is a Jew then,* Darius deduced from the title. Darius scanned the words set lower in the passage and read softly.

"This dream I king Nebuchadnezzar have seen. Now thou, O Belteshazzar, declare the interpretation thereof, forasmuch as the wise men of my kingdom are not able to make known unto me the interpretation: but thou are able; for the spirit of the holy gods is in thee. Then Daniy-El, whose name was Belteshazzar, was astonied for one hour, and his thoughts troubled him. The king spoke and said, 'Belteshazzar, let not the dream, or its interpretation thereof trouble thee.' Belteshazzar answered and said, 'My lord, the dream be to them that hate thee, and the interpretation thereof to thine enemies.'"

Darius broke off his reading. *Why was this man Daniy-El, or Belteshazzar—a slave—concerned for the king's fate, especially since it is known that Nebuchadnezzar was no easy task-master? Why should he have cared what providence beset a man who had laid waste to Jewish cities, ripped his people from their homeland, and mired them in interminable captivity? Why? For the sake of this God who had given him a supernatural ability to discern the times? 'The dream be to them that hate thee,' Belteshazzar had said. Did the Jew not hate him also? After all, had not Nebuchadnezzar threatened to behead all the wise men? Would not this Belteshazzar have also gone to his grave at the hand of this man he now sought to protect? The sincerity of his distress was even known to his king.*

Darius read of the king's bout of madness, a story that many had assumed was nonsense—a ruse concocted to lure potential enemies to their deaths at the foot of Babylon's walls. *How*, he wondered, *had the kingdom been preserved during the king's absence?* The time would have been dangerous. Nebuchadnezzar's leave of wits was sufficient to brew anarchy in his ranks. Such stability in times of trouble was unheard of. Darius surged to his feet, excitement coursing through his tired frame and drawing him erect. *Was not the man Daniy-El yet in charge during this time? This is incredible! he rejoiced. I yet have a hope to corral this lot. The Jew may yet be old, but if he draws breath, I will have need of such a man. The years will have been hard upon a slave but he seems the stronger for it. His God, too—this one whom he bows to as Yahweh, the God of Heaven—He must surely be no trifling deity such as I have known, for such wonders I have never heard of! In Him this Daniy-El must be sustained, for he has survived exceedingly long in this treacherous city of Babylon. He will thus know more regarding the affairs of the kingdom than ten score governors. Nebuchadnezzar had himself testified of the man's loyalty— a loyalty that perhaps was even greater than that of a son of his loins. The wide-ranging reports of his service were unsullied with rebellion or rancor. The ability to foretell the times was a great enigma in itself.*

"Guard!" Darius bellowed. Two soldiers entered swiftly and bowed. "Search the slave quarters of the palace. Find one named *Belteshazzar*, or also called *Daniy-El* by the Hebrews. Take heed. Do not harm him. Bring him hither, but cause him no hurt whatsoever, he cautioned. I have need of his wisdom this night."

And Babylon has further need of his service, he finished to himself. Great need, for in this one man may lay my salvation.

Daniy-El waited amidst the parade of officials who had trooped into the audience hall for the announcement of their anticipated positions in the new hierarchy. Darius sat, imperious and grim-faced, upon the throne. A herald was loudly proclaiming the long list of satraps for the diverse provinces and the extent of their jurisdictions. Other minor officials of the defunct Babylonian regime had been called, as was customary, to attend their new lords. Their familiarity with the minutia of the daily tasks would be indispensable to a smooth transition into governance. It was known that the new king of the Chaldeans had keenly investigated each of the officers who had borne rule under the old system. Some had been killed, others imprisoned. Daniy-El had survived his own encounter with Darius, having spoken with characteristic humility. Nevertheless, he was surprised, and puzzled, to find himself, a slave of waning years, amidst those clamoring for power, and now that the dozens of satraps had been awarded their charges he found himself questioning the reason for his presence at all.

"Let it be known," the herald intoned, "that the Medo-Persian Empire, in the city of Babylon, hereby vests authority in three presidents who shall oversee the kingdom, of whom one shall be first."

Darius stood, his hands extended towards two of the princes. He nodded for them to come forward. They smiled broadly, pleased to be honored before the large assembly. A murmur arose as the remaining princes and officials looked around, eager to know who would be granted the privilege of second ruler. Darius raised his hand, and the hum subsided. The king nodded to Daniy-El who remained rooted to his spot. His brows furrowed in question, and then

Darius nodded once more, his gaze direct and assured as he beckoned him forward. Daniy-El moved slowly, surprise making his steps seem hesitant.

"A slave?" one of the princes muttered to his right. "Surely not?" Though low, the words ricocheted through the silence of the hall. Men turned in bewilderment and grudgingly made way for the approach of the aging man who wore robes of spun wool. His simple garb contrasted their own embroidered silks and flowing, colorful turbans like the crabbed hedge of thorns that grew in the shadow of the velvety hulch lily.

Daniy-El at last reached the dais. He stood, head bowed before the king.

"Come," Darius said with a quiet smile. He gestured to his side. Daniy-El mounted the polished steps and turned to face the gathering.

"Your first president," Darius announced exuberantly.

Daniy-El observed as the host made diffident bows that no one present could mistake for genuine obeisance.

The ensuing feast rivaled the finest in any kingdom, but the expected enthusiasm of the evening was dulled by the supersession that had stunned many a prince. Their day of accomplishment had been thrown akilter by the news, and many ate in silence.

Daniy-El watched their faces, knowing. He had been here before. They would bear the ignominy, but only for a time! The ways of men were predictable. Still, with Darius's confidence, and the freedom of his office, he would be allowed to serve, both men, and God.

16

Entrapment

Look to the rock from which you were hewn

- The Book of the Prophet Isaiah

The upheaval of the realm quieted to sullen whispers. Any trace of the wafting discontent that had risen briefly at Cyrus' news regarding Darius's regency was now shut away behind closed doors. There would be a new master seated atop the coveted throne before long, but for now none dared voice his displeasure lest his light be snuffed out as easily a those of the Chaldean royal court had been. Few of the former advisors remained though many of the slaves were retained. They would continue to serve, for one slave-master was no different from another in the interminable days of bondage.

The reinstituted administration had been rid of the sorceries of the Order, their magic now replaced by a theistic hierarchy. Spells and incantations had availed them nothing during the incursion by Cyrus' force, which forever silenced their aberrant counsel. Yet, as one insidious beast was decapitated, there sprung from the stump several more in its place, equally rabid, eyes glowing with secret hatreds amidst a hoard that was as fervent for domination as its predecessor. There were realms of command yet to be ceded, and the hunger to claim them was such that the creatures of power would abide no whittling of their supremacy. Hence many months did not pass before the petty jealousies of the new princes coalesced into a volcanic core within the administrative halls. The proud men struggled to suppress their opposition to the authority of their Judean president who they viewed as a loathsome remnant from the Babylonian era of Jewish captivity. The Medes and Persians formed the combined might throughout the lands stretching from the Great Sea to the southern coasts. Should a slave now rule them? Darius's selection of the old man lit a fire of rage within them, and despite Daniy-El's efficiency and dedication to his service, their malignance continued to grow. How was it that a subjugated people, cast down to the lowest echelons of the societal plinth, had managed to soar in successive kingdoms? The elevation of the Hebrews to seats of honor, and the quiet reverence shown their God by the king was disturbing to the royal ranks of Media and Persia who had come to Chaldea with high hopes for their own ascendancy, and that of their families.

Prodded by their disappointments and bitter musings, the Persian and Median councilors gathered in secret, distraught by the unwanted presence of the Hebrew who seemed to loom over their affairs. This one, Belteshazzar, overshadowed their counsel to the king with guidance that was too oft contrary, and superior to their own. It was obvious to all that Darius was growing more and more enamored with the man for there was naught in his speech or actions that was duplicitous. Watching the king's curiosity blossom into a solemn and enduring respect made them increasingly uncomfortable with the Jew's headship. The man was aged, and they had quietly hoped that the strain of his significant charge over the kingdom would have curtailed his ability to attend his duties, or at the least, caused him to err in his judgments. Had it been so they could simply accuse him before the king and have him removed. Yet, for all their questing, they could find no occasion meriting Belteshazzar's dismissal from the court. Some had even sought the will of Strobos, who had been granted a notable place within the palace officials, and whose counsel against Belteshazzar stoked their fires even hotter. The room echoed with their collective discontent.

"It is most unsettling. Cyrus made a grave mistake, turning the helm over to Darius."

"However, the kingdom is rich with slaves. Our wealth will not suffer unduly," someone offered in comfort.

"It is not our wealth that concerns me, man. It is the king's lack of good sense in subjecting us to the authority of a common servant! It is totally unnecessary and wraps us about in shame."

"Nevertheless, he had the foresight to choose one who has decades of experience in an administration as intricate as this. The king was obviously moved in his spirit to do this thing, and we should honor his choice. We are in Babylon now, not some hovel of a town that sprung up in the wilderness. Its systems run across many borders and tongues. Even Lydia pales in comparison. We can abide the slight for a little while until the people accept us. Have you not heard? The city is full of Jews, amongst others. They will serve us more willingly with a familiar hand to guide them. This Daniy-El will serve this purpose."

"Come now. It was a purposeful denigration. He could simply have kept the man as an advisor. He need not have placed such a one above our stature. He has willfully bared our necks such that he will be raised that much higher above us. He is pompous, and arrogant. His old back will be difficult to bend our way." Added to this was the unease that settled amongst them like sour bread in the gut. A man's god was his armor, and despite their enslavement, these Jews had not been utterly defeated. They prospered, and unbelievingly well, standing head and shoulders above their Chaldean counterparts. Daniy-El himself had been quiet and unassuming, his presence drawing no notice until he provided due answers, piercing and astute, to the king's queries regarding kingdom matters. His incisiveness drew the admiration and jealousy of most in the assembly of counselors.

The third president squeezed the bridge of his nose before responding. "Still, I believe we should postpone any action until we know more of this Daniy-

El. The king may yet appoint another once we gain our footing securely. We should not commit our footsteps to a rash and foolhardy course."

Several lords agreed grudgingly for the prince was senior amongst the satraps and the favor of the kings oft vanished like the wind, and one's life with it.

"Meanwhile, I suggest we should still consult the one who gained us the leverage we needed in Babylon."

"Who? Do you mean Strobos? He is a dangerous one to continue to court. We should have nothing more to do with him. He—"

"Nevertheless, he has resided here in Babylon for a long while. He can advise us regarding this Daniy-El," the satrap persisted.

A chorus of agreement overwhelmed the prince's objections.

"It is settled then. We shall convene in another week to discuss our position. Until then, we can each seek to know more of this Hebrew. And may his tenure be short!"

A week later, the grouping reconvened around the slender man who held their attention with a vulture's intensity.

"What can I say? The slave has the ear of the king. Darius is convinced that his worth is above a beryl fortress. It is as it was with Nebuchadnezzar and Bel-Shazzar. He poisons the king's thinking with his seemingly meek words that shield his thoughts," Strobos sniffed in irritation. "His service thus far has been beyond reproach. I tell you, we must do more than drop unsubstantial hints of impropriety. It has been nigh impossible to shake the king's confidence in the man. Darius defers to him, and the leading of this God of heaven with an infuriating persistence," Strobos confided.

"No man is above scrutiny," a treasury official chimed in forcefully.

"You should know," Strobos muttered to loud guffaws from several quarters of the room. The official chose to ignore the comment. Few dared match wits with Strobos whose open knowledge of the secrets that many officials had attempted to keep hidden caused them great discomfort.

"Everyone has a flaw, Strobos. Now that your influence has increased, can you not find even one error with which to charge him?" he asked disbelievingly.

"His God watches over him, somehow," Strobos grumbled. "My power to dissuade even the least of his actions unerringly fails."

"Come now, Strobos. Do you mean to tell us that the darkness of your soul is out-witted by the mere prayers of this simple man. He offers no sacrifice at our temple. He burns no incense, as do some of the other Jews. What power can he have that is greater than yours? I should say that his very demise lays in his affections for this God he reveres. After all, is he still not a slave, under our rule—"

"We rule *nothing* if Darius is against us!" Strobos exploded, his sudden fit of anger startling the occupants of the large room. "He is a thorn in your sides as he has been for generations before in mine! Him and his God! Year after year. He bows, and he prays. He bows, and he prays unceasingly in that little room of his. Not one of you has watched him as I have, nor know those things I have endured whilst he prospers. Our regent has even entitled him to resume the use of his Jewish name. Such an honor should not be accorded a slave!" Strobos spat, gesticulating wildly as his words grew more agitated. "We must have done with him, and if we must use his God to lever him from his high perch then so be it!"

The counselors and princes were initially taken aback by his uncharacteristic show of vehemence. It was clear to most of them that his drive to attain authority had reached a stumbling block at the old Jew, but this odium that now oozed upon his words was obviously rooted deeper than mere unfulfilled ambitions. None cared to pursue the matter, however, for it was equally evident that Darius's respect for the Hebrew was growing as quickly as his regard for them was diminishing. Each man's hatreds were his own, as long as they served the purpose of the council and did not threaten its members. This Daniy-El was the common threat that they wished to subdue, and Strobos was the most qualified man to enact their desires.

Strobos calmed himself as quickly as his ire had risen. "We have time still," he continued. "The king's reign has only just begun and he will be tender upon the throne for a while yet. Whilst he continues to bask in the glory of Babylon below his thumb, I shall find the means to rid us of this Hebrew. Permanently. Within a season he shall be no more," Strobos asserted, gleaning the germ of an idea as it grew within the bowels of his animosity. "You shall see," he said, a smile broadening across his lips. "We are but a stones throw away from our accomplishment. The king himself shall repudiate his pet," Strobos sneered. Several of the counselors raised their eyebrows, wondering what sleight of hand was fomenting in his mind. Some leaned forward, eager now for a resolution to their dilemma. "They shall both be caught in a snare of their own making, and we shall be found blameless," Strobos confided amidst a growing hum. "Be quiet, all of you. Would you have us all hung upon the gallows before we have even begun? Be quiet, and listen closely. A false witness will be too easily cast down, for the records speak for themselves. How then can one ensnare a man who is like a clear breeze that enfolds all and offends none, save where it stirs the dusty corners one would rather have forgotten? We must convince the one who holds ultimate power to fashion a wax-sealed box, chiseled from the very mountain from which the air billows. And that mountain, my friends, is Daniy-El's God. Every day this wind returns to its source, and will not refrain from doing so, whatever the cost. Upon this daily homage will we craft the walls of his prison. Furthermore, a new ruler always covets adoration, and, should we treat accordingly, we shall be able to convince the king to embrace a statute forbidding any man from acknowledging any power save that of the king. Assuredly the Jew will be bound to his unerring devotion such that, in his station, he will think to flaunt the edict."

Many of the princes rose to clap Strobos on his back as he strung the tapestry of his proposal before them, its skeins subtle, but deadly. Strobos reveled in the rapt attention given him by the grouping of leaders. *So simple were they. So easily manipulated into evil, he laughed to himself.* Even should Daniel choose to obey the contrived edict he, Strobos, would have succeeded in denying his enemy a crucial lifeline. He disdained the Jew's prayers. Year by year, the man's vaunted righteousness sickened him.

"Surely we must proscribe the time lest we all be found guilty on some future occasion," one official observed."

"One cycle of the moon should suffice," suggested a Mede.

"Thirty days is satisfactory. The Jew offers prayers unceasingly. It is certain that he will be disinclined to withstand the span of days," Strobos asserted.

"We shall toast you at the next banquet, Strobos," the treasurer announced to unanimous approval. "Would that you could have had the Hebrew's place, eh? The First High Prince?" he said, prodding Strobos with his elbow. "The kingdom at your beck and call? Hmm, Strobos? It would be the crowning glory for one as keen as you. But then, you might have each of us drawn upon a spit over Ahriman's hottest fires, lest we abide your will? No?" he said to rowdy laughter from the men.

All, except Strobos, who smiled mirthlessly. He knew that they, blind in their ambition, sought only to use him to their own ends. So many before had thought to do the same.

Indeed! And so you shall be, he agreed. *So you shall be!*

The high council, anxious but resolved, bided their time. They were unwilling to ruin their long-awaited opportunity to entrap their prey. It was difficult to shield such delicate a plot for too long. Hence, the officials rose eagerly when the court affairs evolved to their advantage. Darius was in high spirits and his ebullience made him unusually careless. The selected members of the council huddled together, shielding their shared contrivance. Many now strove to veil their animosity toward their Jewish counterpart who stood out like a white lamb against the dark brush of the waterside, oblivious to the scaled predator watching hungrily from the watery depths. It dared not approach until the appointed time. Perhaps it would have moved away had the contrast not made it seem so leprous—and so vile. In most of the contentions in the court this one, pure and unspotted, had exemplified a level of virtue to which none of the Medes nor Persians could attend—nor had the Chaldeans before them sought to be as blameless or humble as he. Humble. The word grated like a potshard over their cankerous veneer of honor. It also brought reckoning as their culpability was flagrantly exposed to the light of truth. Had the king been less shrewd many deeds would have remained unchallenged, but in the establishment of the new order he had been eager to depart from the sly manipulations of times past. Court engagements in their homeland had been replete with stern penalties. Of late, there was scarcely a reprimand as Daniy-El's diligent and unbiased reports forced the administrators to extreme caution in their affairs and the king grew increasingly disposed to admit Daniy-El's reports alone into the final record.

Now, King Darius sat with pursed lips, nodding in agreement as the princes and satraps presented their writ before him. They watched restlessly as he scanned the congregation, seeing no sign of Daniy-El who they had detained elsewhere. The king frowned but returned his attention to the scroll extended before him. Once more he looked over the men gathered before him in one accord, giving honor to his throne. The king was clearly swayed by their collective show of esteem.

"And all the presidents agree?" Darius asked.

The councilors concealed grimaces, and then one answered guardedly.

"Who could deny the king his due reverence and majesty, my lord?"

Darius nodded again. He smiled briefly before gesturing to the court scribe.

"Hand me my quill," he commanded enthusiastically. All present recognized the flush of pride that lighted the king's eyes as he signed into law the period of worship in his own honor. Darius relinquished the writing implement to the court recorder before flattening the parchment on the table with the jar of wax.

As he appended his seal the princes and presidents in attendance gave broad grins. The councilors exchanged sly glances. Soon the power would be theirs to wield again.

"King Darius live forever," they chorused in unison. The echo of numerous voices reverberated enthusiastically in the court for several moments before the cheer was raised again. The king bathed in the heady glow, mistaking their bold affectation for genuine affection.

"King Darius live forever!"

"King Darius live forever. . . ."

17

Given Over

For my thoughts are not your thoughts,
Neither are your ways my ways, saith the Lord
- The Book of the Prophet Isaiah

When the voice emerged from the darkness, urgent and assailing, its shadowy whispers tumbling forth with imbued terror, he was not surprised. Such a voice always arose in times like these, hoping to snatch away the fiber of one's resolve. Its swelling panic surged at the edge of his consciousness, threatening to wash away his determination. The murk of its presence reeked like the bloated corpses of and animals found bobbing amidst the heaving tide of a typhoon. This storm, brewed artfully over many months, spewed its enmeshed winds toward him, aiming to tangle him in death as mercilessly as it would a hapless creature. The morning that the proclamation was signed he carried out his duties with equanimity, aware of the subversive glances that were cast his way by certain administrators. He knew what they expected. Voices could come, but he would not listen. He would retire to his house for prayer as usual, his windows flung open toward Jerusalem. How could he forsake the One who had never forsaken him?

Daniy-El, Daniy-El! You need not do this. You have read the decree. You should not do this. Consider your life. How much more fruitful it can yet be, serving your

Master. What profit are you to His people if you are dead? He walked on calmly, passing familiar corridors and faces, some showing curiosity, others ambivalent. His passage was marked by a deadly quiet. *It is only thirty days! It is not such a long time to abstain.*

It spoke now with foul assurance. This, his winnowed flesh, was clawing for renewed ascendance in his hour of peril. It had been starved of the sumptuous favors of palace luxury and court power, yet it survived within him, suppressed but still existent. It would not be completely subdued until he was rid of this body, though he had offered in wholehearted service to Yahweh. Its frailties he overcame through obedience. His was a true and unstinting obedience that overwhelmed even the reasoning of a man's flesh and his exalted mind. Reason now said that he should forsake his walk for the sake of self-preservation. However, obedience said *'No'*.

Oh, indeed the flesh was more cunning than any prince of the court could ever be—to convince him of his intrinsic worth should he betray himself and his God to save his life, that he may serve the very One whom he had betrayed. God's forgiveness was great, but for this trespass he would never have forgiven himself.

It is a snare. Do not give those who stalk you the satisfaction of ending your life. Deny them their victory.

He knew all too well that it was a trap, yet it mattered not. Daniy-El had realized also, that were he to renege on his service to God to merely save his skin, then Darius would never know the depth of the evil that plied him with flatteries and false trust. When he knew that the writing was signed he had started for his house. His battle was not against these princes of the court, as it had not been against Nebuchadnezzar, or Nergal-Sharezer, or Bel-Shazzar, or any other authority of the earth. No. The serpent was subtle, and one more king had proven susceptible to its wiles, as had generations of men before them. Darius, he was sure, knew not what he had done. The trust that they had built bespoke a sincere bond between king and servant. Hence, the traitorous act would not have been conceived in the king's heart. Still, the fact changed nothing. Darius was king, and his word would not be gainsaid by mortal men, but Yahweh was sovereign over men and kings—Jehovah Adonai. It was not his first encounter with mal-intentioned courtiers, and even should it be his last, he would not turn aside from this course. No-one who trusted in Yahweh need fear. They would come, and they would find him praising the One who created the heavens and the earth.

You should petition the king for his mercies. Go now. You know that he will hear you, the voice insisted.

No. Any petition brought will be to the King of Kings with whom I now go to fellowship. There is none above Him, Daniy-El affirmed, determined to cast off the press of evil.

Daniy-El reached his chamber and opened his windows to the east as he had done every day since arriving in this land. He took a deep draught and knelt. The voices were banished as he poured his spirit out in worship before Yahweh. He lifted his hands high in surrender, welcoming the presence that was his all in all.

Daniy-El understood that he was not the first, nor would he be the last, to be opposed for the sake of righteousness. Had not King David also been beset by trickery? The ancient scrolls testified that alone in his distress, he cried out to his Lord: *Deliver me, Lord, from evil men; preserve me from violent men, who plan evil things in their hearts; they continually gather together for war. They sharpen their tongues like a serpent; the poison of asps is under their lips. Keep me, O Lord, from the hands of the wicked; preserve me from violent men, who have purposed to make my steps stumble. The proud have hidden a snare for me, and cord; they have spread a net by the wayside; they have set traps for me. I said to the Lord: You are my God; hear the voice of my supplications, O Lord. O Go, the strength of my salvation, You have covered my head in the day of battle. Lord, do not grant the desires of the wicked; do not further their wicked schemes lest they be exalted. As for the heads of those who surround me, let the evil of their lips cover them; let them be cast into the fire; into deep pits that they rise not up again. Let not a slanderer be established in the earth; let evil hunt the violent man to overthrow him. I know the Lord will maintain the cause of the afflicted; and justice for the poor. Surely the righteous shall give thanks to Your name; and the upright shall dwell in Your presence.*

The words echoed their familiarity, and Daniy-El similarly knew that he needed El Shaddai now more than ever. *Be my strength and my rock, my fortress. . . my defense. . . my strong tower. In Thee will I hide myself. With my heart do I honor you . . .*

The king's audience chamber, though empty at first, was filling rapidly with buzzing officials. The king stood atop the dais, regarding the men before him with a look of undisguised fury. Some entering scurried to their seats.

"How could this be? Not Daniy-El!" The king clenched his fists. He scanned the court of vultures from whom he had taken counsel. Now they brazenly encircled their quarry, having already conspired to remove his closest aide. He bristled in anger. By his own hand he had condemned Daniy-El to death—and a death so brutal. *How could I have been so gullible?* he chastised himself. He raked his hand through his hair.

"Daniy-El neither regards you nor the decree that you have signed, making his petition three times a day!"

The king held his hand up in disgust. He had heard enough of their condemnatory report. *They will not have their prize,* he vowed. He would find a way to save Daniy-El from their rapacious clutches.

"I see," he said in a voice that grew dangerously soft. "The matter is now clear. A king can hardly sanction rebellion." His eyes narrowed, realizing that they had watched for this occasion against his first president. The intensity of the king's ire was palpable.

Smug in their apparent triumph, the men stood back. He could see that they had misread his reaction, supposing his anger to be against the Jew. *Fools.*

They were so certain that his hankering pride would drive him to slaughter Daniy-El without question. *No.* Daniy-El was worth more than the lot of them put together. They would discover soon enough upon what the axis of his wrath turned. However, there was much he needed to do before that time. Darius strode from the room, leaving the administrators perplexed. He would deny them their triumph, one way or another.

An administrator entered the counselor's hall on the run. He paused before the milling assembly of satraps, lords, and princes, breathless and stumbling in his anxiety.

"The king has called for the librarians and the lawmakers! He seeks to save the Jew?" he blurted out. The room grew suddenly quiet as their premature congratulations sputtered like sodden oil wicks.

"What have we done?" one of the princes groaned, breaking the stunned silence. "We should not have heeded Strobos's plan. He said nothing would be more important to the king in his pride, but this does not bode well. No. It does not at all bode well—that look in the king's eyes. I first thought it to be his anger at the flaunting of his command by the Jew, but now. . . ."

"Truly," agreed another, grimacing at the recollection. "His eyes burned like coals upon a brazier. One would have thought his own life had been at stake rather than that of the slave. What shall we do now?" he moaned piteously. For all their celebrated stations, much of their pomp and grandeur was wrapped about backbones as thin as a spindle's cog.

"We shall remain calm, and do nothing more. What is done is done. The mark of the king's own signet rests upon it, does it not? He is no less culpable, do not forget. We shall not let him forget either. That it happens to be one of his favored bondsmen is no concern of ours. He should have thought of that before he subjected us to such ignominy. Should we have tolerated that indefinitely? No. On this we all agree. Though he could have, the Hebrew did not forbear. He chose his own destiny. Hence, the king shall have until eventide, at which time we shall remind him of our duty as officers of the Mede and Persian kingdom to uphold the laws. He knows that once enacted they cannot be changed for all time. There is no way out remaining to the Jew. Do not fear. We are in this together. By sunset, the king will have no option but to give us charge to conduct the execution? The furor shall soon pass as soon as the slave has been torn apart by the beasts. It always does."

"You are right. The king's disposition will soon mellow, especially with the aid of a little wine and good company," another prince interjected to lighten the tense mood.

"Indeed," the Second Prince agreed. "We should see that the king is too preoccupied with pleasures to be entertained by the troubles of slaves. The king shall dine in splendor this eve. I want Darius to have no reason to dwell upon this *Daniy-El* ever again."

I shall bless the Lord at all times, and his praise shall continually be in my mouth. As Daniy-El gloried in the peace that only Yahweh could impart the door to the bedchamber crashed inward, splintering on its hinges. It slammed to the floor with a deafening retort. Daniy-El remained with his hands raised in supplication toward the lowering sky. The evening hues were more resplendent than the finest silks. *The Lord's will be done.* He did not turn, but instead bowed in acknowledgement of Yahweh's omnipotence.

Two pairs of rough hands dragged him to his feet. He did not resist as they bundled him callously through the dim passageways. He knew where they were taking him. After an interminable journey, he was tumbled into his prison chamber, its musty air damp and suffocating. There he prayed, not for himself, but for the king. When they had not come to take him during his morning devotions, he had known the king's heart with certainty. His prayers at noontide had also passed without event. Undoubtedly, his persecutors had suffered a discomfiting wait to draw his blood.

There was nothing Darius could have done. His authority had been compromised by men more skilled in deception than he—men whose ears were attuned to the dark, having been given over to lustful seductions. The king was overwhelmed with matters of the kingdom and unable to scrutinize the private affairs of each member of his assembly. He would have viewed this latest statute as a mere dalliance to demonstrate his sovereignty. The foolishness of pride seemed to be a trap for the mighty in power who answered to none but their own hand. Pride inexorably led one to greater sins and justification thereof in one's own eyes. It was for this reason that Daniy-El was glad that his will had been turned over to Yahweh before he had been placed above men. Stoked pride oft caused one to act harshly where temperance was merited, and contemptuously where a judicious decision was needed. Folly rode upon the back of pride, vociferous as it touted itself. They spurred each other on in their bid to subdue wisdom. The people of Chaldea, Media and Persia showed little tendency to piety. Their gods came and went as convenience dictated. Even Darius Hystaspes, whom the Hebrews called *Darjavesh,* besought Yahweh's mercies. He had become known among the Jews for the reverence he held for their God of Heaven whose good graces he thought it prudent to court. Darius was not the first king to seek favor from an unknown god so that he might be shown goodwill in return for good works, and perhaps even receive blessings for his purposed beneficence and gifts to the people of God. Would he ever understand that Yahweh was a God of the heart and not the hand, to be doled meaningless treasures without true sacrifice of spirit? Daniy-El sighed in his bonds. The king commanded the sword, and the sword commanded the loyalties of the people. Fear had superseded reverence and faithfulness in these lands. Decades under the rule of impious kings had bred a people of wayward desires.

Amidst the Jews also, Daniy-El had seen a wavering faith. Ezekiel, a captive and prophet, had been giving rebuke and direction to their people over the years. He stood in Jeremiah's stead, offering cautionary words from the mouth of Yahweh, but who heeded his instruction? Ezekiel had set his face as flint against the stiff-necked tribes who scoffed in rebellion at his utterances. It was painful for Daniy-El to watch as God's people languished in bonds of their own devising.

Daniy-El shook his head. How was it that so few sought His majesty? Their diadems were material, and transitory. The mightiest of rulers upon the earth and within the heavens were all eclipsed by the very shadow of the Almighty, His actual light more glorious than their greatest imaginings. He, Daniy-El, had seen, and he would never forget. All vanities fled away like creatures of the night. He would go wherever Yahweh set his feet too tread.

Yahweh be praised. You have been faithful to me, and I shall be faithful to You.

King Darius slid his heavy robes off shoulders gone stiff from the restlessness that had built throughout the long day and pursued him into the night hours. He could neither sleep nor taste wine. He turned away the servants who brought trays of fruit and meats. He had no stomach for feasting, or for the lull of pleasant music. The entire day he had spent rummaging through the libraries with his servants, seeking a recourse to Daniy-El's plight amongst the annals of the kings. Of what use was his kingship and its celebrated power now. Darius slammed his palm against the bedpost. He had labored to secure a release from the prison of words that he had created. It was the least he could do for this gentle man who had served him more staunchly than his faithless brothers. There was no just recompense to be given, for these shackles had been expertly forged to bind this mild-mannered man whose position was coveted by men of high ambition, but low morals. Darius groaned inwardly, for neither was he blameless in this common quest for self-aggrandizement and people-worship. However, his failure was assured. The law was incontrovertible, as well they knew when they came skulking to ply their wares at his door—jars of spikenard infused with vitriol. Did they think that he did not recognize the product of their malevolent craft? They had meditated upon his weakness, and coddled his ego to his vain delight. They would do so again, should he permit. He was certain that they would slit his throat if he allowed them to grow emboldened.

And I assuredly shall not! He would deal with these miscreants later, but at present, it was the king who would attend the needs of his servant. While he fasted, he would beseech the mercies of Daniy-El's God that He would keep watch over his own. Whom else could he entreat? There was only One in whom he could hope for the deliverance of his friend, and for that the Darius would bow to the King of Kings.

18

Gnashing

The Lord will go before you;
And the God of Israel shall be your rearward.

- The Book of the Prophet Isaiah

Yellow eyes peered feverishly from the dark recesses, gauging the small movements of the form that now lay prostrate several yards away. It did not move for several moments, and neither did the predators. The dust that it had stirred was settling soundless in the dark, prickling the animals' nostrils. Still the predators breathed slowly, and steadily. The large male sniffed the air, absorbing the scent of the two-legged one that had entered their lair, tumbling from the hole that opened to the rocky glen above. The beast, huge and powerful, crooked its head to detect any sounds in the night. Soft breath escaped into the stillness. It waited, sniffing again. There was no tinge of fear pervading the air. The predator raised up on its haunches. It crept forward, wary of its intended prey. Often his own kind had been slaughtered by these feared ones, the *hunter-prey* that lived beyond the plain of grass atop cliffs of stone by the wide streams of water. His own kept to the wilderness reaches, away from this kind. At times, they brought one of their own to the lair, tossing him within, before moving the great stone back into place.

Oftimes, such a one would smell of blood, or urine, and bear deep wounds that told of weakness. Why they came to leave their own was unknown to the predator. He had seen some sacrifice many of their pack to the harsh wilds. The aged, and the infirm all beasts understood, but such as still gave suck, was a mystery as deep as the small lights that pierced the dark high above the land. Some of the strong who entered could yet stand—the young and the virile—they fought, but could not escape past the great stone that blocked their path through the cleft in the rock. This was not the only passage to the plain but the other lay on the far side of the wall of stone, past his hunters. They would not make it there, for the pride had young to feed, and would never permit the crossing.

The yellow eyes remained fixed of the new one, which still had not shifted to its feet. Perhaps it had been stunned by the fall into the cave. The scent grew stronger as the beast neared it. He offered no threat, this one—no glinting teeth to slice his hide. The predator growled to his companions, who paced, eager for his signal to feed. The hierarchy of the pack was clear, and so they waited. They closed in slowly as a low moan escaped the lips of the *hunter-prey*. No matter. There were no others beyond the rock. Their scents had been gone for a while. Hunger was no beast's friend and this one was now separate from his pack. They could feast unhindered. . . .

Bunching taut muscles, it sprung for the kill . . .

Daniy-El lay unmoving, unable to see aught in the pitch-black hollow of the declivity. However, lying with his face pressed to the hard-packed ground, he could hear the soft footpads of an animal prowling beyond. He did not move, assessing his position. He had fallen onto a low ledge after he had been pitched through the maw of the cave. He had braced himself, yet the thudding fall had knocked the wind from his lungs. He had heard others tell of the barbarous practice—men torn limb from limb by the lean cats that fed freely on the human sacrifices offered.

The king had sealed the rock with his own ring, but his visage had been drenched in anguish. Pain had contorted his expression as the guards had dumped their prisoner into the boulder-strewn chasm. Darius's voice had called down to him, a flush of hope overlaying his distress, "Daniy-El, your God whom you serve continually, He will deliver you."

The words of faith had strengthened Daniy-El. Now his peril was immediate. *Jehovah Elohay! Jehovah*—The sudden change in vibration warned him of their lunging attack. He needed to do something, and fast, but there was nowhere to turn. The dark eclipsed his vision and he could as easily plunge to his death over some hidden outcrop. He stemmed the rush of dread that rose like vomit in his throat, threatening to spew itself into his being. *Jehovah Elohay, Jehovah Shalom, Jehovah Shalom*—Daniy-El squeezed his eyes tightly as a searing light scoured the cavern, erasing the darkness in a blinding flash. The glare shone through his closed lids and after a few moments Daniy-El squinted tentatively into the brilliance emanating from a place before him. The vision of the angelic presence was overpowering, and a weight sapped the strength from his limbs. Through the corner of his eye, he could see the maned creatures that stumbled back abruptly, several drawing away in hesitation as the vibrant umbra encircled the two men—one of flesh and the other of everlasting spirit. Daniy-El forced himself to his knees, then pushed himself upright. He gazed toward the feral beasts whose menace was now subdued. The lead male paced for a moment longer in indecision. It bared its fangs then backed away with a snarl of frustration. The lionesses trailed in his wake, merging into the shadowy crevices of the lair.

The angelic warder did not speak, but he watched with eyes as intense as the stars. He would abide until morning when the stone was rolled back in expectation of his charge's death. However, the anticipated carnage would be denied those bloodthirsty men.

God be praised.

Darius urged the chariot driver to reckless speed across the rocky terrain. *God of Heaven, have you preserved your servant? Have you?* The darkness fled away from the sun as it emerged over a peak far in the distance. Before the chariot had fully slowed at the sacrificial ground, the king bounded down, running the remaining distance to the sealed entrance. The startled driver wrenched on the reins, drawing the chariot to a churning halt. Close enough to recognize a place of death, the powerful horses shied at the scent of predators that hovered upon the air. Four guardsmen alighted from their mounts and hurried to reach their sovereign whose face was pressed to a slim crack at the boulder's edge. Darius strained to peer within.

"Daniy-El? Daniy-El?" the king bellowed anxiously. *"Daniy-El!"* he placed his ear to the rock but heard nothing. "Daniy-El, servant of the living God," he cried in lament, his sliver of hope threatening to break, "has your God whom you serve continually, been able to deliver you from the lions?" He gestured weakly for the guards to come. "Move away the stone. Move it. Move it away."

He stood aside as the men came forward, using stout poles to lever the massive rock from its place. "Daniy-El!" the king shouted once again in distress. *Daniy-El.*

There was a sound of scrabbling rock on the other side and Darius backed away a pace, expecting now to be assailed by an enraged roar from an entrapped beast. His trepidation was met with a softly spoken salutation issuing from the darkness of the lair.

"O king, live forever."

Darius was taken aback by the deferential greeting. Despite knowing Daniy-El's humble demeanor he had half-expected to face anger at the injustice meted out to the old counselor. He heard other movements on the far side of the rock then the muffled voice grew clearer.

"O king, live forever. My God has sent His angel, and He has shut the lions' mouths, that they have not hurt me: forasmuch as before Him was I found innocent, and also before you, O king, have I done no hurt."

The king watched fearfully as a guard knelt, reaching into the chasm to take the aging man's arm and hoist him aloft. As Daniy-El emerged unscathed, he laughed a low rumble that broke like a dam of unfettered relief. He shook raised fists as he banished the despondency that had sought to wither the marrow of his bones over the last few hours. The king's mirth caused Daniy-El to grin broadly whilst the guardsmen looked one to another in incomprehension. The king was suddenly freed from the abject guilt that had threatened to suffocate him. Daniy-El was indeed innocent—but there were others who were not. He would not forgive the torment they had caused him, and a faultless man, with their treacheries. Darius was not prepared to let the matter lie. He turned his vengeful thoughts back to the comforts of his old friend. He embraced him unashamedly, inured to the stares of the on-looking servants. He held Daniy-El at arms length. His skin was unbroken and his garments, though rumpled and marred with dust, showed no signs of tearing. Darius released him and marveled. It was as these Hebrews said—a miracle performed by their God.

At Darius's bidding, the warders helped Daniy-El into the king's chariot. Darius climbed in, his mouth hardening into a grim line. He peered at the outline of the city as sunlight caught upon the towers. *There they wait, glorying in their vice.* He looked back toward the lair, which had been closed once more. *It is fitting,* he decided. *They have passed their own sentence. May their God have mercy on them, for I shall not.*

He signaled for the driver to proceed. *There will be changes in Babylon, starting today.*

With only the presence of the court scribe to attend him, Darius envisioned those wonders he had discovered for himself in addition to those testaments that Daniy-El, with quiet intensity, had given of this God, Yahweh. There were marvels that He performed in His majesty; awesome works to which Ormuzd and Ahriman had never attained, nor any other god that Darius had encountered throughout his roving conquests. Recalling Daniy-El's triumph lit an intense fire within Darius that surpassed even the glory of victory in war, for Daniy-El had used neither strength of arm nor superior numbers, yet the victory had come irrefutably. Darius was not prepared to allow the matter to lie with the bones of the perpetrators who had plotted against him and his servant. He would do much more.

Turning his attention back to the matter at hand, the king recounted his witness as the scribe followed his words assiduously.

'Unto all people, nations and languages, that dwell in all the earth; Peace be multiplied unto you. I make a decree: That in every dominion of my kingdom men shall tremble and fear before the God of Daniy-El; for He is the Living God, and steadfast forever, and His kingdom that which shall not be destroyed, and His dominion shall be even unto the end. He delivers and rescues, and works signs and wonders in heaven and earth, He who has delivered Daniy-El from the power of the lions.'

Darius examined the scroll carefully. It was a proper tribute to One so mighty, and also to a servant who was more excellent than all. He nodded in satisfaction before calling for the chief of heralds, who was commissioned to disperse the decree by runner, horse and ship. *Before the day ends, my people will know of the deeds of this day. I myself will never forget.*

He had given Daniy-El leave to retire to his house, after the counselor, though weary, would accept no further ministrations from the king's servants whom Darius had delegated to attend him. Darius thought a long moment. *Had any of my princes served as faithfully and consistently as Daniy-El, I would prosper them beyond measure.* Slave or no, Darius intended to have it be the same for the aging administrator.

Rest well, my friend. You have earned you reprieve. There would be time yet for them to learn more of each other, and of the one true God who was able to save.

19

The Prayer

Remember, O Lord, what is come upon us;

Consider and behold our reproach

- The Lamentations of Jeremiah

As he trudged the long passageways toward his house, Daniy-El could hear screams emanating from the Hall of the Kings, as guardsmen assembled his accusers in the courtyard beyond. Daniy-El knew instinctively that they were soon destined for the terrible place from whence he had just come. The king's retribution had fallen swiftly and ruthlessly upon the men and their families alike. Callous men had roused a beast who they thought to have subdued. Daniy-El knew that the king had been incensed by their brazen act, and would not stay his hand at their pleas. The sounds of mounting terror slowly died away beyond the palace gates as the soldiers herded a large, woeful, group across the plain. Any hope of clemency was now gone.

Daniy-El squeezed his eyes shut and leaned his bowing head against the cold wall. The stench of death exuded from this place. Despite its gold trimmings and glamour, the core of Babylon remained putrid. The superficial calm was too fragile to withstand the forces pitted against it. How long the polished veneer would last remained to be seen.

For the moment, Daniy-El could extend himself no further, and he longed for the refuge of his chamber. He used the wall to steady his steps as he moved down the hall to his bedchamber. He breathed a sigh of gladness as he entered the room that had been his nearing seventy years. The space remained as it had the day before, the windows thrown open to the streaming rays of the sun. Daniy-El walked toward the window, his arms thrown back and his voice raised in a song of praise. He raised his face and closed his eyes. He inhaled deeply and sent prayers soaring to the Master. *Who is like unto You?* He knelt before the sill and worshiped, sunlight bathing his form. He shuffled back and lay prostrate before God.

My *trials are but a pittance before the needs of my people, Lord.* There would be many more *Sons of Belial* who sought the blood of God's people. The spirits of the Children of Judah still cried out like those crossing the wilderness. What more could he do in their aid? Many hardships yet lay ahead before the promise was fulfilled. Concluding his prayers he rose and crossed to his writing desk. As Jeremiah did, he too would give counsel through word. He would note that his people should perish for lack of wisdom. Taking a fresh parchment from a stack on the lowest shelf, he selected an ink pot and quill. He would not lose hope.

It may be a long time yet, but the Prince of princes was coming, and as many as took heed, would be delivered.

Daniy-El resumed his duties with diligence, devoting himself to study during his free hours. Many of the texts that had been looted from the palaces and Holy Temple in Jerusalem now lay buried amidst insignificant writings within the vast libraries in Babylon. Daniy-El sought them out, eager to build his understanding of his people's fate. His mind churned with the visions that he had been sent over the years; the inevitable rise and fall of nations.

Meanwhile, what is our place in His plan? What is mine? Of what value will my knowledge be to my people? They continued to suffer in this land, ripped apart from their heritage and without direction. As he strove within himself, the text of a familiar scroll bloomed suddenly upon the delicate papyrus before him, and Daniy-El bolted upright. He held the paper closer to the low flame, careful not to singe the edges. The words—. How had he not seen this? He reread the writing several times with initial excitement, and then an overwhelming sense of sorrow built within his breast. He had been but a young man when the words were uttered on the lips of the prophet Jeremiah; one dismissed and derided as a blathering fool, thought to be ignorant of the truths of God by the King of Israel and his people alike. However, the prophet had shown himself to be no fool. It was told that one could confirm the truth or fallacy of prophecy in whether it came to pass. In this, Jeremiah's foretelling had been verified above any claim of falsity. The proof was unraveled before their eyes as the Jews were slaughtered mercilessly in their homes by Nebuchadnezzar's conquering armies, and the survivors—the beautiful, the comely and those of excellent trade—were herded like sheep into captivity in Babylon.

Since that time, the desecration of Jerusalem as foretold had belied the derogation of his warnings. So it remained for the past sixty-nine years. Now he read of a promised miracle—the fulfillment of their return to Jerusalem in the seventieth year of their captivity, if only their hearts would likewise return to their God. Realizations surged within Daniy-El as other words came to the fore from centuries past. Had not Moses, even, given similar caution to the Children of Israel generations before?

'When all these things come upon you, the blessing and the curse I have set before you, and you call them to mind among all the nations where the Lord your God drives you, and you return to the Lord your God and obey his voice according to all that I command you this day, you and your children, with all your heart and all your soul, then the Lord your God will bring you back from the captivity, and have compassion on you, and gather you again from all the nations where the Lord your God has driven you. If you are driven out to the farthest parts under heaven, from there He will bring you.'

How could they all have been so blind, and for so long, to cast off their primary source of life and hope? Despite their rebellion, Yahweh had made a way for them to come home to the shelter he had set aside for them before time began.

Daniy-El's thoughts were in disarray but he focused them on the script before him. His remedy in all was to set his face to the Lord and to His things, to seek Him in prayer, and to offer his earnest supplications. The gravity of his people's error pressed upon him, and he groaned aloud, unable to contain the grief that swelled to bursting within him. The depth of their collective malfeasance against the God of Abraham, Isaac, and Jacob, caused him to shudder. The promise of salvation had been there all along, but it would need to be claimed in faith. He fell upon his face in penitence and shame for his people.

"Oh Lord," he cried. "Great and awesome God, who keeps His covenant and mercy with those who love Him, and with those who keep His commandments, we have sinned and committed iniquity, we have done wickedly and rebelled, even by departing from Your precepts and Your judgments. Neither have we heeded Your servants the prophets who spoke in Your name to our kings and our princes, to our fathers and all the people of the land."

Daniy-El stretched himself prostrate as he wept out his earnest confession on behalf of all Israel. "Oh Lord, according to all your righteousness, I pray, let Your anger and Your fury be turned away from Your city Jerusalem, Your holy mountain; because for our sins and for the iniquities of our fathers, Jerusalem and Your people are a reproach to all those around us. Now therefore, our God, hear the prayer of Your servant, and his supplications, and for the Lord's sake, cause Your face to shine on Your sanctuary, which is desolate. O my God, incline Your ear and hear; open Your eyes and see our desolations, and the city which is called by Your name; for we do not present our supplications before You because of our righteous deeds, but because of Your great mercies. Oh Lord, hear! Oh Lord, forgive!"

Daniy-El's plea grew urgent, for the burden of the years squandered in this tormenting land now pressed him sore. If he could but save them all even one added day of trial—

"Oh Lord, listen and act! Do not delay for Your own sake, my God: for Your city, and Your people, are called by Your name."

O Lord forgive. . . .

The prayer issued forth from the depths of the mighty city like a wellspring of crystal, clear water. It breached the cloudy darkness that coalesced to suffocate the light that sought to flow from the heavenlies to the Children entrapped in a prison of their own making. The prayer was awaited—so long in coming—so long and nary a penitent heart to cry healing for the wounds of an embittered people—until now. The instant the first words of the supplication floated up, the heaven's bore record. The prayer would not go unanswered. The angel hearkened diligently to his Master's commands. There would be no hesitation to heed His bidding. His Master's will was paramount and must prevail. As the Word shot forth, the angel took flight. He moved swiftly for the prayer would not be denied reply by His voice.

A force huddled insidiously, watching to steal away the nugget of hope lest its glow pervade the dark city and the war be finished. The war had served its purpose, causing men's hearts to fail in despair of ever gaining freedom. It did not wish an end. There was more that could be paid in blood. The eradication of the Holy City had been a seeming triumph to repay the glory lost when the One had him out from the place of rest. The massacre of his enemy's beloved children satisfied him somewhat. He had basked in the victory. Was it not a sign that he could vanquish them all in the end? That One's love for these weak, mortal men—His wondrous creations—would ultimately be ground into the dust. His enemy had accused him of being proud, but what of these? Were they not the same? Suffering banishment and subjugation rather than accept the mantle of the Master? Yes they were the same. And he aimed to prove it at the last, whence he would mount the coveted steps of the glorious city and claim the crown that had been denied him. His followers would bow before him. They would submit to his radiance and—

A bolt of light—a light that embodied a being of spirit—seared earthward and was gone in a supernatural blaze. Its swiftness left him and his helpers no time to contain its passage. *Gabriy-El! It had to be.* That one had resisted his plans for millennia and had refused to oppose the Master in the day when it all began. He was one of the despised ones, but hated above all were the sons of men who had stolen his promise. He would obtain their deaths at any cost. The One's servant had caught him unprepared this time, but there would be other opportunities. Perhaps he would turn his attention once more to this human below who dared call for the One's intervention. He had sought to crush the old man, to rend him from life as he had so many others in times past, but he had gained no success. It was clear that the Master adored Daniy-El. He would need to watch for a sliver through which he could slip in, and maybe learn what was planned by his former master. Thus far he had been unable to discern the mysteries that revolved around the future of these Jews. Usually the One gave only enough information for any who observed to recognize when His plans had already reached fruition, but not enough to predict and alter the course of His will aforetime. Why the One favored these Hebrews was unknown within his realm, but his minions would combat all who joined their fates to the One in heaven. They would see who stood supreme in the end. It was far from over—very far from over.

Gabriy-El flared toward his destination even as Daniy-El continued to bow in prayer. He sped past the adversaries that cowered in the heavens waiting to deter any whose course defied their foul purposes. He moved unchallenged across the ethereal winds ever aware of the dangers and sly snares, but he traveled safely under the covering of the Almighty.

He entered Daniy-El's room softly, reaching out to touch the one beloved of the Lord God. Gabriy-El had come to impart words of knowledge, for his

Lord has selected this son of man to carry the prophecy to the Jews. To Daniy-El would their end be foreshadowed, until another of equal obedience came forward in service.

"Daniy-El," he said gently, "I have come to give you understanding. At the beginning of your petition the command went out, and I have come to explain all to you, for you are greatly beloved."

The being continued to regard him with compassion. "Consider the matter, and understand the vision: Seventy periods of seven years have been set out for your people and your holy city. In this time the sins of the people shall be contained and judgment enacted. However, a way shall be created through which atonement may be received, and everlasting righteousness issued in. Then, no more will need to be said. A new place will be made and consecrated—the Holy City shall be made anew until the Messiah comes, but after this He shall be cut off, and there shall be proscribed dominion by the followers a false Messiah—one who shall come to usher in a time of immense destruction and sacrilege against all pertaining to the true Messiah. Still, this permitted time of persecution shall be brought to an end as final judgment is passed."

Gabriy-El's explanation of the seasons to come washed clean any lingering uncertainties regarding the visions Daniy-El had previously received. As long as men's hearts were the temple of the Lord God, no destroyer would be able to steal away the worship of the one true King. The imposter would try, but he could not ultimately succeed. On this comfort Daniy-El would rest, and he prayed that all who knew the living God would also find solace in the assurances given. He clasped his hands in thanksgiving. *Yahweh will honor my petition!* Though the tidings were dire and much hardship would beset the future generations of his people, he was overjoyed to know that the re-establishment Jerusalem was at hand. A new season was indeed blossoming for his people, and Daniy-El prayed that they would incline their hearts to Him, trusting in the promise to be fulfilled.

Jerusalem, your people are coming home, and with them, the Prince of Peace.

20

Free

Behold, I, even I, will both search for

My sheep, and seek them out.

- *The Book of the Prophet Ezekiel*

Upon his return from his first campaign after the siege of Babylon, Cyrus met with his second in command in order to strategize. Cyrus was fascinated by the remarkable balance that he found in the affairs carried out in Babylon. He had expected Darius to have spent many long seasons countering trickery, treachery and thievery in their new demesne. Yet the day to day affairs ran as smoothly as any ruler could wish. Much of his success Darius attributed to the steady hand of his First President, who, though aging, was never cowed by the business of corralling the jackals that roamed the administrative halls of power. Further, the Mede's account of his one, unfortunate, edict, and the origin of the deception, even more intrigued Cyrus. The path of Daniy-El's own life, and Darius's report of the visions that the old advisor had brought forth in his predecessor's reign also caught the Persian's attention.

Cyrus felt moved to bid Daniy-El attend him in the royal court, where he was invited to lay bare his vast knowledge of the past, or future, course for the kingdom of Media and Persia. Daniy-El chose to share with the king a portion of Isaiah's prophecies concerning Cyrus himself and the future of

Babylon. Cyrus allowed it, for he was no fool, and he was well aware of the power that existed beyond the realms of men, if they but opened their eyes. *Why should I ignore the truth because it comes from the Jewish quarter?* If he did he might live to regret such pride. Cyrus looked on intently as Daniy-El produced a delicate scroll, which according to the library records, was written more than 100 years before Cyrus was even born yet spoke of Cyrus's own purported future deeds. *Could it truly be so,* he wondered, *that I have been known to these people of Israel before I was known to mother's womb?* He settled back to listen, his curiosity mounting.

'Thus saith the Lord, thy redeemer, and He that formed thee from the womb,
I am the Lord that maketh all things;
That stretcheth forth the heavens alone;
That spreadeth abroad the earth by Myself;
That frustrateth the tokens of liars;
That maketh diviners mad;
That turneth wise men backward;
And maketh their knowledge foolish;
That confirmeth the word of His servant and performeth the counsel of His messengers;
That saith to Jerusalem, thou shalt be inhabited;
And to the to the cities of Judah,
'Ye shall be built, and I will raise up the decayed pieces thereof;
That saith to the deep,
'Be dry, and I will dry up thy rivers. . .'
'That saith of Cyrus, 'He is my shepherd and shall perform all my pleasure;
Even saying to Jerusalem, 'Thou shalt be built,'
And to the Temple, 'Thy foundation shall be laid."

Cyrus leapt up from his seat even as Daniy-El was speaking. "And did we not dry up the Euphrates to claim this city? We did. We did!" he said in amazement. "We did," he whispered, before sitting again. *But what is this of Jerusalem?* His brow furrowed in thought and hands rubbed his lips studiously. Leaning forward the king held Daniy-El's gaze with rapt attention, searching for some hint of duplicity, but he found none. Hand raised and fingers fluttering excitedly, Cyrus urged Daniy-El to continue. Daniy-El recited the history directly to the king, as though in Isaiah the prophet's stead:

'Thus saith the Lord to his anointed Cyrus, whose right hand I have strengthened,
To subdue nations before him;
And I will loose the loins of kings, to open before him the two leaved gates;
And the gates shall not be shut;
I will go before thee and make the crooked places straight;
I will break in pieces the gates of brass, and cut in sunder bars of iron:
And I will give thee treasures of darkness, and hidden riches of secret places;
That thou mayest know that I, the Lord, which call thee by thy name, am the God of Israel.
For Jacob my servant's sake, and Israel mine elect, I have called thee by name;
I have surnamed thee, though thou hast not known me.
I am the Lord, and there is none else,
There is no God beside Me;
I girded thee, though thou hast not known me,
That they may know from the rising of the sun, and from the west,
That there is none beside me
I am the Lord, and there is none else.'

Cyrus had emptied the chambers of scribes and servants while he spoke with Daniy-El alone. The import of the prophecy did not escape him. The God of

Israel, who had proven himself in all His works in Babylon, had called Cyrus to be the deliverer of His people from, and to establish a Holy Temple to Him. As a result, Cyrus would be blessed with might and dominion.

"What more could a ruler ask, eh Daniy-El?" Cyrus had said mirthlessly. "Was there more?"

"Yes."

"Well?"

Daniy-El knew that this was the moment that would change the path of his people, and he had spoken humbly, already with thanksgiving to the God who was beyond knowing, whose ways were a mystery, the Holy One of Israel who had loved His people and made their ways straight from the beginning.

"He has said—" Daniy-El paused, almost overcome with the knowledge and joy. "He has said that He has raised you up in righteousness, and that He shall direct all your ways. That you shall build His city and let His captives go free, but you shall not do it for a price, or a reward."

Cyrus sat, his eyes seeing a world that was beyond the present.

"So it shall be, God of heaven," he said to the air. "So it shall be."

Never, throughout all his years of service as court treasurer, had Mithredath encountered a king so willing to deplete the royal coffers to finance the personal business of slaves—at least, until now. Mithredath had spent days sifting the treasury records, careful not to miss even one item, lest the king of Persia be wroth. Thus far, he had tallied over five thousand precious vessels. Each was checked and returned to the heavy crates, which had been packed and removed from the Temple of Babylon. It was a phenomenal concession for the king to have made, and many in the court wondered at the magnitude of his generosity. Others thought it to be a farce. However Cyrus, King of the entire Persian Empire, had declared his will, and the edict was irrefutable—Cyrus himself was commissioning the building of the Temple of the Lord in Jerusalem, and every Jew from within the Empire who desired to return to his homeland to aid with its renewal, was declared free to leave, unhindered by either master, or bondsman. Furthermore, each Jew was now allowed to receive freewill offerings for his journey from amongst the people of the Empire; every vessel of the House of the Lord in Jerusalem that had been plundered by Nebuchadnezzar would be returned to Jerusalem for the new Temple. Mithredath could not help but consider the host that would be departing—not only would the treasury be bereft of countless riches, but nearly fifty thousand slaves would also be leaving the gates of Babylon and other cities with Cyrus's blessing. An amnesty of such magnitude seemed incomprehensible—an entire people—free? *What could have so stirred the king's spirit to empathy with the Jews? The proclamation had been made so swiftly.* The words still rang in Mithredath's ears:

'Who is there among you of all His people? His God be with him, and let him go to Jerusalem, which is in Judah, and build the House of the Lord God of Israel. He is the God, which is in Jerusalem.'

Could it truly have all been prompted by the obscure prophecy read to Cyrus by the old Jew? No matter. The edict would stand irrevocably. Already the chiefs of the fathers of the tribes of Judah and Benjamin, and the priests and Levites, had risen up, strengthening their hands with all that was willingly offered them. Mithredath sighed. Sheshbazzar, the appointed prince of Judah, would be awaiting the final count and dispatch from the temple courtyard. Cyrus had given the prince the authority of governor, and he would oversee the transportation of the treasures to Jerusalem.

Too much was changing in the city, and its end, he dared not guess. The loss of the slaves would create a pit in the tributes gathered yearly within the provinces—many thousand *drams* of gold and *minas* of silver. Yet he knew that it was not his place to gainsay the king. He would complete his tasks, as would the others, and, for now, leave the business of kingship to the king.

Daniy-El had spent the morning bidding the tribes farewell, his joy tinged with sadness, for many of his friends had departed in their midst. He had been briefly surprised when Cyrus had asked to hear more of the prophecies of Israel concerning Babylon. Still, had not the fulfillment of the prophecy concerning Bel-Shazzar been welcomed, even heralded, by the Persian? Upon reflection, Cyrus's interest was not misplaced. The accuracy of the prophetic words of the Jewish seers had become known to many, and now too, Cyrus. *Our people will still be subjects of Persia, but at last they can go home beneath a banner of peace, and to worship Jehovah Tsidkeenu—the Lord Our Righteousness.* This was more important than all the other sanctions by the king. Cyrus had asked a special boon—that the people lift him and his family to the God of Heaven. They would do so, for his hand acted graciously, and without malice.

Scores of families were represented in the genealogies accounted for repatriation, though several others would remain behind. The majority of the older captives had gone the way of the earth, and it was now their children who were left to uphold the legacy of each family name. Some, though, did not wish to leave the familiar, though not sympathetic, surroundings of Chaldea. Others, however, were afraid to face the pagan tribes that would by now have resettled the lands of Judah. These would not welcome a repatriation of the Hebrews and were likely to be hostile to their homecoming, despite Cyrus' protection. The king would be over one thousand miles distant from their peril, which would be immediate, once they crossed the river Jordan. Each family would need to reclaim the land passed down through his generations for an everlasting possession under the Law.

Each family record had been painstakingly compiled. Through these, it was clear which families had remained pure of intermixing whilst in Babylon. It was critical for those who served as priests not to have intermarried and brought pagan influences into their lineage. This had been one source of division from the first and those who chose to leave were earnest about pleasing God having been given a new hope.

Priests, Levites, singers, gatekeepers, and temple servants were carefully catalogued for service when the new altar was built and the foundations laid. It was also fitting that Levites would be the ones appointed to supervise the construction. Already the diet of those to serve in the temple was being purified. Masons and carpenters had also been identified. It was planned that logs be sent by sea from Lebanon to Joppa. Cyrus had apportioned resources and given the command that they purchase cedar logs from the people of Sidon and Tyre much as Solomon had done in commissioning the first Temple.

Daniy-El would remain to serve the king. The Lord had not bid him go and so he stayed. He uttered silent prayers for their safe journeying. God's promise to Abraham, to make his descendents as numerous as the star, would be fulfilled through these few who were destined to become many. *Yahweh be praised. You are more than faithful.*

21

Sons of El

The champion waited, and he watched. It was no small task safeguarding the sons of men, but he was charged with aiding the establishment of God's kingdom on the earth —the full revelation of the truth guarded within his bosom until it was the time that his Master had chosen. Most men were offered mere glimpses of His purposes, whilst others were granted depths of knowledge beyond earthly realms. One such man was Daniy-El who served the truth with an unswerving passion that called to the heart of God. How many among the sons of men would chasten themselves sore for the sake of others, and for the salvation of a people so given to rebellion? Today he would know even more, for having learnt of the seventy weeks of trial, yet he had not relinquished his yearning for God. His last petition had been heard, and Israel given their deliverance at Cyrus' hand, still the one beloved of Yahweh was not satisfied to rest from seeking his Lord, who saw it fit to send him a message regarding the great war to come, the supreme trial of men. Daniy-El heard, and mourned. In this he would see the end of days and the fires that would assail men. Today he would apprehend much more than men could dream in their fleeting pass upon the rivers of grass, water and stone bounding the earth. This one would bear the burden of the record for whosoever had eyes to see and ears to hear. Many seasons had been proscribed in the heavenlies that bore testimony to the affairs of men; every stone turned and counted, each word made fast in the Book that was written unto life eternal. It would be a dire time when the records became known. Few of these mortal souls would witness His Glory, but whosoever willed may join the throng and rejoice as His majesty flooded all creation. The battle with the adversary was unforgiving in hope of the indescribable rewards to those who chose to stand with the One victor. The consequences of failure were likewise grave. Souls would not be surrendered without a fight. All heaven awaited the triumph that was yet to be bought in Blood, making null all the workings of the enemy that yet gloated over its perversion of the Children of Judah, but it would not be so forever.

The champion stirred at the Word, bidden now to move in defense of the cause set forth below, as the man beloved of his Master drank in sorrow in place of meat and drink. As the warrior came forth he knew —the enemy, too, had been waiting —this one who had been of the Master's own, an anointed cherub with privilege above any other, but doomed to transgress. He had seemed perfect in his ways from the moment that the Master created him, and then hidden perversity uncovered itself, compelling the Master to cast him from the Holy Mountain. This one had plummeted from glory and light to shame, accursed even beyond the beasts of the field, debased and trodden upon. Woe it was in that instant of rebellion. What folly, what pride, to exalt himself so—to seek a place above the stars of God and the Lord of Creation himself. No. You could never be as the Most High. O Daystar—Son of the Morning—how far have you fallen—to be cast so low, having seen the wonder of Eden and walked the fiery heavens. . . . What benefit to inherit a world that would pass away in flame and dust and ashes? —no princely kingdom when compared to the radiance of the Master's glory. No victory was ever in your bid, O Daystar. None at all!

Now this variance enacted so long ago meant that the crossing would be a fight. A fight that he needed to win before he could attend his charge for whom the journey would be one of endings. He must prevail. . . .

The rage of the battle swept the heavens. Were it possible, the adversary would have annihilated him at the first, for the Prince of the power of the air valued himself mighty above all others. The violence of the assault stayed his advance as he was required to pit all his spiritual strength against the fountain of evil set against him. The ferocity of its malice intensified and the wave of aggression crested. Cordoned by malevolence, the being of light could find no eddy through which to slip, and the battle was wearing on. The man of Israel had already been praying in full fast for three weeks, awaiting some answer from his Lord. Cowardice was not at the heart of the warrior, neither was surrender, yet he knew that it could not go on like this. He could not allow the Word to be stayed by the Prince of the Kings of Persia. The adversary would not succeed as long as the glory of God gave him strength to beckon aid. *Mika-El! Mika-El —Glory-of-Yahweh, come!* The angel continued to war the force that pressed hard against him. *He will come as I have called. He will . . . .*

Word and spirit echoed clear across the heavens, and then manifested into time.

Gabriy-El! Champion-of-Yahweh—I have come. The arrival of his counterpart poured righteous resolve into the battle. The angels focused the might of holiness into the vicious struggle for dominion of the air. Mika-El parted a way, slicing asunder the evil so that Gabriy-El could claim straight passage to Daniy-El's side. *Now!* Breaking free of the war, the champion flew upon wings of light, streaming to where the man of flesh waited. Mika-El would hold until his return. No amount of blackness would ever be able to consume God's glory, or sully the holy armor. Hatred and defiance would eventually bow, for no darkness would be allowed to claim the Holy Place. Not now. *Nor ever!*

As his companions flinched with sudden uneasiness, Daniy-El too registered the quavering unsteadiness that crept up his legs, seeming to leech away the life that flowed in his veins.

The men cast about in sudden terror; some stared out over the expanse of the Hiddekel, whilst others turned their back on the dark river, searching the surrounding plain for some source of threat.

"What is it? What is it?"

"I k-k-know n-n-ot," a voice quailed from their midst.

"And shall we wait here like lambs to the slaughter until death has descended upon us? Away!" one man shrieked, hitching his robes as he bolted, heedless of the direction in which he fled. His panicked flight goaded his companions into a stumbling run. A few searched the air at their fleeing backs, convinced now of the impending slaughter by an unseen force.

Daniy-El alone stood still, and the mounting sensation soon rendered him as feeble as a foal, fresh from its mother's womb. He struggled to gain his footing, but he felt as though an overwhelming force pinioned his limbs. Daniy-El's mind reeled, catching at wisps of wind, as he fought a desire to fold into unconsciousness. He had experienced this sundering of volition before—it was at the palace by the Shushan that a force had swept away his natural power as easily as the Euphrates churned flotsam downriver with the winter rains. All that was within Daniy-El seemed to pale miserably before the purity of the vision that now coalesced before him. At last a voice spoke, and it bore down like an onrushing host.

"ARISE!"

An urging impulse came with the command, but Daniy-El's strength fled as quickly as he could draw it to him. His limbs refused to answer the beckoning call and he remained prostrate and still shaking, where he had fallen upon the riverbank. He was unable to resist the terrifying pull upon his limbs. Daniy-El lay still, waiting, and within an instant there was a man before him, body of beryl and loins that shone as the gold of Uphaz. His face. . . ! It was as lightning.

Through the brilliance of the visage, eyes shone out like lamps of fire, regarding him intently. After a moment, Daniy-El felt the slight pressure of a touch that drew him to his hands and knees, yet he could not gain his feet, neither could he speak a word. He stayed immobile, bowed in a crouch.

"Daniy-El —a man greatly beloved, understand the words that I speak to thee, and stand upright for I have been sent to you."

Daniy-El summoned his resolve, and then compelled his trembling limbs to obey. He stood, but only just.

"Fear not, Daniy-El. From the first day that you set your heart to understand, and to chasten yourself before your God, your prayer was heard, and I have therefore been sent to you. But the Prince of Persia withstood me for twenty-one days until Mika-El, the first of the Chief Princes, came to help me, and I remained there with the kings of Persia. Now I have come to show you what shall befall your people in the latter days."

As Daniy-El embraced the stream of visions that were conveyed to him, he could form no words upon his tongue which was struck dumb. Recognizing his distress the Presence touched him gently upon the lips and he found his voice. His words floundered into existence upon the still bank of air surrounding them.

"O—O my lord," Daniy-El whispered, his throat constricting in despair. "By the vision I am overcome with sorrow. I —I have no strength. How can a servant speak with my lord? I have no—no breath—left—to speak, or strength remaining in me," Daniy-El groaned.

Again, the Presence touched him, and he was imbued with a renewed vitality. His shuddering frame straightened. "Let my lord speak," he said, "for you have made me strong."

"Do you know why I have come? Soon I will return to fight with the Prince of Persia, but first I will show you what is noted in the Scripture of Truth, and there is none that is equally strong in these things save Mika-el, your Prince."

At his bidding, the Word came, and it testified of an evolving battle—one that transcended sword and spear. Further mysteries of great kings yet to be birthed were revealed to Daniy-El who absorbed their import with gravity. He watched as tyranny and oppression unfolded in the wake of the incredible deceit that was to be foisted upon his nation—sacrilege and a profane pollution of the sanctuary of God followed his peoples acceptance of an abominable lie. Wherein was the end to the dissembling, the flatteries that warped sovereign after sovereign, and turned generations away for the God that had brought them out of Egypt and claimed them for His own? Base powers falsely claimed His divine authority and vie to corrupt the land and its people with wayward desires and seductive debauchery. The last of such emperors would be vile. Still, he would be received openly by the people of God as a messenger of light. *O Daystar, whose pride could never be assuaged!* So many—too many—would cling to his empty promises in a vain hope of their own fulfillments. Nevertheless, the truth would remain for those from whose eyes the scales of the Leviathan were lifted. Those who did not succumb to his treacherous promises of false peace would survive the breaking of kingdoms through a forged bond with the hope of the world—the Messiah.

The promised outpouring of His unmatched glory flowed like oil over the wound that became Israel. The faithless outnumbered the faithful by a distressing multitude. How many would actually receive the truth, or even recognize its presence? Hope promised that there would be enough souls to make the difference! That the Messiah must depart spoke of harsh days set out before the people. In the midst of this revelation was laid the comfort that His departure would usher in a new light, for He was a God of life and abundance and was wont to leave His people without succor.

"At that time Mika-El shall stand up—the great prince which stands for the children of your people, and there shall be a time of trouble such as there never was since there was a nation, and at that time your people will be delivered, every one that is found written in the Book. And many of them that sleep in the dust of the earth shall awake, some to everlasting life, and some to shame and everlasting contempt. And they that shall be wise shall shine as the brightness of the firmament; and they that lead many to righteousness as the stars forever. But you, Daniy-El—shut up the words and seal the book, even to the endtime. Many shall run too and fro and there will be an increase in knowledge."

Daniy-El understood with finality that the insight he had been given would someday bear record to Yahweh's omnipotence as had the promises given to Abraham, the father of nations. The words would be for a time to come such as Yahweh would reveal. Scintillating glimmers suddenly flared on the edges of the river, and as Daniy-El peered out over the Hiddekel two others appeared, one on either side of the water. The Presence who had revealed all to Daniy-El stood upon the of the river itself, listening as one of the newcomers spoke. When asked what length of time would pass until the accomplishment of God's purposes in the earth, he lifted his hands toward heaven and replied, *"It shall be for a time, times, and a half."*

Daniy-El heard his words, but he did not understand. The ultimate deliverance may be many lifetimes in the making, but at the end of it all, he had given assurances to Daniy-El in the first year of Darius. There would be an end to the transgression instigated by the vile imposter who would seek to stand in God's stead, and He would make an end of the slew of sins so freely committed by men and reconcile those who freely came to Him. After this, he would invoke the time of eternal righteousness and true peace that was so long awaited. The shadow of the Daystar would no longer haunt the realms of men, binding them for his own glory. It seemed that the hour could not come too soon. Still, Daniy-El would not presume to understand all that was encompassed within the plans of Yahweh—all-powerful and omniscient. The day of His return would be beyond knowing for Yahweh was not constrained by the limited spirals of the sun through the heavens that He himself had made. These glimpses were but nuggets of gold along a vast and iridescent plain.

"Go thy way, Daniy-El, for the words are closed up and sealed til the time of the end. Many shall be purified, and made white, and tried; but the wicked shall do wickedly; and none of the wicked shall understand, but the wise shall understand."

The foretelling was grim, but within the nest of ill tidings was couched a blessing—the Jewel of Heaven. Daniy-El took solace from this reassurance. His people would be tested sore, but in answer, the Messiah would twice come, and each time he would irrevocably change the world.

Daniy-El turned as the Presence spoke to him once more, its words conveyed with warmth.

"Go your way until the end, for you shall rest and stand in your lot at the end of your days."

Daniy-El felt a surge of joy at the promised blessing. He was now well stricken in years, and he had seen the manifest glory of God more times than he needed to number. He would willingly bear written witness to wonders past and works to come, that those in whom the Spirit of the living God moved would testify that Yahweh had been faithful to a lowly servant, and to all Israel. There was a home of rest, and when he had done this his last part, there he would go with joy.

22

The Lowering Sky

He shall call upon me, and I will answer him;
I will be with him in trouble
I will deliver him and honour him
With long life will I satisfy him and show him My salvation.

- *The Psalms of King David*

Alone in his chamber, Daniy-El pushed open small, timber casements that looked south across the vast city. He stared wistfully into the thickening gloom. He had endured many trying seasons since the reign of Cyrus had begun, but had gloried in the blessings of Yahweh amidst the upheavals. It had been difficult to watch his friends depart for his homeland along with the thousands others seeking renewal in Jerusalem, and he mourned, not for himself, though he would never return to the land of their birth—Jerusalem lived in his heart like a blossoming fig tree, glorious and majestic. The ruination that had been visited on it by these brutal men whom he now served, did not tarnish the wonder that tinged his memory of home with a golden cast. Nor was it for the knowledge that their companionship be forever lost to him should they not journey back again. Hananyah and Azaryah would offer homage at the new Temple in his stead. Though it could be years before the cornerstone was laid it would be worth the wait. They had paid their price in blood, these Children of Judah who now streamed alongside the mighty Euphrates. No. It was that he prayed that the lessons his brethren had all learnt would not be too easily discarded as they savored the delicate flavor of freedom—its essence would be overpowering as they drew farther from the large city gates that were flung wide to offer them passage.

The cost of our rebellion against Yahweh has been great yet He has stretched out His hand in mercy, Daniy-El considered.

The Jewish numbers, despite their enslavement, had swelled beyond that of any other people who lodged within the city, even as they had so many centuries ago under the Egyptian Pharaoh. *Once more chastised, once more free.*

Even now, his ears still burned with the flaming curses that had flowed from the mouths of former taskmasters who tallied their losses amongst the Jews as though bereaved of their choicest livestock. They gnashed their teeth at the king's decree—'*Free? All of them? Free to depart in peace?*' The kingdom had churned with discontent at the pronouncement of amnesty, but none would defy the hand of the king.

So much had happened since that fateful day when the prince of the eunuchs had come at his king's bidding to search out royal blood amongst the Children of Judah. He had claimed thousands of young men, fair of face and of diverse training, to serve the Babylonian sovereign. None had tasted the bite of a whip on his skin before that day, and they were easily herded like livestock before a cattle driver. The trauma of those perilous days had bound him for many years until the day in the libraries where he had discovered a tightly wrapped scroll amidst a cache of stolen writings from the Temple of Jerusalem. There had been so many texts that it would have been impossible for him to peruse them all, even for a few moments, yet he had found it. And it had quelled some of the anger that he had felt for so long. The words spoken one and a half centuries prior by Israel's prophet were as life to his bones. They were engraved upon his mind now—a warning that had come to life all so harshly . . . . "*All that is in thy house . . . shall be carried to Babylon . . . and thy sons . . . they shall become eunuchs in the palace of the king of Babylon."* It was a humiliation that, for many young nobles, had been hard to bear. He bowed, echoing the words uttered decades before within Hezekiah's palace, "Good is the word of the Lord." He had borne much alongside his companions but he was certain that the hand of Yahweh held the ropes that guided Israel's future in a determined grip. He would not utterly forsake His people. The remnant that He had promised was now on its way home. *Praise be to Yahweh!*

He turned away and knelt beside his palette, knowing that his service was not yet ended. He would not be going with his kinsmen for it was Yahweh's will that he stay. Although the price that he paid had been higher than most of his countrymen, he was not forlorn to be denied the journey home, for he has seen futures that none would ever dream of, and he need not set foot in Jerusalem, or a new Temple to experience the marvel of God's presence at his side.

The air in the chamber grew as warm as the breath that escaped the lips of the old counselor who bowed himself slowly, then lay prostrate upon the thin reed mat. His mouth formed a silent petition. *Thou preparest a table before me in the presence of my enemies. . .* No weapon throughout time had prevailed against the power of prayer; it welcomed the light of the Creator into the dark lairs of men. *He will hear as He has always heard.* The assurance was his, for had not God's purposes triumphed through one man surrounded by adversaries? Nebuchadnezzar, Bel-Shazzar, Cyrus, Darius—mighty men to whom it was proven that there was one greater. The reign of Darius would come to an end, and another would take his place, but the day of the last King still lay before them. *He shall not suffer thy foot to be moved. He that keepeth thy will neither slumber nor sleep. Israel! The hope of Jerusalem is in your hands Lord. You are the Lord—Jehovah Adonai, the Lord our Sovereign. I may die in Babylon, but your plans will be, and they shall be, forever. Jehovah Elyon—Most High God—protect our people from the snares of our enemy. I praise You, God. You are my delight.*

Daniy-El knew it intimately that God was present with His people, as He was with him now. He was assured now of their deliverance and the Promise given—the One to come—the Messiah—and he would always, *always* remember. . . .

Forces swarmed to cast aside the tie that bound this waning light to its Master's cord, tearing at the bonds that linked the spirit of a man to that of his God, but some bonds, forged solid over time, could not be broken, and they were compelled to abandon their quest and to flee. The prayers of a simple servant and the echoes of his life had always been heard by He to whom all life mattered. The wheels continued to churn toward an expected end, but the enemy was not prepared to surrender his desires without a fight. Time was wasted in this place. The quest for supremacy would need to be renewed elsewhere. He would strike at the heart of the Master's homestead and seek the core of his troubles; he would take the fight back to Jerusalem.

23

Last Moves

The glory of the latter house shall be greater than of the former,

Saith the Lord of Hosts;

And in this place will I give peace. . . .

- *The Prophet Haggai*

The shadow slid by as Mithredath, Bishlam, and Tabeel conferred with Rehum, who stood as chancellor. Shimshai had agreed to be their scribe in the matter.

"What news, Shimshai?" Rehum questioned.

Shimshai smiled broadly, hitching his robe slightly. "Thus far we have the support of the Dinaites, the Apharsathchites, the Susanchites, the Babylonians, the Archevites, the Dehavites, the Tarpelites and the Elamites. Even those from Samaria whom Asnappar brought over to lodge in their city, have joined their voices to ours. I have a copy of the letter that we sent to King Artaxerxes. I believe it shall accomplish our purpose. Here. I shall read it to you."

He smoothed the parchment before him.

"Be it known to the king, that the Jews which came up from you to us have come to Jerusalem, building the rebellious and bad city, and have set up its walls, and joined the foundations. Be it known now unto the king, that, if this city is built, and the walls set up again, then they will not pay toll, tribute, and custom, and so you shall endanger the revenue of the kings.

Now, because we have maintenance from the king's palace, and it was not meet for us to see the king's dishonour, therefore we have sent this certification to you, that a search may be made of the book of the records of the fathers, and in it you shall find confirmation that this city is indeed a rebellious city, and hurtful to kings and provinces; furthermore, they have made sedition there in the past, because of which the city was destroyed. We can assure the king that if this city is rebuilt, and the walls set up, that you shall no longer receive your portion from this side of the river."

Shimshai sat back in smug satisfaction, relishing the news he had thus far withheld.

"And the king has replied."

"What? So soon!"

"Yes," he handed the sealed case to Rehum. "It came this morning."

Rehum broke the seal and read aloud.

"The letter which you sent unto us has been plainly read before me, and I commanded that a search be made. It has been found that this city of old time has lifted up itself in insurrection against kings, and that rebellion and sedition have been made therein. There have been mighty kings also over Jerusalem which have ruled over countries beyond the river, and toll and tribute and custom were paid to them. Therefore, make a decree to cause these men to cease, and that this city not be built until I give another commandment. Take heed now that you do not fail to do this. Why should damage grow to the hurt of the kings?"

Tabeel shook his clenched fists, savouring the victory wrought over the Jews.

"This is exactly what we need."

"We shall now be able to act. Zerrub-babel and Jeshua shall not dare scoff at us now."

"Indeed."

224

Indeed. The shadow slunk away, satisfied that its will had been accomplished. It savoured the anticipated frustration that would sap the strength of the servants of God as the command was revealed. He would oppose the One who sat on high until the last battle was set and His servants would gain no quarter.

"It is not right!" the man wailed, his distress sounding through the thick walls to the courtyard beyond. "How can we stop now when we have come so far? We are almost at a height. How can they do this to us now? We—"

"We *must* stop! There is no one to aid our cause in Babylon. There is neither governor nor prefect left in the court of Assyria to herald our cause. In times past it is true that the one Belteshazzar pleaded the case for our people before the mighty kings of the east, but the one prophet left for his greater home many seasons ago. He was our fortress in Babylon through the reigns of our enemies. Now he is gone, and we have not another. Yet we trust in . Never fear. Victory will be wrought at the last."

"Still! How can they be allowed to do this to us? Have we not paid enough? How can we willingly bear this injustice?"

Murmurs coursed through the elders as the senior most among them sought to quell the tide of anger that swelled within their midst. Such emotions if let free would lead to open rebellion, which would do little to aid their cause. Jerusalem could not afford to have such words wafting to the ears of the new king.

An elder rose to speak. "Listen. . . . *Listen!*" These governors have sought the ear of the king. It matters not that they speak lies and go against Cyrus' decree and their own law. Cyrus no longer lives to testify of his hand in our work. Yes, they are like cockatrices, laying eggs in the brush. When we first came they gathered with our neighbors, offering 'aid'. The man spat on the ground. Were it not for the mercies of Yahweh and the urging of His hand upon Jeshua and Zerub-babel here, and all of the chief elders likewise, to reject their sweet words we would be in the pit even now, slain by their machinations. Every man with his hand to the anvil and chisel would have found a dagger in his side ere he could defend himself. We must trust our God to deliver us as He has always done. We shall wait as we have learned to do. He shall preserve our work upon the temple. You shall see. Did they not hire counselors against us, and try to weaken our hands? Yet we prevail."

The grouping bowed in respect of the words of the chief elder.

"We wait."

Zerub-babel, son of Shealtiel, governor of Judah, sat in silence as the prophet Haggai spoke solemnly. He yearned to hear words of encouragement for it had been sixteen years since they had been ordered by the king to stop their construction of the Temple and they yearned for direction. He had been given the name 'Offspring of Babylon', but he was eager to show himself a true son of Israel and servant of the Most High God. Jeshua, son of Jodech, stood with him to hear the prophet's words.

The prophet spoke quietly at first as he addressed them. "Thus says the Lord of Hosts: *'The people say that it is not time to build the House of the Lord. Is it time for you to dwell in your houses with ceilings while this House lie waste? Consider your ways. You have sown much, and bring in little. You eat, but you do not have enough. You drink but you are not filled. You have clothes but no-one is warm. You earn wages and put it in a bag that has holes! Consider your ways. Go up to the mountain, and bring wood, and build the House, and I will take pleasure in it, and I will be glorified.'"*

Zerub-babel's countenance lifted. *The Lord wants His people to build His House. He is with us. He is with us!* Zerub-babel rejoiced.

Haggai need say no more. Zerub-babel lifted up his hands in praise.

"Jeshua. Gather the people. The work on the Lord's house shall begin today!"

Zerrub-babel noticed the men approaching, their faces wreathed in malice. He had expected that they would come. Not only had Haggai come again to lift up the work on the Temple, but so too had Zechariah, son of Iddo. Zerrub-babel had been assured of God's presence, and he knew no fear. He stood erect before the men. Tat-nai, the newest governor of the king, came abreast of his companions, his visage fierce.

"Who has commanded you to build this house, and to make up this wall?" he demanded.

Zerub-babel came forward boldly. "We are the servants of the God of heaven and earth, and build the House that was built these many years ago, which a great king of Israel built and set up. But after our fathers provoked the God of heaven unto wrath, he gave them into the hand of Nebuchadnezzar, the king of Babylon, the Chaldean who destroyed this House, and carried the people away into Babylon. But in the first year of Cyrus, the king of Babylon, that same king Cyrus made a decree to build this House of God. And the vessels also of gold and silver of the House of God, which Nebuchadnezzar took out of the Temple that was in Jerusalem, those did Cyrus the king take out of the Temple of Babylon, and they were delivered to one whose name was Sheshbazzar, whom he made governor, and said to him; 'Take these vessels, go, carry them into the Temple that is in Jerusalem, and let the House of God be built in His place.' Then Sheshbazzar came and laid the foundation of the House of God. And since that time til now it continues to be built and still it is not finished!"

Tat-nai was taken aback. He glanced with uncertainty at Shethar-boznai who had accompanied him to question the elders of Judah.

"We shall investigate these things that you claim," Tat-nai said woodenly. "If it is not as you say. . . . Well. We shall see."

Zerrub-babel watched their retreating backs with relief.

God will be our shield, he affirmed, and returned to his task upon the building, singing a song of praise to the Most High. This time, there will be no stopping.

Tat-nai was aghast when he read the king's reply regarding his urgent letter requesting intervention in the erection of the Temple. The king had checked the records at Achmetha, in the palace located in the province of the Medes, and found confirmation of Zerub-babel's history of events. The king had also learnt that his predecessor, Cyrus, had himself proscribed the size of the future temple: three score cubits in height and breadth. The expenses for the new timber and stones had even been commissioned out of Cyrus's reserves.

Tat-nai re-read the king's instructions, quailing as he absorbed the depth of threat that it carried:

"Let the work of this House of God alone. Let the governor of the Jews and the elders of the Jews build this House of God in His place. Moreover, I make a decree concerning what you shall do to the elders of the Jews for the building of this House of God; that of the king's goods, even of the tribute beyond the river, that expenses be given forthwith unto these men, that they be not hindered. And that which they have need of, both young bullocks, and rams and lambs, for the burnt offerings of the God of heaven, wheat, salt, wine and oil according to the stipulation of the priests in Jerusalem; let it be given day by day without fail, that they may offer sacrifices of sweet savours to the God of heaven, and pray for the life of the king and of his sons.

Also I have made a decree, that whosoever shall alter this word, let the timber be pulled down from his house, and being set up, let him be hanged thereupon; and let his house be made a dunghill for this. And let the God that has caused his name to dwell there destroy all kings and all people that shall put their hand to alter and destroy this House of God which is in Jerusalem. I, Darius II, have made a decree; let it be done with speed."

Tat-nai let the parchment fall from his fingers to the desktop. Shethar-boznai , picked it up anxiously and read, his face growing pale. The two stood a moment in silence, then hastened to carry out the mandate of their sovereign. *Long live the king.*

When the temple was dedicated 5 years later, in the month of Adar, there was no shadow to eclipse the joy of the celebration as sin offerings were given for all Israel. The feast of unleavened bread lasted seven days, and the people rejoiced. The last vestiges of captivity were lifted and hearts sung again with spirits that knew true freedom. Their garments were again white as snow, for the God of heaven had accepted them again, as the stain was washed clean on new holy ground.

EPILOGUE
Second Chances

The Spirit of the Lord God is upon me;

Because the Lord hath anointed me to preach good tidings unto the meek;

He hath sent me to bind up the brokenhearted;

To proclaim liberty to the captives,

And the opening of the prison to them that are bound. . . .

- The Book of the Prophet Isaiah

Polemus closed the pages and placed a hand to his brow where beads of perspiration had gathered despite the coolness of the evening. He recalled vividly the beasts rising from the sea, tearing at each other in a bid for dominion . . . and the battle-weary ram brutally torn gored by a more vicious animal. . . .

How could the Hebrew have known? Ohhhh! Polemus shook his head. *As told, Grecia was playing out its foul part in this far-ranging war, its conquests monumental!*

The celebrated defeat of the Persians at Marathon had come almost a century before, but the threat from the northern conqueror yet loomed. Many other battles had ensued between the territories, as fighting over the spoils of war burgeoned amongst their ranks. Athens had only recently survived a bitter battle with Sparta, and to what end? Power fluctuated between the nations as each usurper vied to be uppermost, cleaving innocents asunder, for these were indistinguishable in the quagmire of hate that had been cultivated. And yet another would come that was greater than Chaldea, or Media and Persia, or Greece. . . . Each new ruler died, fading into oblivion as some more brutal predator abounded. It did not seem to matter now whom it would be, for ultimately the Prince of princes would ultimately rule. Prowess and wisdom had availed each conqueror nothing, for the true victor was always unclear as the lands were washed in blood.

Polemus yearned to escape the writhing morass that strove against itself, for he could feel himself being sucked under, destined to be drowned along with thousands in the perversities and excesses that were suffocating the people of Greece. Polemus had long since recognized that his was no simple physical need that could be assuaged by extravagant meats, strong drink, or the company of women. Nor could the exercise of his body and mind in contests of endurance cleanse him from this malady. All these things he had achieved, yet a darkness lay within him, gnawing resolutely at his willpower to defy it. And why should he, if there was naught else to life?

Now, however, he perceived something new. *I have been granted every boon that men desire, and I know that it is not enough.* His heart did not pulse with the ebullience of achievement that he had anticipated. He could pretend, when he saw Father, that all was well, for it was expected, but behind closed doors, his mask abruptly shattered. Only Daccarus knew of his disappointment with what his life had offered. Wherein was the end? Neither Babylon then, nor Athens at this hour with its celebrated trophies could hold the future captive. Where was Babylon now? And what of Persia, and Greece? Each nation bucked in its death throes, straining to resist an inevitable calamity. It was more evident to Polemus now that nothing had changed thus far in the course of history, but something would. The Son of Man— One who was destined to protect His people at the end of days. Polemus could already feel new understanding growing inside him, and with it came an unaccustomed sense of calm. He considered the revelations carefully: *Daniy-El placed his trust in a living God, who aided him by giving peace to his spirit despite the bondage of his body. He found the freedom that I yet seek; though our bonds may differ, I see death in disguise all about me. Still, this God—the God of Daniy-El, the God of Miysha-El, Hananyah, and Azaryah—shone a light that beckoned him from above the miry chaos, promising a way out. Could it be that my way out lies upon the same path? Perhaps Daccarus will know. If I abide until my brother returns, my decision will ultimately be clearer,* he decided.

Surely it could wait until then.

Three days hence, Polemus was startled from his contemplations by a low voice that called within the lower chamber of the entrance hall downstairs. The heavy oak panels of the door leading to the stairwell muted the sound. He cocked his head, perplexed. He was not scheduled to appear within the magistrate's court for several days yet, but he had taken the liberty to stay within the quietude of his quarters that lay within a stone's throw of the courthouse instead of returning home; it would provide a needed hiatus from the bustling family estate. Polemus had been determined to complete his brother's manuscript and peruse the other records without the frequent disturbance of servants and chamberlains. He had thus sent a missive to his father telling him of Daccarus's plans, and his own intention to remain within the city.

Polemus rose to his feet and moved to the next room. "Evander, is that you? Come on up." He then paused to listen, but discerned no audible reply. Perhaps the court scribe required a missing record, as would sometimes occur. The shuffle of feet sounded on the floorboards beyond the portal, and the young man awaited his visitor who likely brought more work to add to his growing stack.

However, Polemus was surprised to see his aging father enter, his countenance dour.

"Father, you needn't have climbed all those stairs. You could have had Valos send for me!"

His father waved away his concern. "It does not matter. The carriage waits outside. I came myself because there was news from the seas. One of the boats that supply the estate sent word. There were terrible storms, Polemus. Terrible— terrible storms—" His father's voice grew suddenly choked and Polemus felt a twinge of alarm stab at his breast. He forced aside the crush of images as his father forged on.

"Several vessels were tossed and broken on the rocks near Crete. Styra's ship has not made port, and Daccarus—" The old man collapsed against the doorpost, weeping. "Daccarus—" he could say no more as his frame shook with racking sobs.

Polemus bolted to his father's side to steady him. He helped him to a padded bench then quickly poured a glass of water. "Drink, Father." The aged gentleman sipped weakly at the proffered cup.

"I needed to tell you myself. It took all my strength to make it here, but I could not have Valos bring you such news. I am sorry Polemus. I—"

"Shhh, Father," Polemus said softly, laying the graying head against his chest. "What is to be done?" he smoothed his father's hair as the man drew strength from his son. "Father," he said tentatively, knowing his father's disposition to religion. "I shall call upon the God Most High to spare him." Polemus declared.

"Which god? Poseidon?" He shook his head. "No, my son. I fear the God of the Sea will not hear our cries. Daccarus is already lost!" His father continued to weep.

Polemus said no more, but turned his mind to the hope he had found. "I will collect my things and accompany you home, Father."

Polemus took a small bag from the corner and placed the book, along with the neatly wrapped transcript within it. He hands moved numbly as his thoughts were thrown into disarray by his father's words. *Styra's ship? Broken on the rocks?* His elation of discovery, and the renewed solace acquired over the past days, was erased in a moment. *How can this have happened? And why now? Are you real, Lord, Most High? Am I too late to call upon you? You must be real! Daccarus found*

You, and he has sent You to find me. Please. Please. Deliver Daccarus from the seas, as you delivered these men of Judah. In You I put my trust. Please!

Polemus languished at the estate for several weeks, unable to return to his duties at the court. He had pored over the transcript that Daccarus had translated for him. *Daniy-El's faith is not mine*, he brooded, *but I can yet trust with such faith as I now comprehend. What had Daniy-El done when he was grieved? He had prayed.* And so too did Polemus. However, his faith began to wane with the passage of the days. He grew more restive, and the room at once seemed confined, adding to his distemper. Seeking to escape the restlessness swarming about him, he saddled a mount from the stables and rode toward the city. Astride a horse, he might find some surcease to his churning thoughts. *Help me?* he cried. *Help me Lord, Most High? You are no myth. My brother found you, as did I, through him. Help me?* He set the horse into a full gallop, hoping that the bite of the chill air would soothe him. After several miles, Polemus felt warm within, despite the chill wind that screamed past. He slowed the horse to a canter and patted its neck. "Sorry, Lussa," he said leaning down to whisper to the mare. "I needed to run for a while. We shall walk the rest of the way."

The horse tossed its head and gave an understanding snort. Within reach of the outskirts of Athens, he noted a lone rider plodding tiredly along the road. Polemus clicked his horse to a stop and squinted into the glare. Eyes growing wide, he sat upright suddenly, heart pounding. *Is it?* He gathered the reins excitedly. "Once more, for me, Lussa," he shouted, "Once more," and he threw the horse forward, racing toward the rider who, upon hearing the pounding of hooves, raised up in his saddle.

Polemus came alongside the approaching mount and threw himself out of his stirrups even as the mare slowed. Tears flowed down his cheeks as he reached up to embrace the man who leaned from his saddle, disheveled and weary.

"He is real. The Lord Most High—He is real!" Polemus laughed between sobs of joy.

"Indeed he is," Daccarus replied with shared knowledge. "I was forced to change ships in Phoenicia. Styra's ship was overloaded, and it sprung a leak. The ship menders sent for extra pitch to make repairs before setting sail. A retinue of the king's soldiers arrived at the dock whilst the ship was delayed and commanded passage. After this, there were no cabins to be had, so I was forced to wait for another ship. Meanwhile, the coast was ripped by several gales that blew in swiftly. Most of us who had stayed back took shelter to wait out the tempests. I prayed for the ships that had gone on, though, when the winds tore the quay asunder I feared the worst had come upon them. I heard of the calamity as we made port." He hung his head for a moment before raising it again, new light shining out from eyes that were yet tinged with the sadness of loss. "But here I am, Little Brother." He threw his arms about Polemus who shook his head and laughed.

"I almost doubted," Polemus admitted. "Let us go tell Father that his sons have found true life—the both of us."

Polemus turned his horse, and the brothers trotted back along the path that Polemus had come, chatting animatedly of fire, and lions, and of a hope in glory.

THE END

Key Titles

Abed-Nego —Servant of Nebo: Azaryah

Arioch —Lion Like: Captain of the Guard

Ashpenaz —Prince of the Eunuchs / Chief of Eunuchs

Azaryah / Azariah —God Strengthens: Abed-Nego

Bel (Baal) —God of Babylon

Belteshazzar—Favored by Bel / Keeper of Bel's Treasure: Daniy-El

Bel-Shazzar / Belshazzar —Bel's Prince

Daniy-El / Daniel —God's Judge

Darius / Dara / Darjavesh —Lord King

Evil-Merodach —Merodach's Fool

Gabriy-El —Champion of Yahweh

Hananyah / Hananiah —Jah is Kind

Jehovah Tsidkeenu —The Lord Our Righteousness

Jehovah Adonai —The Lord Our Sovereign

Jehovah Elyon —Most High God

Jehovah Shalom —The Lord Our Peace

Jeshua —Jehovah Saves

Mika-El / Michael —Glory of Yahweh / Like God

Miysha-El / Mishael —Who is What God Is

Nebo (Nebu / Nebo/ Nego) —God of Learning and Letters in Chaldea, Babylonia, and Assyria

Nebuchadnezzar - Nebo the Mighty

Meshach —Guest of a King / Ram (Sun-god of Chaldea): Miysha-El

Nebuzaradan - Favors: Captain of the Guard

Nergal-Sharezer / Rab-Mag —Champion of the Gods / Prince of Fire: Chief Magi

Sarsechim-Nebo / Samgar-Nebo —Cupbearer

Sheshbazzar —Fire Worshiper

Shethar-boznai —Star of Splendour / Persian Officer

Shadrach —Royal

Strobos —Shadow

Tat-nai / Tattenai—Persian Governor / Satrap

YHWH / *Yahweh* / *Jehovah* —The Lord God

Zerub-babel —Offspring of Babylon

Select Historians

Histories regarding Babylon, and King Cyrus, were compiled from deciphered texts and translations by the following historians:

Berosus: 3rd century BC

Ctesias of Cnidus 5th century BC

Flavius Josephus: AD 37-93

Pliny: AD61-112

Rawlinson: 1819-1895

Strabo: BC63-AD21

About the Author

Ruth Durant, an award winning novelist, has been gifted with an extraordinary literary penchant that has produced truly inspirational writing. As a world-traveler and ministry leader, her books have been deeply enriched by her journeys through the Holy Land, Israel. Her voyages have inspired captivating novels, each of which unfurls a vibrant weave of characters, some enduring enemies, others unshakeable friends. New realms of intrigue unfold, where nobility blooms amidst the tumult of treachery and rebellion and honor supremely triumphs. Through her writing Ruth continues to magnify the Lord for His enduring and wondrous works.

Ruth is a graduate of the Harvard Graduate School of Design and has produced a range of publications as editor and graphic illustrator. She now resides in the Caribbean with her husband Terrence and their daughters.